THE HOUSE AT DEVIL'S NECK

THE HOUSE AT DEVIL'S NECK

A JOSEPH SPECTOR
LOCKED-ROOM MYSTERY

TOM MEAD

THE MYSTERIOUS PRESS
NEW YORK

To my parents
and in loving memory of my grandparents

CONTENTS

DRAMATIS PERSONAE

Imogen Drabble,	a reporter
Francis Tulp,	a believer
Madame Adaline La Motte,	a spiritualist
Virginia Bailey,	a mother
Fred Powell,	a driver
Clive Lennox, ⎫	present occupants of the
Justine Lennox, ⎭	House at Devil's Neck
Rodney Edgecomb,	a controversial figure
Maurice Bailey,	a shade
Walter Judd,	a detective
Lidia Rees,	a psychiatrist
Estelle Rainsford,	a private secretary
Mr. Horsepool,	a valet
Robbie Atkins,	a constable
Allan Pepperdine,	a solicitor
Alastair Quinn,	a financier
George Flint,	a Scotland Yard man
Jerome Hook,	his second
Joseph Spector,	a professional trickster

PART ONE

INVOCATION

It was a place shunned by the people of the village, as it had been shunned by their fathers before them. There were many things said about it, and all were of evil. No one ever went near it, either by day or night. In the village it was a synonym of all that is unholy and dreadful.

—William Hope Hodgson,
The House on the Borderland

A certain number of coincidences of a particular sort have occurred: did they or did they not occur by chance?

—Edmund Gurney, F. W. H. Myers,
and Frank Podmore,
Phantasms of the Living

CHAPTER ONE

A BAND OF TRAVELLERS

It does not do to trust people too much.

—Charlotte Perkins Gilman,
"The Yellow Wall-Paper"

August 31, 1939. 3 P.M.

L oping through the steady hammering rain, splashing through puddles without care, panting like a maniac, the man in the beige mackintosh reached the bus depot just in time. Imogen Drabble watched him from the coach window and wondered about him. He was heading in their direction and must have made frantic eye contact with the driver, for the driver waited, hand poised on the ignition key.

The man in the beige mackintosh—his trilby hat dented and misshapen—advanced and rapped on the glass door, looking like a damp and miserable wraith. The driver took his time leaning forward to deploy the door lever; there was something bitter and vengeful in the tardy passenger's gait as he clambered aboard.

"Is it McGinn or Edgecomb?" said the driver, reaching for his clipboard. He, too, had a face for funerals. The crimson ribbon on his peaked cap was a single slice of frivolity in an otherwise cadaverous aspect.

"Judd," said the man, "Walter Judd." He was out of breath, and his shoulders heaved up and down as he waited for the driver to confirm his booking. In his right hand he clutched a crumpled ticket, and in his left a small traveller's case. He'd evidently had a hell of a rush, and had made it only just in time.

"You're not on here," said the driver, indicating the clipboard.

"Then it's under 'Edgecomb,'" said Judd.

The driver looked again and nodded brusquely. "Any other luggage, sir?"

"Just this," said Judd, indicating the travelling case.

"All right then. Take a seat, we'll be underway in a moment."

Imogen watched Judd lumbering along the aisle, eventually settling in a vacant seat a couple rows in front of her. He did not even remove his mackintosh, and the seat was no doubt drenched in rainwater. He immediately began fumbling in his pockets, emerging with a cigarette packet and book of matches. The cigarettes were dry, but the matches were, unsurprisingly, soaked and limp.

Judd grumbled under his breath, the unlit cigarette clutched in his teeth.

"Excuse me," said Imogen, half rising and leaning forward across the vacant row, "care for a light?" She had nimbly extracted her lighter from the bag in her lap, and now proffered it to the irritable traveller.

"'kyou," he said, turning his head so she could ignite the tip of the cigarette between his lips. She got her first full look at his face then, in the shadowed relief of that flickering flame; glaucous skin dappled in orange light, his chin a grey-black fuzz, his half-open eyes swollen with sleeplessness, looking for all the world as though he were already quite dead.

"Lousy day," she said.

"Mm," he grunted, then turned away from her. Puffing on the cigarette, he felt around in his pockets once more and now emerged with a somewhat tattered-looking envelope. He removed and unfolded three sheets of notepaper, densely packed with hand-written words. By the wholly inadequate light of the slate-coloured sky, he began to read.

Imogen liked to think of herself as a collector of interesting persons, and there were plenty on this little coach. Unfortunately, the person she was travelling with was not one of them. She glanced at the old woman beside her on the bench seat, who had been snoring ever since she boarded. It was going to be a long, long journey.

Adaline La Motte was an expansive and gregarious sleeper. Like every other aspect of her life, she tended toward maximalism. Her dress was tentlike and funereal; her astrakhan coat as heavy as mammoth hide; a scarf was tied around her head and her throat was cluttered with paste jewellery. Her bulldog jowls flapped and rippled with each intake of breath, and her mouth hung open, revealing small, brown teeth.

The driver (Imogen had not yet learned his name) fired up the engine and it started on the first attempt, which came as a considerable surprise. The coach was a juniper-green Leyland Cub, a 22-seater, and in decent nick. It coasted away from the depot and into the street, headlamps casting blades of yellow light through the rainfall.

There were seven of them on that coach, including the driver, which would no doubt make for a lively trip. These were "characters," thought Imogen. Just the sort of people she *ought* to be writing about.

Aside from Walter Judd, about whom Imogen had yet to make up her mind, there was a middle-aged lady in beads and an unfortunate hat, who was now sitting at a conscious distance from her fellow passengers. She and Madame La Motte knew one another—indeed, it was at this woman's behest that Madame had joined the excursion—and yet they were not sitting together. There was a curious uprightness to this woman's gait, as though she were making a conscious effort to remain impassive. She wore a long black dress with a white jabot pinned at her throat by a pearlescent brooch. Her hair was a tight, cinereous snare of curls, her eyes ringed by crow's feet like cracked porcelain. Her bearing, the way she walked, the way she carried herself on surprisingly light feet; it all gave her a curiously ghostlike aspect. She had a large canvas bag in her lap, into which she peeked periodically, as though checking its contents were safe. Her name, Imogen knew, was Mrs. Bailey.

Across the aisle from the silent lady was a young (perhaps late twenties) and handsome man whose raffish appearance was belied by the ungainliness of his movements and the childlike way he fidgeted in his seat. He looked like an adolescent who has grown up too quickly and is now unsure quite where to put his long limbs.

He wore a dun-coloured suit and a grey, limp-brimmed trilby; the waterlogged felt had the texture of a lily pad. His face was pale, smooth as a soft-boiled egg, and even-featured—save for a slightly receding chin.

At the very rear of the coach sat perhaps the most unlikely (and therefore interesting) passenger: an old man, again dressed all in black (what a morbid cabal this had turned out to be!). He had a thin, hollow-cheeked face with creased, papery skin and pale blue eyes. He held a walking cane with an ornamental silver handle; it took Imogen a moment or two to realise the handle was in fact shaped like a human skull. The more she looked at this old man (furtively, from the corner of her eye), the more she wondered whether he *was* in fact old at all. Though spindly and slightly hunched, he had a kind of tight muscularity, like a coiled spring. His hair was silver, and his homburg hat was black and slightly askew atop his altogether impressive head.

Madame La Motte, the woman who could sleep through a hurricane, stirred as the coach left London. ". . . Telephone," she burbled, the last vestige of her dream drifting from her.

"What's that, Madame?"

"Answer the telephone."

"You were dreaming, Madame. We're on the coach."

"Mm? Was I? Where are we?"

"Just outside London."

"Such a long way to go," said old Madame La Motte, settling back and leaning sideways with her forehead pressed against the window. She closed her eyes, and within moments was snoring softly once again.

They made good progress despite the weather, largely thanks to the driver's eager acceleration, which saw them bumping and jolting through plenty of dips in the uneven roadways. An especially deep depression sent a small round object sailing from the young male passenger's hand. It came rolling along the aisle toward Imogen; she stopped it with her foot and leaned forward to pick it up. It was a lens cap; she had worked with photographers often enough to recognise it.

The young man was on his feet in an instant, peering round agitatedly. When he spotted Imogen holding the cap up to the light, he sighed with relief and came lunging toward her. Settling in the vacant seat across the aisle, he spoke in low tones, to avoid waking Madame La Motte.

"Nice catch," he said. "Thought I'd never see it again."

"Are you a photographer?" asked Imogen.

"Of a kind. A rather specialised kind."

"Meaning what?" She had not yet handed back the lens cap and made a show of idly examining it.

"Forgive me," he said, holding out his hand, "my name is Francis Tulp."

She shook the hand. "Imogen Drabble."

"You look rather familiar, Miss Drabble. Perhaps we've met somewhere before?"

"Perhaps we have," she said, finally handing back the lens cap. Tulp pocketed it.

"May I ask what it is you do for a living?"

"I'm a writer," she told him.

"Of fiction?"

Her only answer was a smile.

Francis Tulp blustered a little. "I'm actually a scientist, I suppose you'd call it. Or an investigator."

"Of what?"

"Of . . ." He gave a little wave with his right hand. "Phenomena."

"Ah," she said, slightly disappointed. Another of *those*. It explained the camera, at least.

"Tell me, is that Adaline La Motte?" he said, nodding toward the sleeping old woman.

"It is. I'm her . . . companion, I suppose you'd call it."

"I thought you were a writer?"

"So what brings you out on this trip?" Imogen said, changing the subject.

"I imagine the same thing that brings Madame La Motte. There are so many stories about this place. When I heard they were opening up to the public, I jumped at the chance."

"And you're travelling alone?"

"I'm a one-man band these days," said Tulp. "I used to be with the OPC."

The Occult Practice Collective: Imogen had heard of it, though it seemed to be little more than a drinking club, albeit with remarkably deep pockets. She speculated that a young man like Tulp would not have relinquished membership willingly—the loss of funding would be crippling to any serious researcher.

"I saw you loading your belongings into the luggage bay," Imogen observed. Tulp had insisted on doing this himself, to the driver's obvious chagrin.

"Some of my equipment," he explained. "Rather fragile. Not to mention costly."

And purchased with the OPC's money, she speculated.

As they had been speaking, Imogen was conscious that Tulp's gaze was drifting over her shoulder, toward the old man in the very back seat. "Do you know him?" she asked.

"Yes, I rather think I do. I didn't spot him when I first boarded. But yes, we've certainly met before."

"You practice spirit photography?" Imogen prompted in an effort to draw Tulp back into conversation.

"I do," he offered eagerly. "I have one of the most sophisticated setups in Europe, and I've produced some of the most compelling results. Even ardent sceptics have struggled to dispute my findings."

"Really? Strange that I've never heard of you before."

He was a little affronted. "Perhaps you're reading the wrong kinds of journals. But then, I don't do what I do in order to be famous. I am no Madame La Motte." He uttered the old lady's name with a certain sharpness. Was it resentment of her celebrity? Or antipathy toward her showy manner, and the embarrassing amounts of money yielded by her high society séances?

Imogen, who had little sympathy for the old charlatan, found this rather amusing. "You mean you really *believe*?"

He frowned. "Of course. I shouldn't be here otherwise. I take it, then, that you're a *non*believer, Miss Drabble?"

She gave him a disarming smile. Before taking this job with Madame, Imogen had known next to nothing about the supernatural. Now that she had been at it for a while, she felt as if she knew even less. She had sat through copious readings and healings and communications, and had come away from each feeling as though she'd witnessed nothing more than a cynical confidence trick. She had begun the escapade as an agnostic; she would finish as an outright sceptic.

"Let's just say I'm still waiting for that conclusive evidence to erase the last doubts from my mind."

"Well," said Francis Tulp softly, "perhaps this weekend you shall find it."

His gaze was trailing off over her shoulder again. It was as if, knowing that she was not fully committed to a belief in ghosts, he was permitting his attention to drift.

"Who is he?" asked Imogen.

Tulp leaned in close, as though wary of attracting the old man's attention. "His name is Joseph Spector. Have you heard of him?"

She shook her head.

"He used to be a music hall magician."

"Yes," said Imogen thoughtfully, "he looks the part."

"Now he's . . . well, he's like me. That is, he has an interest in the unexplained. The inexplicable. He wrote an excellent monograph on the Pittenweem witches."

"How did you meet him? The OPC?"

"No, no." Tulp half chuckled. "We met through work. We were both called in to investigate certain *happenings* at a place just outside London; an old house called Coldwreath. Do you know it?"

She shook her head again, slightly discomfited by her own ignorance.

"Well, it was rather mysterious, but not supernatural. It meant I got to see Spector in action, though. That strange brain of his. I wonder if he remembers me?"

"You know a lot about everyone on this coach, it seems," said Imogen, making an unwritten note to speak with Spector later.

"What about the gentleman in front of me?" she said, lowering her voice to a whisper. "Walter Judd?" They both looked, and saw that Judd was still hunched over the rain-damaged notepaper, studying it carefully.

"Is that his name? Can't help you there."

"How about the widow?" She indicated Mrs. Bailey.

"What makes you say 'widow'?"

Imogen pouted her lips thoughtfully. "Just the look of her. She seems as though she ought to be in a pew at a funeral somewhere."

"Well, when you put it that way . . ." Tulp offered with a smile, settling back in his seat.

Imogen resisted the urge to prolong the conversation. She had often found it more beneficial to eke these things out. People tended to be more forthcoming that way.

She turned in her seat, and jumped a little when she saw that one of Madame La Motte's eyes was half-open. The old medium had been awake the entire time, no doubt listening to the whole conversation. The errant eye snapped shut again, and she let out a low, tasteful snore.

Imogen could see little beyond the windows. The rain was so heavy that only greys and whites were perceptible amid the deluge. No shapes; only colours. The road, the buildings, the land.

So she returned her attention to her fellow passengers. Not Madame La Motte; she'd already had quite enough of the old lady. But Walter Judd, who was now glancing around distractedly, as though trying to attract someone's attention but unsure how to go about it. And Mrs. Bailey, who was looking straight ahead, her lips moving slightly, as though she were praying, or reciting an incantation. And Francis Tulp, the young parapsychologist. And, glancing over her shoulder, she studied Joseph Spector.

What were the odds, she wondered, of all these unlikely and eccentric persons descending on the same location for the weekend?

She turned her thoughts to their destination. Of all the "haunted" locations she had visited with Madame, this was the one about which she knew the least. She understood it had been used as a military hospital during the War, and that it had since fallen into disrepair. But its very dilapidation had fuelled rumours of its ghostly happenings and made it a prime spot for ghost hunters and apparitionists. It had recently come under new ownership, and it had been these new owners' ingenious idea to open the place up to paying guests.

From what Imogen had managed to determine in advance, there was very little in the surrounding area to appeal to tourists. Countryside, she supposed, though she didn't consider that much of an attraction. She was raised in a tiny village, and now had little patience for the quaintness of the country. Perhaps that was why she found working for Madame La Motte so unpleasant. The old woman was like a vulture, preying on the superstition and naivety of her "clients." It was grotesque, but also somehow . . . parochial.

Usually, Imogen managed to circumvent the question of conscience by focusing on her salary—which was healthy. She was doing inordinately well for one so young. Maybe when this trip was over she would bid the unpleasant Madame La Motte farewell for the last time, and take a holiday somewhere. Her friends often chided her that she was too cynical and jaded. A nice, refreshing voyage to the continent might be just the ticket.

Moderately comforted by the thought, Imogen let her imagination wander. For a little while, at least, she need not be in this miserable coach, but on a beach somewhere—perhaps Greece. Somewhere warm, away from the driving rain.

The coach slowed. The driver swung the wheel, and they were off the road and in what was presumably a lay-by of some kind. Imogen was still unable to see.

"Ladies and gents," the driver announced, "this is a scheduled fuel stop. If you'd like a quick leg stretch, I'll be setting off again in ten minutes. But personally, I wouldn't recommend it."

Imogen sighed. Her fleeting fantasy was now dispelled. She was inescapably *here*, in this coach, with these people, pressing on like lunatics through the punishing weather, toward the house at Devil's Neck.

CHAPTER TWO

THE PHANTOM BELLHOP

'Tis strange what a change comes over masses of
men as they gaze upon a dead body.

—James Malcolm Rymer, *Varney the Vampire*

August 31, 1939. 3 P.M.

O ccasional slivers of sky permeated the charcoal cloud plumes.
George Flint turned up the collar of his greatcoat and
stamped his feet to ward off the unseasonable chill. His face was
ruddy from the walk, and his moustache particularly bristly. An
unlit pipe hung from his lips—the rising cost of tobacco meant he
could only sporadically afford to refill it. And besides, he found
that the simple act of chewing on the pipe assisted his concentration and all-round cognition. On a day like today, it was essential.
Only midafternoon, and already the darkness was gathering.

"Did you try round the back?" he asked his sergeant, Jerome
Hook.

"Yes, sir. Locked up tight, just like the front."

"All right," Flint sighed, "worth a try, I suppose." Then he mounted the steps and hammered on the front door once again. "Police," he barked, "open up."

The house was a corner property at the end of a long terrace of virtually identical Victorian homes, each comprising three storeys and crowned with teetering chimney stacks. The bricks were grey and sturdy, with the façade framed by elaborate cornicing. This was a nice street; the sort of street where Flint hoped to move one day.

The case was a strange one; the call had come in about an hour ago of a madman waving a loaded revolver, threatening both his secretary and his valet. They had cleared the place sharpish, and the assailant—who was reported to be middle-aged and otherwise unassuming—had locked himself in the house. It now fell to Flint to try and smoke the bugger out.

"The place is surrounded?" he said to Hook.

"Yes, sir. Three constables at front and back." As the house was on a corner, a simple wooden fence—about eight feet high—shielded it from the road on the right-hand side. Constables had made short work of the gate, gaining access to the long, narrow garden behind the building.

"Good." Flint grunted. "Better safe than sorry."

"Right you are, sir."

"He's alone in there?"

"As far as we can tell. There was a housekeeper who cooked his meals, but she's on holiday."

Flint nodded. "Then we'd better get moving. No time like the present. And we may as well strike while the light's still on our side."

It had just begun to rain too, which could complicate matters. He could feel it drumming on his bowler hat. It was likely in for the day now, if those drooping clouds were anything to go by.

After a moment's thoughtful chewing on his pipe, Flint said decisively, "Very well. On my signal."

Hook strode along the paving stones outside the house till he was in sight of both sets of constables—those lurking across the road, and those in the rear garden. Then he locked eyes with Flint, waiting for the signal.

Flint held up his gloved hand, glanced toward the house once more. He let the hand drop to his side, as though starting a race. The men advanced on the house from all sides—uniformed constables converging in a balletically choreographed pincer movement. When the place was fully, impenetrably surrounded, Flint himself made for the front door, mounted the four stone steps, and pounded the brass knocker.

"Open up!" he bellowed, growing tired of repeating himself. "Police!"

A moment's silence, crackling with anticipation.

Then came his favourite part of the entire operation: with the sole of his hobnailed boot, he buckled the door and led the charge on the absurdly commonplace, dreary little suburban residence. Constables filed into the dark hallway, the only sound the regimented pounding of their footsteps. They spilled into the side rooms—the kitchen, the lounge, the pantry—systematically searching the ground floor.

Hook caught Flint's eye and shook his head.

"Upstairs," Flint instructed.

As the men were pounding their way up the wooden staircase, there came a sudden, thunderous *crack* from somewhere on the second floor.

The constables waited. Silence. On the second-floor landing, a closed door faced them across from the staircase. Flint sidled past the uniformed men and was the first to set foot on the upper floor. The gunshot, he determined, had come from behind that door.

He approached and tried the handle. It was locked. He rapped on the wood with a leather-gloved knuckle. "Police!" he announced. "Don't do anything foolish. Put the weapon down, and unlock the door."

He pressed his ear to the wood; silence. After the fact, Flint convinced himself he had smelled gunpowder. The landing was unlit, so Flint drew a book of matches from his pocket and attempted to strike one so he could examine the handle and lock. After three attempts, the match refused to light, so he simply gave up and shouldered open the door. It caved in easily, and he stumbled into the room, pipe still gripped between his teeth.

The room was a small, carpeted study lined with bookshelves bearing austere, leather-bound volumes. A bureau was angled along the right-hand wall, with a man sitting behind it, slumped forward. His position was alarmingly unnatural, with his head cocked to his left but his body leaning conspicuously to the right. Between his feet lay a revolver and a spent cartridge.

Flint sighed. "It's all right, gents," he announced to the constables assembling rapidly at the top of the stairs. "I'm afraid we're too late."

He approached the dead man and leaned over to get a better look at him. There was a punctiform, black-rimmed wound in the right temple. The other side of the chap's head was hidden by shadow, but Flint did not need to see it to know that the exit wound was a bloody mess, a pulpy crater, with skin, bone, and brain spattered over the shelf to the man's left. Flint's attention was also caught by a long scar that commenced at the widow's peak and disappeared into the mop of hair.

This was, Flint supposed, a disappointment. And yet it was not entirely unanticipated. When he was told the name of the man who had frightened away his private secretary and valet by brandishing a loaded revolver, Flint had recognised it immediately, though it was a name he had not heard in roughly two decades. It was this name that had brought him out here, dragging the unwitting Sergeant Hook along with him. This name dated back to Flint's earliest days at Scotland Yard, near the end of the War, and was inextricably linked to a bizarre unsolved mystery—the mystery of the Aitken inheritance.

—⁓—

The story began over twenty-five years ago. On April 15, 1912, as everyone knows, the RMS *Titanic* sank in the northern Atlantic Ocean en route to New York City. Flint was only nineteen at the time, and not yet interested in the police. He did not discover his vocation until after the War, which changed his life in so many ways. But he nonetheless remembered the *Titanic*, with all its romance and tragedy.

As with any major disaster, other comparatively minor disasters spawn therefrom, and so it was with the Aitken inheritance. Wealthy London financier Dominic Edgecomb was among the first-class travellers reported dead—he had been travelling to New York for business. This death alone would have caused untold damage to global stock markets; in conjunction with the *Titanic* tragedy, it presented a veritable cataclysm—not least in the life of Edgecomb's younger brother, Rodney. As the eldest, Dominic had been slated to receive a prodigious fortune when his ailing maternal uncle, Harold Aitken, bedridden since the winter of 1910, finally died. With Dominic himself now dead, all that money would come to twenty-two-year-old Rodney instead.

Harold Aitken died in May of 1912, and no one was especially surprised. He was found by his nurse one morning, his eyes sealed shut as though with wax, and his toothless mouth yawning open. The cyanotic blueing of his fingers and lips indicated he had been dead some hours. As deaths go, it was ultimately unremarkable, save for the occasional whisperings about the man who visited the house during the night, the young man identified by some as Rodney Edgecomb. There was even talk of poison (Rodney had a degree in chemistry), though simple suffocation seemed more likely. Nothing came of these rumours, however, and Rodney received his inheritance, estimated at close to twenty-five thousand pounds in value.

Rodney Edgecomb's profligacy was the stuff of legend, and he had a tendency to fritter away cash in the illicit gambling clubs of London, particularly one underground establishment in Saffron Hill, bailiwick of the notorious Cortesi brothers.

Just as an unfortunate twist of fate had set the *Titanic* on its deadly course toward the iceberg and killed Dominic Edgecomb, another unfortunate twist of fate brought him back again. In the spring of 1913, a man surfaced in a London hospital answering to the name of the dead financier.

This threw the legacy of Uncle Harold into question. It placed Rodney Edgecomb in the invidious position of owing money to the Cortesi brothers (in the person of their vicious lieutenant, Titus Pilgrim), whilst simultaneously losing the entirety of the fortune that had been within his grasp, which would now transfer to Dominic, the rightful heir.

But it also raised questions: Why had Dominic Edgecomb been absent ever since the sinking? Why had he not declared himself alive and well straightaway? The answer was doubly unfortunate for all concerned: he had suffered a head injury during the sinking and had lost his memory. An amnesiac! And just when it seemed the resemblance between this case and the plot of a Victorian novel could not be more pronounced, there was the fact that his illness had robbed him of his appetite, causing him to lose over a hundred pounds of weight, and that his heavy beard had also been shaved at some point in the interim. This left him virtually unrecognisable to his erstwhile associates. Indeed, for each individual who would swear that this Dominic Edgecomb was *the* Dominic Edgecomb, and a legitimate claimant to the Aitken inheritance, there was another individual to dispute it. Numerous in-depth newspaper reports examined photographs of Dominic Edgecomb pre- and post-sinking, presenting compelling evidence for both sides of the argument. This case proved startlingly divisive, and it seemed that everybody had an opinion on it. Ultimately, though, the "deciding vote" was left to Rodney Edgecomb. After all, surely the testimony of Dominic's own brother could not be disputed?

Then, in a court of law, he was asked outright whether he could confirm or disconfirm the identity of the "Edgecomb Claimant."

"My Lord," he declaimed, "that man is no brother of mine."

Amid uproar from the gallery, he explained, "The man who has presented himself to this court as my brother, Dominic Edgecomb, is not my brother. He is an impostor. A liar. A fraud."

And there the matter might have ended.

This "Dominic Edgecomb," however, remained an enigma. Several doctors were on hand to testify that whether or not this man *was* the real Dominic, he undeniably *believed* himself to be Dominic Edgecomb, and thus could not be accused of deliberate imposture. And now, even in the aftermath of his public humiliation, he remained adamant that he *was* Dominic, that he had always been Dominic, that he ever would be Dominic. His entreaties grew increasingly desperate. Then, in April 1914, almost two years to the day since the sinking of the Titanic, he shot himself through the side of the head, killing himself instantly. The suicide took place in a room at the Hotel Maurienne in central London, where he had been living since his unlikely resurrection.

The circumstances of the suicide caused another brief sensation, though there could be no doubt that it *was* a suicide. He shot himself in a sealed room, with the key in his pocket. The only other key, the master key, was under close watch behind the front desk. Or so it was assumed at the time.

Since the claimant could not be buried under the name of Dominic Edgecomb (Rodney would never have permitted it), he was buried in an unmarked grave. By August of that year, the question of whether the dead man was Dominic proved trivial. Atrocities at Leuven, Tamines, Dinant, and other Belgian towns provoked Britain to action, and the Great War was underway.

It would be another four years before George Flint became involved in the case. Rodney Edgecomb had just been released from hospital (he had the scar on his head to prove it), and he seemed weary and confused as Flint explained the reason for his visit. It had been a brief, unpleasant encounter.

That day in the autumn of 1918, Flint had been accompanied by an old man named Barnaby Osgood. Osgood was a curious character: a South African diamond merchant, or so he claimed, who had been staying at the Hotel Maurienne the night Dominic Edgecomb died in 1914. He had seen something that night, he said, a bellhop that did not belong. But the significance of what he saw had not become clear until years later—three years, to be precise. He first made himself known to Scotland Yard in 1917 with what he called "new information" on the Dominic Edgecomb case: proof that Rodney Edgecomb was a liar, and that the young heir had murdered both his uncle and his brother to get his hands on the Aitken inheritance.

There were plenty of holes in the old man's story, but like a bad smell he lingered until 1918, periodically showing his face and generally making a nuisance of himself. That was when a frustrated sergeant referred him to the newest of new recruits: Constable George Flint. And Flint found himself reading up on the story of the ill-fated inheritance, wondering if perhaps the old man might be onto something after all. Because why else should he keep cropping up all these years later, and with such a strange story of what he had seen at the Hotel Maurienne that night? Flint was eager and industrious in those days; it had seemed like an opportunity to really *do* something. These days, he would have been more cautious.

That bleak interregnum, the War, had changed everything. Hundreds of thousands of men were now dead; the money squabbles of toffee-nosed brothers were scarcely more than a tawdry distraction. Besides, Rodney Edgecomb had since served on the Western Front, where he (presumably) killed his fair share of men. Adding one or two extra tallies to his grand total did not seem so dreadful amid the pervasive cynicism of the post-War years.

Inevitably, society scandals such as this one lost their lustre. Barnaby Osgood returned to South Africa and died of some obscure illness. The Aitken inheritance and its controversial legatee were eventually lost to time. Even Flint, who prided himself on his memory, had begun to let the story slip from his grasp.

That is, until lunchtime on August 31, 1939.

—⁓—

PC Robbie Atkins, as dependable as they come, was meandering along his patrol route at an unhurried pace, when he happened to pass the mouth of Crook O'Lune Street. As he did so, he glanced along the row of terraced frontages, only to find himself met by an unwelcome sight: a middle-aged woman hurtling toward him with horror in her eyes.

"Constable! Constable, thank God. He's gone mad. Locked himself in. He's got a *gun* . . ." Though out of breath, she was entirely coherent, and whilst he was tempted to treat her as he would any ordinary hysteric, PC Atkins hesitated. There was something about this woman that he found inherently credible; whether it was the sensible tweed attire, the practical bob of her greying hair, or the round, gold-rimmed spectacles on the bridge of her slightly hooked nose, he couldn't say. Perhaps she reminded him of his mother.

There was also the matter of the man in the waistcoat, dressed up like some kind of butler, who came following her at a light jog, panic nonetheless etched in his face.

"Steady on now," said Atkins. "What's going on here?"

"The master, sir," said the butler. "He seems to have . . . gone mad."

"And what's this about a gun?"

"I regret to inform you that he is armed. A service revolver, fully loaded. He has threatened both myself and Miss Rainsford here, and now he has locked us out of the house."

—◇◇◇—

That was how, on a miserable afternoon at the tail end of a drab summer, George Flint found himself thinking about the strange circumstances of the Aitken inheritance once again.

"Well," he said, examining the corpse, "all that money, and look where it's got him."

This was the most obvious and inescapable case of suicide one could ever wish to encounter. The room was locked on the inside. The windows were bolted. The weapon lay at the dead man's feet. And he, Flint, had been the first to enter the room and come upon the undisturbed tableau of a man with half his head blasted away to buggery. It was as intractable and unquestionable as the stars in the sky.

Perhaps for that very reason, Flint caught himself looking for holes in the story. Over the years, he had developed an acute suspicion of any situation as clear-cut as this one. He had let himself be fooled too many times in the past.

Despite the obvious and irrefutable indications that the suspect had taken his own life, Flint pondered the possibility of murder. Strolling around the room with the contemplative air of a tourist in an art gallery, he constructed elaborate scenarios in his head, all of which culminated in the unidentified second man (whose face was, by necessity, a blur) placing the barrel of a revolver against the side of Rodney Edgecomb's head and pulling the trigger.

What then? Flint had heard the shot. The door had been in view of his men the entire time. No one had emerged from the room. No more than two minutes had elapsed between the moment the shot was fired and the moment Flint stepped into the study. By rights, any assailant should have been standing there, positively *asking* to be caught. But he wasn't. And there was no place in this small, unassuming study for him to hide.

Nonetheless, Flint wondered. He had learned to distrust appearances, a lesson he owed to his friendship with Joseph Spector. Many times the old conjuror had offered his unique insight and logic to the detection of some bold or unusual crime. More often than not, the most complicated cases had the simplest solutions, while those with apparently obvious circumstances tended to be deceptively complex. Even without Spector around, Flint had learned to ask the kinds of awkward questions that could occasionally cast a case in a new light.

And yet, on this occasion, the longer he spent in that study, the harder it became to characterise this as anything other than a wretched man taking the coward's way out.

An idea struck him. Flint returned to the body and peered at the half of its upturned face that was visible. Canny killers were often out to pull identity tricks; to fake their deaths by butchering some poor patsy in their place. And yet—here he was. This body was indisputably that of Rodney Edgecomb, the younger Edgecomb brother, who had been the object of so much pernicious gossip in his time. Even with half his face blown away, what features remained were obviously those of the man Flint had met in 1918. Above all, there was that distinctive scar. There could be no room for doubt.

But still, Flint doubted. He had come upon numerous death scenes that had seemed too perfect; too pat; too predictable. And the most important lesson he had received from Spector was that when something seemed a little too obvious, it usually was.

By now, the rain was drumming the side of the house. "At least," said Flint, "we can put this business to bed, anyway." But he was not entirely sure that he believed it.

CHAPTER THREE

A TIME BEFORE THE GHOSTS

Do what thou wilt shall be the whole of the law.

—Aleister Crowley

August 31, 1939. 4 P.M.

As they had been travelling for only an hour, Imogen was surprised when everybody filed past her, out of the coach and into the rain—even Madame La Motte. When she was alone, Imogen sighed and stretched her arms above her head.

Now they were stationary, she could make out the dingy outline of the roadside garage, with its sentinel-like petrol pumps. Everybody piled into the adjoining shop, including the driver.

Imogen closed her eyes. She knew she would not be able to sleep while they were on the road, but she might be able to doze a little during these few brief minutes. It was when her eyes were closed, though, that she realised she was not in fact alone at all. Everyone had stepped off the coach—except one. She glanced over her shoulder at the shape of the old man in the corner; the man called Joseph Spector.

"You don't seem especially enamoured of Madame La Motte." His voice was quite soft and melodious, yet it carried a certain authority.

"I beg your pardon?" she rejoindered sharply.

"The curse of aging," he offered somewhat whimsically. "One notices things one oughtn't, and feels a compulsion to announce them to the world."

"Not sure I follow," said Imogen. A doze was now out of the question. She turned all the way around in her seat and looked at him properly. He was leaning forward in a slightly stooped, inquisitive attitude, his long fingers threaded round the silver skull that topped his cane. Imogen wondered if he was really as old as Francis Tulp thought he was. Perhaps he feigned a certain degree of decrepitude to wrong-foot people. It had certainly worked on Imogen.

"I understand you are something of an occultist," she said.

"An investigator," he amended.

"Not a believer, then?"

"Oh, I believe in many things. Belief is integral to magic, after all."

Imogen considered this, and concluded it was no answer to her question. "You know Madame La Motte?"

"Her work, certainly. And I used to see her at OPC gatherings. These days she tends to run with an altogether different crowd."

Imogen adopted a different tack. "So what brings *you* to Devil's Neck, Mr. Spector?"

"I first visited the place decades ago. I'm long overdue for a return visit. Ghosts get lonely, after all."

"So you *do* believe?"

"In ghosts? Or spirits?" Spector asked wryly. "As Madame La Motte points out, the two are not the same thing."

This was the sort of statement Adaline La Motte made with disconcerting frequency. She did it when challenged by a sceptic at one of her "readings." Imogen smiled at this little in-joke she now shared with Spector. "You haven't answered the question."

"No," he conceded, "I haven't, have I?"

"And what about Francis Tulp? He says he attended one of your 'investigations' in the past."

"I thought I spied Francis. He's ever so keen. And he really *does* believe. It's a shame to see a sound intellect squandered, though I suppose it's understandable."

Imogen smiled. Spector's cynicism was oddly refreshing. "I imagine you have certain opinions regarding Madame La Motte."

He grinned in return. "Well, she's a bloviating con artist, as I'm sure you know. But then," he spread his fingers, "so am I."

"What about the other passengers?"

"You're curious about the man who arrived late, aren't you? I saw you watching him."

"His name is Walter Judd. Have you ever met him before?"

Spector shook his head.

"Quite a mismatched crowd, to be spending a weekend in a haunted house," Imogen commented.

"Indeed," said Spector.

At that moment, the driver boarded the coach once more and resumed his seat at the wheel without a word. He was followed sharply by Francis Tulp, who made a show of recognising Spector and came over to shake his hand.

"Mr. Spector, I thought I spotted you back here. I see you've met Miss Drabble."

"Please join us," said Imogen.

"Glad to see you again, Francis," said Spector.

Francis Tulp sat, his expression a little sheepish. That is when it occurred to Imogen that not only did the young man hold Spector in high esteem, he was also a little frightened of him. Why, she wondered? He seemed to her a harmless old ham.

"I had a feeling I might see you on this trip, Francis," commented Spector. "Devil's Neck has a lot to offer the inquisitive, and the fearless."

"There are few places quite so notorious," agreed Francis, "save Borley Rectory, perhaps."

"The last time I came out to Devil's Neck," said Spector, "it was in the company of Harry Price. The place will have changed a great deal since then, naturally. After all, there has been a war in between. But I imagine the atmosphere will remain . . . as it was."

"You know a lot about the house, then?" said Imogen.

"I believe I know as much about the place as anybody alive."

"Why is it called 'Devil's Neck'?"

Spector grinned widely. Evidently Imogen had followed her cue to the letter. "It's an interesting story. At least, I find it so. The house was constructed in 1640 by Adolphus Latimer, the mystic. Until that time, no one had dared to build on that precarious bit of land. But that was Latimer—ever the nonconformist. He was an alchemist, so they say."

At that moment, Spector struck a match to light the end of his cigarillo. It gave his face, underlit by the thin flame, a sinister, Mephistophelian look. Tulp and Imogen exchanged a glance.

"They say the ultimate goal of alchemy is the unification of opposites," the old conjuror continued. "And not long after he settled at Devil's Neck, Adolphus Latimer encountered *his* opposite: the Puritan witch finder Samuel Draycott. The two men were bitter enemies from the start. Where Latimer was licentious, Draycott was abstinent. Where Latimer possessed an inquiring mind, Draycott was as cloistered as they come.

"On the mainland, all kinds of stories about Latimer's activities spread among superstitious residents. There were rumours that he conjured demons, that he devoured human flesh as a means of prolonging his life, and that he used syncretic spells to divine the future. Naturally, this attracted the attention of Draycott.

"Samuel Draycott, incidentally, was a soldier of the Civil War. He made a name for himself as a ruthless assassin and a savage on the battlefield, in spite of his young age. They say he orchestrated the Tadstone Massacre, which endeared him to Oliver Cromwell. When his father died, Draycott inherited a tidy sum and set himself up as a country squire of sorts. He was of Puritan stock, so when the Essex Witch Trials took place, I imagine he felt duty bound to participate. Soon enough, he established a reputation as the scourge of heretics. A fierce iconoclast. He began travelling the country, hunting witches. That is what led him to Devil's Neck."

"But you haven't told me how the place acquired its name," cut in Imogen.

"I am about to. Draycott became a little too ambitious. He hunted down a supposed coven of witches in a nearby town and oversaw the hanging of some forty-six women in the square. He then seized the opportunity to deliver a fire-and-brimstone sermon in which he vowed that the next neck to break would belong to the devil himself. It was this affront, supposedly, that attracted the unfriendly scrutiny of Adolphus Latimer.

"Rumours spread that Latimer had placed a curse on Draycott. Eventually, the witch finder came out to the house to confront Latimer in person. He came on horseback, riding out across the causeway. And, in spite of various warnings, he did so without his retinue. Evidently he was overtaken by a wave of righteous fury, and felt compelled to act swiftly." Spector smiled. "Perhaps he should have waited.

"You see, he did not quite make it to the house at Devil's Neck. He was traversing the narrow causeway when he encountered . . . something. Something terrible. The few eyewitnesses on the mainland gave descriptions of a man rising from the water; a man in strange garb—a robe of rich purple. A spectral figure, waving its arms. And his face (so they said) was a mask of blood. Whatever it was, this phantom figure, it startled the horse, causing the creature to rear up, bucking Draycott clear off its back. He landed in the water and was washed away before anyone could get to him. And, when his body washed ashore again days later, the head was lolling loosely, the neck cleanly broken."

"So it's a lesson in hubris," Imogen commented, ignoring Spector's gleefully gruesome description.

"One could interpret it that way, perhaps. But it might also simply be a reminder of the immutability of evil. It goes without saying that no trace of the spectral figure was ever found. And yet the descriptions given by the eyewitnesses were so vivid, and tallied so exactly. A curious mystery. Thenceforth the island was commonly called Devil's Neck. It's had a reputation ever since—a place where the devil holds sway."

"What happened to Adolphus Latimer?"

"A very good question. I wish I could answer it. Unfortunately, nobody knows precisely what became of the alchemist. The death of Samuel Draycott led to considerable consternation among the God-fearing residents of the mainland, and a mob of sorts was convened. Flaming torches, all the usual trappings. But, by the time they got out to the house, the place was completely empty—not a living soul around. Latimer's servants, too, had all vanished. It was a remarkable scene. The house was otherwise completely undisturbed, as though the residents had simply stepped outside for a moment or two. There were candles burning, there was a stew bubbling away on the fire. And in Latimer's study they found his book."

"What book?"

"After his disappearance, it emerged that Latimer had been writing a book called the *Liber Daemonum. The Book of Demons.* There is only one copy in existence; the same copy that was found at Devil's Neck that day. It is bound, so they say, in human skin. The covers have a rough, leathery texture . . ."

"You've held the book yourself, then?"

"Held it? My dear Miss Drabble, I own it. When we get back to London, feel free to pay me a visit in Putney and I shall be glad to show it to you. My library consists of all manner of incunabula; Elias Ashmole's *Theatrum Chemicum Britannicum*, the *Picatrix*, the *Pseudomonarchia Daemonum*—that one contains a list of sixty-nine demons, complete with methods for summoning them. Then there's Johannes Hartlieb's *Book of All Forbidden Arts, Superstition, and Sorcery*, Giordano Bruno's *On Magic*, the *Secretum Secretorum . . .*"

"Do you believe Latimer killed Draycott?" Imogen asked sharply, before the conjuror could grow too attached to his new subject.

"That's not for me to say," he answered. "But something did."

"So you think he was some kind of necromancer?"

Spector shrugged. "That is as apt a description as any. I feel a certain empathy for Adolphus Latimer, you know. He and I share a fascination with the unexplained. Though I have a suspicion that our underlying philosophies were somewhat different."

Francis Tulp, who had not spoken in a little while, seemed compelled to interject. "There are certain *things*," he put in, giving undue emphasis to the latter word, "which nobody can explain, nor ever will."

"Spiritualism is pervasive, like a parasite," Spector said brutally. "Bear in mind, Mr. Tulp, that every single spiritualist of the last hundred years has been exposed as a fraud in some capacity or other. The very first, the Fox sisters, admitted their table rapping was really just controlled clicking of their joints. Then there were the Davenport brothers, pioneers of the 'spirit cabinet' illusion, subsequently exposed by the great John Nevil Maskelyne, and even condemned as 'humbug' by P. T. Barnum. As for Daniel Dunglas Home, on his travels in St. Petersburg he 'dematerialised' a splendid set of emeralds, only for the 'spirits' to refuse to give them back! Make no mistake: it is a shoddy, shabby business, designed purely to exploit the gullible."

"Surely magicians do the same thing?" said Imogen, feeling an urge to stir the pot.

If Spector was affronted (she had thought he might be) he didn't show it. "With quite different ends, Miss Drabble. Quite different. I have never claimed to be anything but an illusionist. And a well-executed illusion *is* magic in the way that a great symphony or a Shakespearean soliloquy is magic. A glimpse into a better world. Understand this: Magic and spiritualism are not bedfellows. They are enemies.

"Take a look at this," said Spector, producing a coin before Tulp could argue. "An ordinary double-header. See?" On one side was the king's head, and turning it over on his palm, Spector revealed a second identical head. "Now watch." He gripped the coin between thumb and forefinger of his right hand, then gave it a flick with his left forefinger, causing it to spin. When it stopped, the king's head was upside down. He performed the operation again, and now the head was facing upward, nose to the sky. Once more, and it was looking downward. "See," he took the coin and bit into it, revealing it was solid metal. "The coin is hard as rock, and yet the head changes position with each spin."

"How?" asked Tulp.

"Easy enough. Sleight of hand, the magician's greatest ally. The *illusion* is that both sides of the coin are identical to begin with. In fact, while one head faces to the left, as on a normal coin, the other faces upward, as though His Majesty were lying down. In other words, positioned at a ninety-degree angle to its opposite. Then, careful placement of the thumb and forefinger controls the axis on which the coin spins, and therefore the final direction in which the head is facing. So, the coin itself attracts the eye, when really it is the performer's fingers that control the illusion. Like all magic, it relies on an assumption."

"Which is?"

"That you may believe the evidence of your own eyes," said Spector, pocketing the coin.

"And what of the actual, tangible evidence? There's plenty of it to go around, you know, Mr. Spector."

"Oh, I'm sure."

"Take the famous Combermere Photograph, for instance," Tulp persisted. "The shadowy figure in the chair at Combermere Abbey. You know that photograph was taken the very day of Lord Combermere's funeral? Perhaps even the moment his earthly remains were being lowered into the earth. You can't seriously claim it to be a trick of the light—the very image of the dead man appearing in his chair *during* his own funeral?"

"It was not an image of the man," said Spector. "It was the image of *a* man. A thin, translucent outline of a bald head and a beard. You do know that the photograph was taken almost fifty years ago? That it required at least an hour for the exposure to take, and that anyone might have entered the room and sat in the chair while that was going on?"

"The entire household was at the funeral!"

"Evidently not."

"All right—so you don't accept the Combermere Photograph. What about the Raynham Hall one? The Brown Lady? That was only three years ago, for heaven's sake."

Spector nodded, accepting the challenge. "Yes. The 'Brown Lady'—so called because of her brocade dress, isn't that so? She has been seen plenty of times over the last century. I think there is a story that she is Sir Robert Walpole's sister, am I right?"

"Yes. But you can't claim that it's just suggestion. I interviewed Captain Provand, who took the photograph. I saw the negatives! Nothing untoward there."

"No? I must say, Mr. Tulp, photographic evidence in these cases is seldom to be trusted. There are such things as double exposure, you know, to account for a spectral shape. And even if that is ruled out, it's been suggested that a blob of grease on the camera lens could have created the amorphous outline of the late Dorothy Walpole . . ."

But Tulp was not to be bested. For each refutation, he fired back with a new and (to him, at least) damning piece of evidence. They sparred for a while longer, while the rain hammered the coach. Eventually, and perhaps wisely, Spector changed the subject. "You are a little young to remember the Great War, I imagine."

Tulp was nonplussed. "Yes," he said, "I was only six when it started."

"Too young for active service, then." Spector smiled. "I suppose one could say you've always lived in the shadow of that great tragedy. That's where you and I differ, you see. *You* cannot remember a time before the ghosts."

"It's a different time, that's true. But a time when more things are possible than ever before. Technology enables us to accomplish so much. Did you know Thomas Edison was hard at work on an electronic device which would enable him to converse with the spirits when he died?"

Spector offered a sly smile. "That sounds very fitting. No doubt the great inventor found the easiest way to speak with the dead was to become one himself."

"Scoff all you like, Mr. Spector," said Tulp, glancing somewhat irritably in Imogen's direction. "As far as I'm concerned, the pursuit of knowledge is one of the noblest there is."

"I agree completely," said an equable Spector. "However, it's also important to note that knowledge and the *pursuit* of knowledge are not the same thing. An unanswered question is not proof of anything."

"There are plenty of answers out there," said Tulp, determined to be argumentative.

"There are," agreed Spector. "There are plenty of right answers, and also plenty of *wrong* answers. Reason enables us to distinguish between the two."

Imogen concurred with everything the old man had said, and yet she'd begun simultaneously to nurture a sneaking admiration for Francis Tulp, who spoke with such conviction.

Spector, sensing that he'd won the argument—for now, at least—lapsed into happy silence as the bus rumbled to life, and the band of travellers resumed their ill-fated journey toward Devil's Neck.

CHAPTER FOUR

"MY WICKED SHADE"

The boundaries which divide Life from Death are at best shadowy and vague. Who shall say where the one ends, and where the other begins?

—Edgar Allan Poe, "The Premature Burial"

August 31, 1939. 4 P.M.

O nce the photographs had been taken and the surfaces dusted, Flint ordered the study to be cleared of constables.

"What about the body, sir?" asked Hook. "They're waiting to move it."

"Tell them they can wait a while longer. And go to the telephone box on the corner, Hook, and see if you can get hold of Spector."

When he was alone with the corpse, Flint made a very slow and considered circuit of the room. It ought to have been such a simple thing. A man with a troubled past snaps one day, frightens off his household, then blows his brains out. But there were curious echoes—the death of Dominic Edgecomb in 1914, a murder disguised as a suicide. And now the prime suspect (indeed, the only suspect) in that twenty-five-year-old murder lay dead in identical circumstances.

Flint stood and wondered.

At first glance, it was impossible. Flint was the first across the threshold into a house that was locked and bolted on the inside. And inside that house, at the top of the stairs, the study was *also* locked on the inside. He paid close attention to the arrangements of the furniture but spotted nothing untoward. The bureau along the right-hand wall, with the dead man slumped over it. A fireplace opposite the door, with a cast-iron fireguard. A slightly smaller desk to the left of the door, presumably where the secretary had sat.

Finally conceding defeat, Flint left the study and descended the steps at a heavy-footed trudge. The secretary, Miss Estelle Rainsford, had been readmitted to the house and was currently in the kitchen drinking hot, sweet tea. She had been informed of her employer's death. Flint judged this an opportune moment to make inroads with his questioning.

"Miss Rainsford," he said, pulling up a chair at the kitchen table, "mind if I pour some tea?"

"Please help yourself," she answered.

Flint filled a cup and scooped in three cubes of sugar. "You've had quite a day," he commented.

"I have. And now Mr. Edgecomb is dead. It's a shame, of course, but in a way I suppose he's better off."

Flint was shocked. "What makes you say that?"

FLOOR PLAN:
RODNEY EDGECOMB'S STUDY,
CROOK O'LUNE STREET

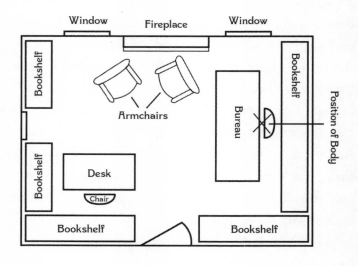

Window   Fireplace   Window

Bookshelf

Bookshelf

Armchairs

Bureau

Position of Body

Bookshelf

Desk

Chair

Bookshelf   Bookshelf

"Oh, it doesn't do to speak ill of the dead, of course. But there was something very wrong with Mr. Edgecomb. If *this* hadn't happened, it would only have got worse."

"What was wrong with him?"

She glanced right and left, like a schoolgirl telling a fireside ghost story. "His mind, Mr. Flint. He was going mad."

"How so?"

She braced herself. It was evidently an unpleasant topic, and one she would never have dared broach in her employer's lifetime. "He'd been talking a lot about someone coming after him. Hence the revolver. And all the strange new security measures. But it was all in his head. He had these nightmares, you know. They woke him up screaming. He'd been seeing a *psychiatrist*." She uttered the last word in a whisper, as though this were the dirtiest of the late Edgecomb's secrets.

"Oh yes? Do you know the name?"

"Of course. I made all of his appointments for him. It's Dr. Rees, over in Dollis Hill."

Flint nodded and made a note, though this was purely for show. He was already acquainted with Dr. Rees.

Miss Rainsford sipped from her steaming teacup, and at that moment the valet, whose name was Horsepool, came into the room. A preliminary statement had been taken by one of the constables, and he, too, had been readmitted to the house.

"Ah," said Flint, "Mr. Horsepool. Good of you to join us."

A brief yet telling look passed between valet and secretary.

"Won't you sit at the table?"

"I'll stand if it's all the same to you, sir."

"As you like. I understand you've both provided statements to one of my constables, so now I should like you to give me a more—how shall I put it?—*personal* account of today's events. What about you, Horsepool? Care to set the ball rolling?"

The valet steeled himself. It was clear he was unaccustomed to being the centre of attention, and that he did not care for it in the slightest. "I packed his things, Inspector. He had informed me that he was planning a weekend trip."

"Where to?"

"I'm afraid I couldn't say for sure, sir. It was all rather hastily arranged."

"*I* can tell you where he was going," put in Miss Rainsford, "because I arranged the ticket myself. *And* made the reservation."

Flint waited, eyebrows raised.

"He was going to an old house called Devil's Neck."

"I think I've heard of it," said Flint. "Wasn't it a hospital in the War?"

"That's the one," said Miss Rainsford. "When Mr. Edgecomb found out the place was newly open to paying guests, he asked me to make the arrangements as quickly as possible. Well, he didn't exactly ask. He demanded. He said it was a matter of the utmost importance."

"Why?"

"That is where my knowledge falters. But I have reason to believe he spent some time there as a patient during the War. He had that scar on his forehead, after all."

Flint nodded. "All right. So he was to be going out there today?"

"The reservation was made for a seat on the three P.M. coach."

"And he didn't tell either of you *why* it was so imperative that he visit the old hospital?"

"No."

"All right. Then why don't you tell me what *did* happen?"

The secretary and valet glanced at one another again, and then the valet began: "The morning started in a perfectly ordinary fashion, sir. I was not aware of anything untoward when I took the master his breakfast. He said he would be working in the study for a while."

"Working on what?" Flint turned to Miss Rainsford.

"He dictated a few letters," she explained, "to his solicitor."

"The solicitor's name, please?"

"Mr. Pepperdine, of Pepperdine, Struthers, & Mull. But he also made a few notes in his journal. And he did begin to grow somewhat distracted as the morning wore on. The post arrived at ten thirty, and there was a letter which seemed to disturb him."

Flint pounced on this. "A letter? What letter?"

"I'm afraid I don't know the contents. It was a handwritten letter, I know that much."

"*I* delivered the letter to him, sir," said the valet, "and I saw that the envelope bore no return address, and a local postmark. There was nothing more to it than that, I'm afraid."

"I see. And you think there was something in this letter that drove him mad?"

"I didn't say that," added Miss Rainsford, "only that it was *after* the letter's arrival that he began to act strangely."

"What happened to the letter?"

"He burned it. Put a match to it, and let it curl and blacken in the ashtray on his desk. That was rather unusual, as Mr. Edgecomb was normally most assiduous when it came to keeping his correspondence in order. He would not have burned a letter unless its contents were particularly . . . unwelcome."

Flint nodded and made a note of this. "What happened after that?"

"He began to grow visibly nervous, Inspector. He got up and started to pace, whereas previously he had simply sat at his desk to dictate. He kept glancing at the clock. He seemed to be waiting for something."

"But he gave you no indication as to what he was waiting for?"

She shook her head, then turned to the valet, who briefly took over the account. "In recent days the master had been somewhat . . . susceptible to his imagination. He perceived threats where there were none."

Flint looked curiously at the two employees, then said, "How can you be sure of that?"

"Only the evidence of my eyes," said the valet.

"And what happened then?"

Miss Rainsford resumed the story. "It was twelve noon. The clock on the mantelpiece began to chime, and Mr. Edgecomb got out of his seat and peered out the window. He was looking out at the garden, and he was muttering something."

"What?"

"It sounded to me like 'not yet, not yet.'"

"And what was he looking at?"

"I'm afraid I don't know. I was sitting at my typewriter, so I couldn't see."

Flint turned to the valet. "And you? Did you see anything outside the house?"

"I'm afraid not, sir."

Flint turned to Hook, who had tried and failed to reach Spector by telephone. "Get one of the men to have a look around outside. See if there's anything to indicate anyone approaching the house via the garden."

Hook leaned in close to his superior and said confidentially, "There won't be much left, sir, what with the rain, and the constables' boots tramping through."

"All the same, I'd like you to look."

"Yes, sir." And Hook withdrew again.

Returning to his two witnesses, Flint decided on a different tactic. "Did you know that Edgecomb kept a revolver in his desk?"

Miss Rainsford shook her head, but the valet just said, "Yes, sir. It was his service revolver. From the War. He was a captain, I believe."

"But you, Miss Rainsford, you'd never seen it?"

"No. I never had cause to look in his desk."

A lie, Flint supposed. "And when did he produce the revolver today?"

She seemed to blench at the memory. "It was . . . shortly after that. Shortly after he looked out the window, I mean. He was listening, as though he could hear footsteps. But I couldn't hear a sound. He told me to stop typing and to continue taking notes in pencil. But then he told me to stop that, too, so that he could hear. Finally, he reached into the drawer and came out with the revolver. I just screamed, I didn't know what to do. Then he pointed the thing at me, so I got up and ran."

"I heard Miss Rainsford's scream," put in the valet, "so I came to see what the matter was. I was just in time to see her descending the staircase and disappearing out the front door."

"What did you do then?"

"I—foolishly, perhaps—went to the study. I could hear the master in there, marching up and down."

"You knocked on the door?"

"I did."

"Then what?"

"He came out onto the landing. There was a certain . . . mania about him. It was most disquieting. We exchanged a few words—"

"Such as?"

"I rather think I said, 'What seems to be the matter, sir?' and he simply told me to get out. 'Out,' he said, 'or you'll be next.'"

"And what did he mean by that?"

"I'm sure I couldn't say, sir. I had little choice but to obey his wishes—I left the house in Miss Rainsford's footsteps."

Flint nodded. This story was a messy patchwork of information; he needed to step back from it to observe the fullness of the tapestry. "When did you begin working for Mr. Edgecomb?" he asked Miss Rainsford.

"About a year ago. He seemed quite all right then, Inspector. A little subdued and secretive, but that was all."

"Did he ever talk to you about his past?"

"Not really. Wasn't much to tell, I don't think."

"He never mentioned his family, or his life before the War?"

"Nothing like that, no."

"Do you know what he did for work? Or where his money came from?"

"His business dealings, I assumed. He always had that air about him."

"Have you ever heard of the Aitken inheritance?"

"Why, no. Ought I to have done?"

Flint smiled reassuringly. "No reason why you should. It was just a thought." He turned his attention to the valet. "And you? What did you know of his finances?"

The man coughed slightly awkwardly into his balled-up fist and said, "I'm afraid I cannot say for certain, sir. It did not seem germane to enquire."

Flint nodded, though this was highly unsatisfactory. "All right. Let's return to the circumstances of Mr. Edgecomb's death. The study was locked on the inside when we entered the house. Presumably you both have a spare key?"

Horsepool and Miss Rainsford nodded.

"And where are these keys?"

"Mine, sir," answered Horsepool, removing a thin brass key from his trouser pocket.

"And mine," said Miss Rainsford, extracting hers from the hip pocket of her dress.

"You both had your keys about your person at all times?"

The two nodded. They were both outside the house when the shot was fired, making illicit ingress improbable, perhaps even outright impossible. If, as Flint was coming to suspect, the death of Rodney Edgecomb was not self-inflicted, the solution lay elsewhere. Because there was only one key inside the house in Crook

O'Lune Street when Edgecomb died, and it was the key that now protruded from the lock of the study door; protruded, in fact, on the inside.

There are plenty of means by which a door may be unlocked and then resealed from the outside. Some are so simple as to be outright insulting (the key gripped through the keyhole with tongs, and turned from outside, the lock manipulated through the wood with a strong magnet), while others are subtle to a fault (a careful arrangement of objects to simulate a locked door—wedges and the like—or perhaps a skilful misdirection on the part of the murderer to guide attention elsewhere *after* the room has been accessed, so that a stolen key may be replaced, or substituted, or . . .).

"Mr. Horsepool," Flint said suddenly, "may I ask for your key, please?"

The valet relinquished it willingly, "And now yours please, Miss Rainsford." She handed it over. "Your keys are *always* about your person?" he repeated. "They never leave your sight?"

When pushed, neither could swear to it. This meant that there could (*could!*) have been a switch at some point. An assailant *may* have pilfered the key from either of them, had a copy made, and returned the original at some later point. But nobody could have done this without leaving a trace.

"Were there any other regular visitors to the house?"

"None spring to mind," said Miss Rainsford.

But Horsepool was not so immediately forthcoming.

"Horsepool?" Flint prompted. "What say you?"

"With due respect to Miss Rainsford," he said haltingly, "there *was* someone."

A mysterious visitor! At last, a development of some practical use. Even, perhaps, a suspect. "I see. And who was it?"

"A gentleman named Judd, sir."

Flint scribbled the name. "Judd. Who is he?"

"I'm afraid I cannot give any particulars, sir. But I can tell you that he began visiting Mr. Edgecomb last month—always at night. During the last week or so, he has stopped by every evening. He arrives at nine o'clock sharp—after Miss Rainsford has retired to bed, of course."

"Did he have a first name, this Judd?"

"I am not aware of it, sir."

"So it's safe to say these little meetings were conducted in secret?"

Horsepool nodded. "I believe I was the only one apart from the two gentlemen who knew about them."

"And what did they discuss?"

"I cannot say, sir. While I facilitated the meetings by admitting Mr. Judd to the house, I was never present for the actual discussions. *They* all took place behind closed doors, in Mr. Edgecomb's study."

"And was there a meeting last night?"

"Yes, sir."

"Do you know if one was arranged for tonight?"

"I do not, sir. Mr. Edgecomb did not tend to share such plans with me. But I should not be at all surprised."

"And you saw this Judd? Got a good look at him? What I'm driving at is, could you identify him if you saw him again?"

"I believe so, Inspector."

"Good. Good. I want you to give a description to Sergeant Hook here. All right?"

"Of course, sir."

Flint made notes of all this new information, but he seemed to have reached the summit of his witnesses' knowledge concerning their late employer's comings and goings. Next, he gave the order for Edgecomb's body to be removed. He waited at the bottom of the stairs while two constables carried the shrouded cadaver down the angular staircase and out through the front door to the ambulance. Then he headed back up to the study and found that Sergeant Hook had beaten him to it.

"You're thinking what I'm thinking, aren't you, Hook?"

"No suicide note, sir."

Flint nodded, sidling over to the desk. "And he seems to have been a prolific correspondent in other quarters of his life." Heaped atop the bureau were numerous leather-bound journals. "These will make interesting reading, I imagine." He seized the topmost volume and skimmed through it.

The room was crammed with ledgers, papers, and books, though most of these proved wholly useless. There were only a few items that might have any conceivable relevance to Edgecomb's death. The most obvious was a diary. Flint took it over to the fireplace and settled himself in an armchair to give it his sedulous and undivided attention. It began as a record of appointments. As he leafed through the pages Flint found that Edgecomb had started to use the book as a place to scribble the occasional idea or passing thought.

MAY 3RD: Strange dream.
MAY 7TH: Bethnal Green. 217???

The abundance of question marks caught Flint's eye. And what of Bethnal Green?

As the year progressed, Edgecomb's musings grew more substantial, though less coherent. He seemed preoccupied with his dreams.

> *JULY 12TH: Woke up most dreadfully afraid—drenched in sweat—the same dream—must do something or shall go mad.*
>
> *A visit from my wicked shade—what is to be done about him? He will be the death of me, I know it. He haunts me like a spirit. I shall never be rid of him, I know, unless I take certain actions in the matter.*
>
> *Dreams again.*

Aside from the occasional ramblings, there emerged a few other instructive details. August 12 had "Meeting w. Pepperdine."

There was no mention anywhere of the gentleman called Judd.

Closing the diary, Flint took another look around the room. It was a study like so many others he had visited, even down to the artfully woven Aubusson rug with elaborate crimson-and-gold latticework pattern beneath his feet. The chandelier above was unlit, but Flint observed its crisscrossed branches strung with teardrop-shaped crystal shards. There was a notable absence of human faces on the walls: no photographs, nor even a painting of some long-dead ancestor. The only ornamentation of this variety was a japonaiserie lacquer panel on the left-hand wall depicting a hummingbird. Flint, who had come across countless similar arrangements in his time, approached the panel and—delicately—pried it from the wall to peek behind. But there was nothing there. Only a slightly paler pink rectangle where the surrounding wallpaper was begrimed with dust motes.

The remaining walls were only bookshelves, floor to ceiling. Flint, who had never quite outgrown adventure tales of secret passages and smugglers' coves, could not resist the urge to remove a book or two from a shelf at head height, but nothing happened; no sudden moan of ancient clockwork mechanisms; no dark occlusion yawning open behind a concealed door. All told, it was a room of positively painful ordinariness. Flint's often educative conversations with Joseph Spector over the years had taught him that rooms like this usually harboured the most startling secrets.

He went over to the door, which now hung open, and examined the keyhole. The key still protruded on the inside. He removed it carefully, with a gloved hand, and inserted the key which had been given to him by Horsepool. It turned freely. He repeated the procedure with Miss Rainsford's key; again, the lock yielded. So there had been no substitution. At least, not after the fact.

Still crouched and peering through that keyhole, he called over Sergeant Hook. "Go downstairs and fetch Horsepool, will you?"

Hook did, and returned with the valet a moment later. Flint got to his feet. "How easily may the windows be opened?" he enquired.

"From the outside, with great difficulty, sir," answered Mr. Horsepool.

"Not impossible?"

"I shouldn't care to speak definitively on the subject, sir. But I should deem it unlikely."

"Quite so." Flint peered out and saw there was no convenient drainpipe up which an assailant might have shimmied, nor even the odd declivity in the brickwork that could have acted as a hand- or foothold. "It's bolted on the inside, and the one over there is the same. Is there any means you are aware of by which these windows *could* be accessed from outside, no matter how improbable it might seem?"

The answer was a resounding negative.

"And what about the fireplace?"

"Completely inaccessible," Horsepool assured him. "You see, the fireguard is screwed into the wall."

"Why?"

"There was an incident, sir," said the valet. "Last spring, a pigeon flew down the chimney and entered the study, creating a considerable fracas. Mr. Edgecomb was keen to prevent that from recurring."

Flint nodded to himself. "All right, Horsepool, you may go."

When the valet was gone, Flint pulled shut the study door so that he and Hook were alone in the murder room. Hook continued his assiduous but aimless business of cataloguing all the books on the shelves. Flint began to pace. He was chewing on his pipe again, and his contemplative amble took him over to the large, ostentatious stone fireplace. It was shielded from view by a cast-iron fireguard, secured to the wall on either side by spring clips attached to eyelets which were cemented in place—just as the valet had described. There was a gap of only four or five inches between the top of the fireguard and the underside of the lintel.

"Has this fireguard been checked for fingerprints?" he asked Hook.

"Yes, sir."

"Anything?"

"No, sir."

Flint turned to scrutinise his sergeant. "Nothing at all?"

"No, sir."

Flint removed one of the spring clips and eased the guard away from the fireplace. As he did this, he felt a slight dent in the upper part of the metal frame, as though a hard object had collided with it at some point. The fire itself had been burning pleasantly when they burst into the room, but had since gone out. All that remained now were blackened logs—or so it appeared. At the very back of the fireplace, just below the mouth of the chimney flue, lay a handful of chipped pieces of brick which Flint sifted with interest. Where had they come from? He felt around, and soon discovered that they had broken free from the underside of the lintel, as though dislodged by some unusual force. This was a striking detail. Then, probing the fireplace detritus further, he came across several shards of glass. He delicately picked up one of these shards between his gloved fingers and examined it beneath the chandelier. It looked to have been part of a bottle.

"And there were no fingerprints on the fireguard," he repeated. He was speaking slowly and methodically, enunciating each word with the kind of precision that Joseph Spector was known for.

"Nobody could have got in or out that way, sir," Hook assured him.

"I don't doubt it. But I suspect it was not a *body* that was used in the trick. Would you believe it, Hook—I think I may have learned something in all my years with Spector after all. And I'm *convinced* this wasn't suicide. It was murder." He had returned to the desk and was looming over the dead man.

"How come, sir?"

"Our killer is not as clever as he might like us to think. Take a look at this." He swooped to retrieve the spent bullet cartridge from the floor. "See how one end is sort of crimped? This came from a *blank round*. And if this cartridge matches this weapon—which I reckon it will—then it means the shot fired from this pistol *wasn't* the one that killed Edgecomb. I think this suicide was staged, and a blank shot fired in an effort to convince us that the revolver was the murder weapon. In fact, I'd say the killer took the *real* murder weapon with him."

"Why? And why leave a blank cartridge behind, rather than the one from the actual shot that killed him?"

"Maybe Edgecomb wasn't even killed in this room. Maybe his body was carried here. There are plenty of possibilities."

"And what about the gunshot we heard? Was that the blank?"

"I have an answer for that as well. I believe that the sound we heard was not a gunshot at all. The fireguard is the clue. It was secured to the wall, and yet a glass bottle has obviously been recently dropped into the fire. The absence of fingerprints indicates it wasn't Edgecomb who dropped it in there, as of course he would have needed to remove the fireguard. Which would have left fingerprints."

Hook nodded slowly.

"I believe Rodney Edgecomb had been dead at least half an hour when we heard what we assumed was the fatal gunshot. An object was introduced into the room at an appointed moment in order to create that sound. A glass bottle, stoppered with a cork, containing a mixture of dry ice and water. Popularly known as a dry ice bomb."

"Blimey! That would make a hell of a noise."

"It would and did. The heat from the fireplace caused the bottle to explode, dispersing the carbon dioxide and leaving only the broken glass in its wake. The killer must have been on the roof, waiting for us to enter the house and gather outside the room. He could easily have got out there via one of the unsecured windows outside the study. It's only the *study* window that was inaccessible, after all—not the ones on the landing. He would have timed it to perfection, I'm sure, then dropped the bottle down the chimney. The fireguard was necessary to contain the explosion, otherwise there would have been bits of glass all over the place."

"All right . . ." Hook was gradually coming around. "But what about the locked door? The room certainly seems to have been locked on the inside, sir."

"Hmm," Flint rumbled. "*Seems* that way. But remember, if our killer used dry ice to create the sound of a gunshot, what's to stop him using it to lock the door?"

"But how?"

"Easily enough, I should have thought. If the key were encased in dry ice, with only the hasp protruding, that ice could be fashioned into a thin, pencil-like point which could be inserted into the keyhole so that it emerged from the other side. Then, with a gloved hand the killer could have twisted it from outside on the landing, locking the door with the key still on the inside. This would take a matter of seconds, and of course the ice would melt before any physical trace of it could be found. All that remained would be an invisible cloud of carbon dioxide in the air of that cramped landing—and you noticed, didn't you, that I tried to strike a match outside the door *three* times without success?"

"Sir!" Hook burst into spontaneous applause. "Sir, that's bloody marvellous. Spector would be proud."

"He might, at that," said Flint, smiling behind his moustache. "All the same, it gets us nowhere. The only thing it tells us is that somebody killed Edgecomb. And that this 'somebody' has a bit of flair about them. What's that word Spector uses? *Panache*. Get to work, Hook. There must be something in this room that tells us *who*. We've got a suspect already, of course: this mysterious 'Judd' chap. And I'll need to speak with the solicitor, Pepperdine . . ."

He paused, a look of sudden excitement crossing his face.

"Wait a moment," he said, taking another sweeping gaze about the room. "Something appears to be missing. Miss Rainsford mentioned Edgecomb was planning a trip out to Devil's Neck—a coach trip. She said the reservation and the bus ticket were in the bureau. Well, they're not there now."

"What do you think that means, sir?"

"Isn't it obvious? It means that whoever shot Rodney Edgecomb took the papers and made off with them. Perhaps they even joined the excursion under Rodney Edgecomb's name."

Hook nodded frenetically. "Yes, sir. There must be something out there that the killer's after."

"It makes sense, I suppose. But I wonder what it could be? What the hell could *anyone* want out at that old hospital all these years later? Either way, you'd better make a telephone call, Hook. See if you can get hold of the present owners of the house. Tell them we'll need to pay them a visit. But whatever you do, don't let on that a member of their weekend party is a suspected murderer."

CHAPTER FIVE

ACROSS THE CAUSEWAY

> When I had prayed sufficiently to the dead, I cut
> the throats of the two sheep and let the blood run
> into the trench, whereon the ghosts came trooping
> up from Erebus.
>
> —Homer, *The Odyssey*

August 31, 1939. 7 P.M.

The coach chugged on through the blistering rain, leaving behind cities, towns, villages, until they were deep in the salt marshes, with nothing but flatlands all around. It felt as though this unlikely little band of travellers was approaching the outermost edge of the civilised world. If one were impressionable, it would be easy to convince oneself there was something uncanny about this barren stretch of salt water and mud.

As they neared the coast, the driver expertly navigating the narrow lanes, they began to encounter the occasional hamlet of cottages, no doubt occupied by oystermen and other local tradespeople. The coast was messy, riddled with coves and damp little inlets. The land itself was both empty and curiously cluttered; bereft of people and life, yet simultaneously teeming with history, and memories. Imogen could sense the stories here; stories dating back millions of years. They were positively etched into the shells, fossils, and ancient rocks; they whistled through the tufts of grass battered back and forth by the wind.

Soon the coach was travelling uphill—the driver kept his foot a little heavy on the accelerator, causing the engine to whine shrilly—and then they were nosing their way along ragged clifftop roads while the sea battered the rocks below. As they reached the prow of the hill, Imogen caught sight of Devil's Neck for the first time. The house was a hulking shape, a creature waiting at the valley's nadir. In that deceptive darkness it seemed adrift on an island, separate from the tattered mainland, but Imogen knew there was in fact a causeway—scarcely wide enough for a horse cart, it had nonetheless been optimistically laid with cobblestones at some point over the centuries. Perpetually awash with seawater, the causeway was often totally submerged. If they were not quick enough, the bus itself might be carried away, dragged down into the depths, never to be seen again.

Imogen could see how Devil's Neck had achieved its fearsome reputation. She felt positively sick at the sight of it. The notion of spending the weekend here now felt truly demented. She fidgeted in her seat and glanced around at her fellow passengers. They seemed a band of pitiful misfits, and she was hopelessly ill-suited to their company. Because who but a misfit would willingly visit this awful place?

The bus descended into the valley, past clusters of tumbledown fishing cottages. Brittle drystone walls were the only defence against the onslaught of vicious tides. Just before they reached the causeway, Imogen glimpsed a parked car at the roadside, a grey Alvis. It was in a patch of mud, surrounded by tufted grass, and yet there were no tracks leading from its tyres; of course, Imogen half-consciously thought, it had been parked up long before the rain started. Even the Lennoxes, it seemed, had not been foolhardy enough to tackle that serpentine road on four wheels. They must have walked the causeway, before the storm.

She closed her eyes as the coach took to the cobbles, trying not to think of Samuel Draycott's strange fate, or of the figure in the purple robe, whose face was a mask of blood.

It was a bumpy few minutes and Imogen convinced herself she could hear the creaking as the wind took hold of the bus and almost lifted it off the ground entirely. In an instant, she knew, they might be washed away amid the swells and gyres of the advancing waters. Worryingly, the driver seemed a little too comfortable—even lackadaisical—with the road conditions. He kept only one hand on the steering wheel; the other looked to be hanging at his side. To distract her worried mind, Imogen turned to Francis Tulp. "What do you know about the Lennoxes?"

"Nothing" was the discouraging answer. "Don't think there's anything much to know."

"Really? I'd have thought a couple that bought a place like Devil's Neck would be inordinately interesting."

"Well . . ." For some reason he spoke in a low, confidential tone. "*Apparently* they didn't. Word has it they're just the caretakers;

they were hired by somebody else. The real owner of Devil's Neck."

"And who's that?"

He raised his eyebrows. "Your guess is as good as mine."

But before she could ponder this, the caretakers in question came into view. At least, the outline of two figures appeared through the windscreen as the coach reached the land and drew haltingly toward the house. It was a man and a woman, waiting beneath a stone portico.

Pulling the coach to a stop, the driver switched off the engine and got slowly from his seat, stretching his arms above his head till the bones cracked. He looked exhausted, which seemed at odds with his devil-may-care approach of a few minutes ago. Then he pulled the lever to open the door and stepped out.

"Nasty night out there," he said, or rather shouted, the rain stippling from the brim of his cap, drenching that curious ribbon and its bronze *croix pattée* pin.

"Quite so," answered the man.

"I wasn't sure we'd make the crossing."

"I wasn't sure either," said the man.

"Mr. Powell, is it?" said the woman. Her demeanour was chilly, her lips pinched tight so that she could scarcely move them to form words.

"That's it, ma'am. Fred Powell."

"Well, I am Justine Lennox. And this is . . ."

"Clive Lennox," said the man, who was considerably more chipper than his wife. Or was it perhaps nervousness? His eyes flitted about uncomfortably as he shook the driver's hand. "Well, let's get them inside, shall we?" Mr. Lennox was bald and unimpressive, with a pinkly sclerotic face and a toothbrush moustache. He looked quite short—shorter than his wife, at least—with narrow, slouching shoulders. His wide mouth, bulging eyes, and plump belly reminded Imogen of a melancholy toad.

Mrs. Lennox, meanwhile, was slim and rather tall—taller than her husband, anyway. Her expression matched her wardrobe—conspicuously bland.

The guests filed out of the coach and into the vast hall. Blinking the rainwater from her eyes, Imogen glimpsed an ornate brass knocker as she passed through the doorway; it was fashioned into the shape of a snake chewing on its own tail. "Ouroboros," said Spector. "The alchemical symbol of universal oneness. I would hazard a guess that this knocker dates back to the time of Adolphus Latimer."

Imogen's teeth were chattering as she strode deeper into the firelit hallway. She caught a glimpse of herself in a large antique mirror hanging above the mantel: of her small, sharp chin, thin mouth, and very dark eyes. Her hair, which was usually a sleek blonde wave, was embarrassingly fluffy in the inclement weather. Indeed, she struggled to keep her beret in place. She hugged her trench coat tight around herself but it didn't do much good. The damp and sheer misery of the place was not merely skin deep. It burrowed into the bones.

Joseph Spector had trailed behind her and was looking excitedly at the various carvings along the high walls. "You see these hexafoils etched in the stone?" He indicated a row of strange shapes—glyphs, she supposed. "They are sigils, for protection.

You'll find them placed all about the house, in certain strategic locations. For Latimer, this place was a kind of mystical fortress. I imagine he believed he could get away with anything out here, within his own circle of protection." She was only half listening, but that was all right. Spector was only half addressing her. Rather, he seemed to be speaking mainly for himself, positively overflowing with the excitement of being here, in the environs of this strange and horrible house.

Imogen moved away to listen in on another brief exchange between Clive Lennox and Powell, the driver:

"Staying the night as well are you, Mr. Powell?"

"Not much choice. The causeway'll be flooded out by now."

"Quite so. Well, the more the merrier seems to be the order of the day . . ." Though his words were friendly, his voice had that same edgy brittleness to it. "Now, if you'll excuse me."

Mr. Lennox bounded up a couple steps then turned to face his guests. "Ah-*hem*," he coughed. "Ladies and gentlemen, I'm sure you are already familiar with the history of Devil's Neck—" he began, but his words did not sufficiently project into the recesses of the echoing hall, and the guests struggled to hear him.

"Speak up, won't you?" called Madame La Motte.

Mr. Lennox flushed bright red, then cleared his throat a second time. "Of course. Do forgive me. Perhaps my *wife* would care to say a few words? She does it so much better than I . . ."

He mumbled a few more things as he skulked back down the steps, and Imogen felt mortified on his behalf. Mrs. Lennox, looking imperious, took his place. "Welcome to Devil's Neck," she commenced. "Constructed in approximately 1630 by Adolphus

Latimer, the famed mystic, the place has gone through all manner of changes over the years. On this murky land, with only a causeway tethering it to the mainland, it would be easy to abandon or forget about such a place. But, against all odds, Devil's Neck has weathered the storm. Most recently, it was used as a convalescent home for wounded soldiers during the Great War, and was in some respects a fully functioning hospital. Pioneering surgeons from all across the country were brought here to rebuild the bodies, minds, and faces of our heroes." She recited all this somewhat gloomily, and it was obviously a spiel which had been rewritten and edited at some length.

"The hospital closed in 1925. Since then—for fourteen years, in fact—it has lain empty, waiting for the right people to bring it back to life."

Her eyes drifted over the faces of those assembled, suddenly distrait. They settled on Joseph Spector, who gazed back impassively.

"No doubt you're tired," she concluded, "and would like to get some rest. Your rooms are prepared for you upstairs; however, tea will first be served in the drawing room."

"Tea . . ." said Madame La Motte, suddenly clinging to Imogen's arm as though she might collapse. "What *I* should like best is a cup of tea . . ."

Fred Powell sized up Mr. Lennox. "You can help with the luggage," he said. Lennox flinched a little, uncomfortable that he should be the object of attention again.

"Of course, of course . . ." he murmured, following the driver toward the door and out into the rain.

"I'd better tag along," said Tulp to nobody in particular. "I'd hate to see my equipment bashed about." He trailed after them.

Madame La Motte had already disappeared into the lounge, followed swiftly by Walter Judd and Joseph Spector. Imogen's attention drifted in the direction of the only traveller who had not spoken a word throughout the entire journey: the mysterious Mrs. Bailey. Mrs. Bailey smiled at her, but Imogen did not return it. They went into the lounge to join the others, pursued by Mrs. Lennox.

The lounge was as large and unfriendly as the hall, yet some effort had obviously been made with the soft furnishings. Imogen found herself perched on a divan with surprisingly luxuriant upholstery, looking at a baby grand piano in the opposite corner. Whose idea was the piano, she wondered? The other furniture was shabby enough to be authentic, but not appealing enough to be an antique. It was, she supposed, "lived-in." A drinks cabinet, a coffee table, assorted lounge chairs arranged around the fireplace. While Justine Lennox served the tea, Imogen found herself looking at Mrs. Bailey again and wondering about her.

She tried to picture the house as it would have been during the War, with rows of hospital beds, crisp sheets, bedpans. Now, the place was plain and empty, though clearly somewhat battle-scarred. The floorboards between the elaborate rugs were damp and scuffed. Imogen closed her eyes briefly, and imagined the *swish* of nurses' starched uniforms, the rhythmic *clunk* of crutches on the ground . . .

She opened her eyes, and at that same moment the entire house was smothered by a scrim of darkness—every light in the place was extinguished at a stroke and there was only the shuffle of bodies, the grumble of voices, the spatter of rain on the windows, and the sudden closeness of the dark. Even the fireplace embers did little to alleviate the dense blackness. During those moments—which seemed interminable—Imogen began to panic. It was the darkness of the grave, she convinced herself; the darkness of death. Instinctively she rose from her seat, raised her hands, and felt her way forward a few steps. She stopped when her fingertips brushed a man's shoulder.

"Who's that?"

"It's Francis." Tulp sounded as distressed as she. He must have entered the lounge just as the lights went out.

Finally, her eyes began to adjust. She made out the shape of Tulp, and of the driver, Fred Powell, standing by the door.

"There ought to be a generator around here," said Spector's voice from the other end of the room. "Mrs. Lennox . . . ?"

Before their hostess could comment, there came a shriek in a high, trilling tremolo. "He's here! He's here!"

"Who, for God's sake?" That was Walter Judd.

Madame La Motte was leaning her back against the wall, breathing in a panicked, erratic manner. She was the one who had screamed. "There," she said, pointing with a quivering, crooked finger, "by the piano. He was there."

"What did he look like?" asked Spector.

Madame La Motte, who had now caught her breath, said, "A man in a soldier's uniform. He wore a mask. It covered his face."

"A uniform and a mask," Spector ruminated. "How closely did you see him? Can you describe the mask?"

"It was one of those . . . portrait masks. The ones they made for the men with wounded faces."

Mrs. Bailey's hand flew to her mouth and she let out a cry.

Spector narrowed his eyes. "Mrs. Lennox, is there anybody else in this house apart from your husband and those who arrived by bus?"

"No, sir. Nobody."

"And do you happen to know what's wrong with the lights?"

"Generator, sir," answered Powell. "Lennox has gone to look at it."

Then, on perfect cue, the lights flickered back on. Mr. Lennox came into the room, slightly out of breath, and said, "So sorry about that. Took me a little while to find the generator. Is everything all right? I think I heard a scream . . ."

Madame La Motte was now fully composed once more. "Please, all of you, forgive me. I should not have screamed like that. Sometimes, however, the visitation takes even the medium by surprise. There is most assuredly a presence in this house. I saw him as clearly as I see you all now. The veil is thinner here than any other house I have visited. The spirits are among us. They have been waiting a long time. Evidently there is something they wish to say to us."

Mrs. Bailey, who had not spoken a word the entire time, was now quietly weeping. She got to her feet and inched toward the door. En route, she stumbled, her foot catching the edge of a large rug, causing the contents of her canvas bag to spill across the floor. The oddments came skittering out in a clatter: a comb, a purse, a makeup compact. But what immediately caught Imogen's attention, and the attention of all the other assembled guests, was the mask. Hastily, she dropped to her knees and scrabbled to retrieve it, but not before it had brought all other conversation to a halt. It was a lightweight metallic construction like so many that were issued from the so-called Tin Noses Shop after the War. It bore smooth, handcrafted features in dull enamel, and its design would cover the entirety of a man's face. Imogen could only imagine the injuries it must have concealed. It had little wire arms akin to those on a pair of eyeglasses, which would slip over the patient's ears and hold the features in place. The unfortunate fellow who wore this would have been able to remove his face as easily as spectacles. If the mask was an indicator of what had been lost beneath, then this man had lost everything. His eyes, the bridge of his nose, his mouth. A face held together with bits of string, a clay approximation of what the man had once looked like, peppered with real hair and eyelashes for added verisimilitude. No matter how meticulous and skilled the artisans were, the abiding impression was one of absence—of the empty space beneath the Plasticine and galvanised copper. The uncanniness of looking into a face that was not a face at all.

Walter Judd was standing curiously still, his gaze fixed on the mask where it lay. He took a step or two closer, as though attempting to get a better look at the features. Imogen watched the expression on his face change, but she had never been particularly adept at reading faces. Nonetheless, there was a certain indefinable alteration that lasted a second or two. Then he stooped to retrieve the mask and return it to Mrs. Bailey.

"Here," he said. She took it from him and slipped it back into the bag.

"Thank you," she said, before turning to address the generally assembled company. Her face was still streaked with tears, but she spoke clearly. "The young man you saw, Madame La Motte—I'm positive that he meant no harm. But I know why he's here. It's because of me. You see, I'm his mother."

PART TWO

MANIFESTATION

Whether the reader belongs to that majority who are incredulous upon the subject, or to that increasing minority who accept the evidence, he can hardly fail to be interested in the circumstances in which the whole strange psychic movement arose.

—Arthur Conan Doyle, "A Rift in the Veil,"
as published in *The Edge of the Unknown*

Olympia's waxen, deadly pale countenance had no eyes, but black holes instead—she was, indeed, a lifeless doll.

—E. T. A. Hoffmann,
"The Sandman"

CHAPTER SIX

A CERTAIN LEGATEE

There are always some lunatics about. It would be a
dull world without them.

—Arthur Conan Doyle,
"The Red-Headed League"

August 31, 1939. 5 P.M.

H ook had tried and failed to reach Joseph Spector via telephone, so Flint was wondering whether to send the sergeant
out to Putney in person to look for Spector at his habitual watering
hole, the Black Pig public house. Before he could act on this, however, a constable handed him a piece of paper.

"What's this?"

"Victim's personal effects, sir. Pathologist thought you'd like
to see it."

"Right you are." Flint squinted at the cramped handwriting.

Clothing
Jacket—wide lapels, three buttons (second button recently
replaced—black thread instead of navy).
Shirt—white cotton, cuff links (gold, 9ct) monogrammed:
RE
Necktie—sky-blue silk, loose Windsor knot
Trousers—turned-up cuffs, inner-waistband buttons (6)
Underclothes—vest, underpants
Dress socks—white cotton, held in place by elasticated garters
Shoes—leather dress shoes, right sole lightly scuffed, tied by
right-handed individual (evidenced by thumb loop technique)
Miscellaneous—Parker pen, inside breast pocket (jacket)
cigarette packet, Pall Mall, containing cigarettes (3),
right-hand pocket (jacket)
silver fob watch and chain, right-hand pocket (trousers)
leather wallet, left-hand pocket (trousers)
signet ring, little finger, right hand—gold (18ct), carnelian
intaglio stone bearing Edgecomb family crest

"A sharply dressed gentleman," commented Flint, pocketing the paper. He was satisfied with the locked-room murder theory, and before he left the house in Crook O'Lune Street he ordered a few constables to go door-to-door, enquiring whether the neighbours had seen anything unusual immediately *prior* to the gunshot, such as a figure on the rooftops, or traces of an intruder in one of the back gardens. This was admittedly optimistic. Rather, the likeliest explanation was that the murderer had escaped in disguise—perhaps even a police uniform. Flint reflected somewhat ruefully that even he could not say for certain how many uniformed officers had been present at the scene. A killer in disguise might easily have slipped away unnoticed. All the same, Flint did not care to let the trail go cold if it could be helped, and so he initiated a manhunt, not knowing precisely what sort of man he was after. An ordinary-looking sort, he supposed. Most killers were.

Sergeant Hook drove him out toward Maida Vale, where the offices of Pepperdine, Struthers, & Mull occupied a large, modern sandstone edifice. The office would soon be closing up for the day, a bored-looking secretary informed him when he entered the foyer.

"Not to worry," he said with some approximation of a smile, "I won't keep Mr. Pepperdine but five minutes."

After considerable vacillation from the secretary, Pepperdine was informed via intercom that there were two policemen here to see him. The solicitor grumbled something unintelligible, then said with an air of defeat, "All right, send them in."

Allan Pepperdine's barrel-like belly, no doubt sloshing with claret, strained tightly against his waistcoat as he sat with his fingers threaded meditatively across his navel, looking for all the world like a living incarnation of Buddha. "And how may we assist you today, Inspector?" the lawyer inquired punctiliously.

"A client of yours, name of Rodney Edgecomb. What can you tell me about him?"

"What would you like to know?"

"First of all, how well did you know him?"

"*Did* I know him? The past tense is ominous. I know him quite well, I should say. The fact is, he has been a client of ours since 1920. I breach no confidences by telling you that."

"You ought to know, Mr. Pepperdine, that Rodney Edgecomb is dead. He was murdered this afternoon."

"How positively dreadful." A flat, emotionless declamation. "And you, Inspector, are hot on the killer's tail. Please: ask your questions."

"Did he have any enemies?"

"We did not discuss such matters."

"Are you aware of any friends or associates Mr. Edgecomb may have had?"

"No."

Flint changed tack. "Have you ever heard of a man named Judd?"

Pepperdine shifted slightly in his seat. "Why do you ask?"

"Please answer the question, Mr. Pepperdine."

The solicitor huffed irritably. "Judd is the name of a gentleman I have had cause to employ on a freelance basis in the past."

Sensing the inspector's dissatisfaction, Pepperdine continued, "Judd's services are engaged in the event of any particularly . . . sensitive enquiry."

"He's a private investigator?"

Pepperdine sighed. He had obviously wished to avoid using the term. "Correct."

"Did he ever have any dealings with Edgecomb?"

A lengthy silence ensued, during which Flint fixed Pepperdine with an intense, unmoving stare. Finally, Pepperdine succumbed. "He asked me if I knew any private investigators. Since he has always been a good client, and I have never had any trouble with Judd, I did not hesitate to recommend his services."

"When was this?"

"A few weeks ago. I don't recall the date offhand, but my secretary will have it in her notes."

"All right," Flint said with a nod. "Did he give any indication of *why* he wanted an investigator?"

"No, no. Nothing of the sort. It was not my business, and so I did not ask. All I did was hand over Judd's business card. You will need to speak to Judd himself if you want further information."

"Do you happen to have another of his cards?"

Pepperdine produced it wordlessly from a drawer in his desk and handed it over. "Now, that really is all I can tell you on the subject of Judd's dealings with Mr. Edgecomb."

"Very well," Flint acceded, pocketing the card. "Perhaps we might change the subject slightly. When was the last time you saw Edgecomb?"

"Three days ago."

Flint frowned. "He came here?"

"Correct."

"And what did you discuss?"

"He wished to make a change in his will."

"What sort of change?"

"The removal of a certain legatee."

"Their name?"

"Mr. William McGinn."

"And who is Mr. McGinn?"

"He is not a client. My only knowledge of his existence comes from Mr. Edgecomb."

"How much would he have received on Edgecomb's death?"

"I would need to check my figures, but certainly somewhere in the region of five thousand pounds."

Hook whistled, but Flint was somewhat bemused. The Aitken inheritance, he knew, had totalled over twenty-five thousand. Weren't these rich types supposed to be adept at turning money into more money?

"That's a lot to lose out on," Hook observed.

"My thoughts exactly," said Allan Pepperdine.

"Can you tell me who replaces Mr. McGinn as the primary legatee?"

"With pleasure. The Salvation Army."

Again, Flint was puzzled. The Salvation Army? This ruled out money as a motive for a lone killer. Unless, of course, Will McGinn had not *known* he was no longer remembered in Edgecomb's will. Five thousand was certainly enough to provoke murder. All the same, Flint couldn't escape the notion that there was something a little *off* about the dead man's financial arrangements. "Who managed Mr. Edgecomb's money? I presume he didn't undertake the task himself."

"A sister firm of ours. A gentleman named Alastair Quinn."

"Where can I find Quinn?"

"He has an office across the street, in fact."

Flint nodded pensively. "All right. We'll be in touch. Come on, Hook, let's head over to see Quinn."

They traipsed across the road to an almost identical building, spoke with an almost identical secretary, and were eventually admitted to an almost identical office. Alastair Quinn, however, was the total physical opposite of the full-bellied Allan Pepperdine. Quinn was lean and athletic, clean-shaven and pomaded to within an inch of his life. Like Pepperdine, he did not seem particularly surprised at receiving a visit from two police officers; even less so when he learned the reason for said visit.

"My name is Inspector George Flint, Scotland Yard. I have a few questions about a client of yours; a Mr. Rodney Edgecomb."

"What would you like to know?" No offer of drink or cigarettes; it was as if he already knew they wouldn't linger. Perhaps Pepperdine had telephoned ahead with a warning.

"I'd like to know," said Flint, adopting the other's laconic air, "what exactly happened to the Aitken inheritance? It seems to have depleted to the tune of twenty thousand pounds."

The financier was not piqued by the line of questioning. "Unwise expenditure," he said candidly. "Mr. Edgecomb is unwilling, or perhaps unable, to heed the sound financial advice for which my office is rightfully esteemed."

"Gambling?" Flint ventured. After all, it was gambling that had caused all Edgecomb's problems back in 1914.

"Alas, no," the financier sighed, "such vices may be mitigated against. No. I'm afraid Mr. Edgecomb's problems with money are more *ephemeral* in nature."

"Meaning what?"

"Meaning he has a tendency to give away his money."

"Charitable sort?"

"Dear me, no. Again, such vices may be mitigated against. I'm afraid the recipient of Mr. Edgecomb's generosity is considerably less salubrious in nature."

"A woman?"

"Not for me to say. But the fact is, regular payments of increasing value have been made by Mr. Edgecomb on a monthly basis for well over a decade. He is frivolous—positively wanton—with his money."

"Where does it all go?"

"A bank account in Nice. And I must tell you, sir, that if it were not for my frequent intervention, the sum of Mr. Edgecomb's holdings would be significantly less than five thousand. May, in fact, have depleted to zero. Recently, the payments have simply been cashed. I would hazard a guess that the situation in Europe has made it rather difficult to facilitate transactions. It seems likely that cash payment is made instead."

"Sounds very fishy, Mr. Quinn. Like blackmail, or something similar. Why didn't you come to the police?"

Quinn remained expressionless and spoke in the same measured tone. "Because I was forbidden to do so by Mr. Edgecomb himself."

"We'll let that go for now, but you'll have more questions to answer on that topic, I assure you. You seem to be inferring that the owner of that French bank account is now *here* in England."

"Or an emissary of same." Quinn shrugged.

"How long has this been going on? The cash payments, I mean."

"Not long. A matter of months. Perhaps recent developments on the continent have prompted the payee to make the adjustment."

The situation in Europe. Developments on the continent. These euphemistic phrases sent a chill through Flint. "And there's no way you can tell me who the payee actually is?"

"Not here. Not me. But the details of the transaction may be used to trace the account. Which will of course take time."

It most certainly would—time which Flint was not altogether sure he possessed. And yet he needed that name. "And you're positive all that money has gone into one bank account?" he pressed.

"Well . . . not quite. There are other, ordinary expenses of course. And certain singular extravagances . . ."

"Such as?"

"Well, the house."

"What about the house?" Flint was picturing the place in Crook O'Lune Street, which was painfully drab and démodé. He could not imagine any particular amount of money being frittered thereon.

"Ah—I believe we're at crossed purposes. I do not refer to Mr. Edgecomb's primary residence in Crook O'Lune Street. I speak of his other, recent acquisition—the house at Devil's Neck."

Flint looked at Hook, who waggled his eyebrows questioningly.

"Devil's Neck is an old house out on a causeway in the wilds of Essex," Quinn explained. "Been there hundreds of years, but it's fallen into disrepair ever since it was used as a military hospital during the War."

"All right," Flint affirmed with a nod. "But what about now? Why on earth would Edgecomb spend money on the place?"

"Well, it seems the house has acquired a bit of a . . . reputation. Hauntings and such. The Harry Price brigade likes to make themselves at home there."

Quinn was able to give a brief account of the circumstances under which Edgecomb acquired Devil's Neck. The dead man had taken great pains to ensure his name did not appear on any documentation pertaining to the deal. The financier informed Flint that a company had been registered for just this purpose—it was the name of the company which appeared on all sales documentation.

But this was not all the eccentricity that Edgecomb had demonstrated in his activities relating to the house. He had also struck upon the odd idea of opening the place up to paying guests. To that end, he employed a married couple—the Lennoxes—to act as caretakers. It all begged a simple yet profound question: Why?

"What do you know of the Lennoxes?" asked Flint.

"Nothing whatever, I'm afraid. I was responsible only for the drawing up of the contracts. But the applicants were carefully chosen by Mr. Edgecomb. They came with the finest references from previous employers."

"Do you have those references on file?"

After several minutes, the references were in Flint's hand. Clive and Justine Lennox, a married couple, had previously worked as caretakers for Lord Congleton, acting as custodians of the Congleton estate. Declining fortunes had seen Congleton forced to sell up, but not before providing a glowing reference for the couple. They had been in his employ for seven years, he wrote, and he would be greatly sorry to see them go. Lord Congleton had recently left the country altogether, evidently none too keen on the way the wind was blowing in Europe, and had settled among a community of expats in (of all places) Kenya. He was therefore out of reach. If Flint wanted more information on the Lennoxes, he would need to find it elsewhere.

"More evidence of Edgecomb's financial inexperience," put in Quinn. "He paid considerably higher than the going rate to convince the Lennoxes to take the job."

"Why was that, do you think?"

"Your guess is as good as mine. More of that troubling erratic behaviour. And yet he's not a bad sort, you know, Inspector. I'm positive that with the right guidance his circumstances may yet be turned around."

"I dare say they might," said Flint, before breezing out of the office.

―⁓―

"What now, sir?" asked Hook, raising his voice over the sound of the hammering rain as the two men left the building.

"You pay a visit to the private investigator, Mr. Judd," said Flint, handing over the business card. "See if you can find out why Edgecomb hired him. These gumshoes can be rather obstreperous, so you'd better lay it on thick about this being a murder enquiry. Take the car—I'll hail a cab."

"Where are you off to, sir?"

Flint called out an answer as he dived into a waiting taxi, but Hook could not hear over the sound of the rain. Before he could ask his superior to repeat himself, the taxi was roaring away, its rear wheels casting wide fans of rainwater in its wake.

What Flint had said was "Dollis Hill."

―⁓―

One of the reasons Sergeant Jerome Hook and his superior got on so well was that Hook knew when to ask questions and when to simply shut up and do as he was told. This was one of the latter occasions, and so he made no bones about tracking down Judd's office, which was actually not too far from Maida Vale. Almost equidistant, really, between Crook O'Lune Street and the solicitors' offices. *This* office, however, was considerably less salubrious than the one he had just left.

The secretary had a patch over her right eye and, with her good left eye, was squinting at a sliver of paper protruding from the top of the typewriter. At ever-lengthening intervals, she prodded one of the keys. The look on her face was one of profound concentration, and she scarcely glanced away from it when Hook entered the office. He sidled up to her, waited a moment, and—when it became obvious that she was not going to acknowledge him—rapped on the desk with his knuckle. She sighed at length, then looked up.

"Office closed at five," she snapped.

"You're still here."

She scowled, the corners of her lips downturned. This last comment was not worth a reply. She was about to return to her typing—was in fact cracking her knuckles ready to prod another letter—when Hook said, "I'm here to see Judd."

"He's out."

"Where?"

"*Out*," she reiterated sharply.

It was Hook's turn to sigh. He perched on the edge of the desk and lit a cigarette. "What's your name?"

"Who wants to know?"

"Jerome Hook. Scotland Yard."

Another sigh. "Can't you lot just leave us alone? A bloody pain is what you are. He's got his licence. Everything in order. This is persecution, is what this is. Do you want me to put you in touch with Mr. Judd's solicitor?"

"As a matter of fact," said Hook, puffing smoke, "it was a solicitor that sent me to Mr. Judd. I'm not here to make trouble. I'm here on a different matter. I need to talk to Judd, so *you* need to tell me where he is."

"Look, all right, there's no need for the third degree. I don't *know* where he is. Last I saw of him was lunchtime, he said he was going out, that he was on a case and he might be away for a few days."

"Does he do that often?"

She shrugged. "Comes with the territory."

"And he's left you to hold the fort."

She looked pointedly at the heap of papers. "I have my duties."

Hook changed tack. "It's about a client."

"Well, that's different. I don't know nothing about clients."

"Indulge me. His name is Rodney Edgecomb."

"Haven't you lot got enough to do? Aren't there enough problems in this country, what with fascists in the streets?"

Hook made a show of stubbing out his cigarette in the ashtray. "You know damn well that he hired Judd."

"Do I? Must have slipped my mind. Comes with age."

Now Hook grabbed a chair and sat down at eye level with the secretary. "Edgecomb hired Judd a few months ago. I need to look at any files you might have, and I need you to tell me everything you know about Rodney Edgecomb."

"Why should I?"

"Edgecomb is dead."

For the first time, the secretary seemed close to perhaps comprehending the gravity of the situation. She folded her arms, the typewriter forgotten. "Ah-*hah*. And you think Judd is involved? Reckon he's on the run, maybe?"

"Nobody's saying anything about that. All I want to know is *why* Edgecomb hired Judd. Can you tell me that?"

"Maybe." She turned in her seat and consulted a filing cabinet, riffling through the steel drawers and eventually emerging with a document and scrutinising it closely. "Ah," she said, "here."

Hook reached out for the document, but the secretary had no intention of relinquishing it. Instead she said: "Rodney Edgecomb. He first came to the office last month. July '39. He requested background information on two individuals, and he was offering a retainer."

"Tell me about the two individuals."

"Two soldiers, apparently he served with them in the War."

"Names?"

"One was McGinn. The other was a Maurice Bailey."

"Will McGinn?"

"That's the one."

"What about him?"

"Edgecomb was after a full report. Background, associates, the whole shebang."

"All right. And the other fellow?"

"Maurice Bailey—a private. He died in 1919."

Hook got up and headed over to the window. As he peered out at the rain, he spoke over his shoulder. "Tell me about McGinn."

There came the shuffling of papers as she sifted through the detritus. "Not much to tell. Bit of a mystery man. But Judd found out a few choice nuggets. Far as he could tell, McGinn first met Edgecomb when they were invalided home from the Somme."

"What's the story there?"

"Captain Edgecomb was in a car that struck a land mine; miraculously no one was killed, but Edgecomb caught a terrible head wound that knackered his brain. Lost his memory, is what I mean."

Hook nodded. "I see."

"This was in early 1918. Edgecomb was treated at a field hospital, then shipped back to England. He was in and out of hospital for a long time—several months at least. And while he was at a place on the coast, Will McGinn was also being treated for shell shock. So Judd started with the war records."

"Go on."

"McGinn was a private, born in a village in the Cotswolds, son of a blacksmith and a midwife. He never would have come into contact with someone like Edgecomb if not for the war. They were from different walks of life, you might say."

"But they met in hospital."

"Right."

"Did Edgecomb tell you *why* he wanted to know about this Will McGinn?"

"We didn't ask. Edgecomb paid his dues, so Judd did as he was told."

"So what else did he find out?"

"Whatever there was to be found. After the War, McGinn lived on the continent."

"And what of his friends? Associates?"

The secretary fixed him with a steady glare. "That information will be in Mr. Judd's files."

"Would you check, please?"

"No. I don't have a key to the filing cabinet. Mr. Judd keeps the results of his investigations confidential."

"Did I tell you that this was a murder case?"

She gave an insolent shrug. "Nothing I can do about that. I don't have a key."

Hook sighed and decided to pursue a different avenue of discussion. "What about the other man? What was his name? Hailey?"

"Bailey. Maurice Bailey."

"And what is there to say about *him*?"

She shrugged. "More, at least. Used to tread the boards. He was a conjuror of some kind."

Hook turned back to her. "A conjuror? Are you sure?"

She was affronted. "Course I'm sure. What do you mean?"

"Nothing. Never mind. Where does Bailey fit into this?"

"Nowhere. He's a dead end. In every sense of the word. He died in 1919. Drowned himself, you know."

"How come?"

She shrugged and gave a ghoulish little smile. When he thought about it later, Flint shuddered. "Probably on account of getting his face blown off at Ypres. Want to see the photographs?"

"What are you talking about?"

"He was in the papers at the time. A miracle of modern surgery, they called him. Fat lot of good that it did. Built him a new face from scratch and the silly bugger goes and sticks it underwater till he's stone-cold dead."

"Let me guess—they operated on him at the same hospital where Edgecomb and McGinn were treated?"

She smiled at him, enjoying leading him along the winding path toward the truth. "You're catching on."

"Where's the hospital?"

"A place called Devil's Neck."

CHAPTER SEVEN

THE STEPNEY LAD

'Tis no fable—beings able—Rap-tap-tap upon a table.
—"Spirit Rappings," popular song, 1853

August 31, 1939. 8 P.M.

"You understand why I had to come here," said Mrs. Bailey, as Mrs. Lennox plied her with tea. Madame La Motte gave a slow, sagacious nod.

The guests were seated around the fireplace, which was wide and welcoming. Mr. Lennox and Fred Powell had unloaded the luggage and heaped it in the hall; they were now in the kitchen drying themselves after braving the deluge.

Madame La Motte had positioned herself to the right of the bereaved woman and clasped her hand in her own. "Such suffering, my dear," she offered in a voice like butter. "You have endured so much."

"His name was Maurice," said Mrs. Bailey. "He fought on the Western Front. He did so well—made it almost the whole way through without a scratch. Wouldn't that have been a miracle? But his luck didn't hold out. First thing I heard, he was driving an armoured car that hit a land mine—he got out unscathed. What luck! Just a mild concussion, they said. But they took him to one of those field hospitals. Fourrière, I think?"

"Fleurrière," said Fred Powell. When all eyes turned to him, he explained, "I served myself."

"Oh yes? Then you must have heard about what happened to Fleurrière?"

Powell nodded solemnly. "It happened all the time."

"A stray German shell," Mrs. Bailey resumed. "The hospital was obliterated. Odds of survival virtually nil." A little smile played across her lips. "But again, Maurice made it through. It's just that this time his wounds were more . . . serious."

"The Fates can be so cruel," commented Madame La Motte. "A hospital—a place of healing—turned into a charnel house. A circus of death."

"And you see, by rights he shouldn't even have been there! But he went along because he'd been ferrying around this hotshot young captain who got hurt when the car hit that mine. But then a stray shell wiped the whole hospital from the map. And robbed Maurice of everything he had . . . You can't imagine the relief when I heard that he was alive! Alive, but injured. How bad can an injury be, I thought? They shipped him home and brought him here. Convalescence, they said. That was the word they used. They made it sound so . . . benign. I came out here, to Devil's Neck, and they showed him to me . . ." Her eyes closed and she covered her mouth with a quivering hand.

"They kept him in a private room, all to himself. They ushered me in through a side door, so that I wouldn't bump into any of the other patients. I should have known then that they were trying to tell me that he wasn't *like* those other patients. And he never would be again. There was just nothing left. Most of the time he wore bandages, but they got him that mask to try and see about getting him back into the world. To try and turn him back into Maurice again instead of just 'Patient 217.' But it didn't take . . ." She stopped and dabbed at her cheeks with a lace handkerchief. "He lasted that way for a year. He couldn't see, couldn't speak, couldn't do much of anything. Couldn't hear; they reckoned the explosion had made him deaf. So they kept him here, they kept trying things, God bless them, though none of it took. But I never gave up on him. I think he knew that." She sighed softly. "He killed himself in 1919. Threw himself into the water twenty years ago tonight. He wasn't the only one, of course. It happened a few times over the years. Patients just . . . went."

"Disappeared," said Spector quietly. "Like Adolphus Latimer."

If Mrs. Bailey heard this, she did not acknowledge it. "He left this mask behind with his personal effects." She swallowed. "Now it's all that's left of him."

"There must be more," Imogen heard herself say.

"What do you mean, young woman?" Mrs. Bailey asked sharply.

"Forgive me. But there must have been other people in Corporal Bailey's life. Didn't he have a sweetheart?"

Mrs. Bailey's posture stiffened. "He had a sweetheart, yes. But she abandoned him as soon as he got hurt. Probably for the best."

"What makes you say that?"

"It wouldn't have been right. I didn't want anybody but me to see him . . . as he was."

Imogen chewed her lip. "What was the sweetheart's name?"

Mrs. Bailey screwed up her eyes, as though struggling to remember. "Maude."

"Do you know what became of her?"

Mrs. Bailey shook her head.

"Did she come to the funeral?"

"I wouldn't have allowed it, even if she had wanted to."

A moment's silence followed this, and Spector was the one to break it. "Tell me, Mrs. Bailey, when did you first 'see' Maurice again?"

"Last year. I had never believed in . . . this sort of thing. I was always most profoundly sceptical. But how can one dispute the evidence of one's own eyes?"

"Perhaps you'd care to tell the story?" Spector cajoled gently.

"Oh, I should like nothing more. I was at home, as usual, and my servants had left for the night, so I was alone in the house. It was perfectly dark outside, but the road was lit by streetlamps—it's Duckett Street, in Stepney. It was a clear night. I had made myself some cocoa for the evening and was just about to take it up to bed when I happened to linger a moment by the landing window. There was a man outside; a figure beneath the streetlamp directly opposite the house. He was standing perfectly still, and I saw him as clearly and unmistakably as I see you now. He was looking up at the house with an expression of . . . longing, I suppose you'd call it."

"And you recognised him as your son?"

She nodded. "There could be no mistaking it, Mr. Spector. There are things in this world that a mother knows. She cannot fail to recognise the face of her child, even after all these years."

"He was as you remember him, then? Before the war?"

"Naturally," Madame La Motte interjected. "A man's spiritual form is the effigy of his earthly love," she said. "If a man has spent his life loving, it will show in his spirit-face. Likewise, if he spent his life hating, then that will show there too."

"Maurice was very loving. So loving," said Mrs. Bailey, a tear coursing down her cheek and lingering feebly on her chin before dropping into her lap. "And of course I didn't know what else to think. That's why I got in touch with Madame La Motte, who was particularly keen to assist me. But our séances at my home yielded nothing"—Madame let out a frustrated sigh—"so it occurred to me that the *location* might make a difference. And it seems already that I was right."

"You *are* right," interrupted Madame La Motte. "This place is effervescing with psychic energy. In fact, I would suggest we begin our communion as soon as possible."

"A séance . . . before dinner?" Clive Lennox was hesitant.

"There is not a moment to waste," said Madame La Motte, sounding like a Saturday morning serial. She would truck no argument. "Well for goodness' sake, what on earth are we waiting for?" she declared. "Our great work is just beginning. Mrs. Lennox. Mr. Lennox. No doubt you are aware of the reason for my visit here—it was *not* merely to sample your hospitality. I am here to make *contact*."

Madame La Motte had taken unassailable control of proceedings in the drawing room, relishing the attention of the other guests. Imogen was the only one among them who let her gaze wander elsewhere, toward the dingy corners of the room, and toward the piano where the phantom soldier had stood.

Indeed, Madame was now adamant that a séance must be performed as soon as humanly possible. The Lennoxes were trying to talk her out of it, arguing that the other weary travellers no doubt wished to fill their bellies before venturing beyond the veil. Imogen knew well enough that this was one of Madame's favourite tricks: to take advantage of her subjects' distraction and weakness. It was painfully obvious, and yet so many fell for it. Imogen wondered how it would play here, in the unfamiliar territory of Devil's Neck.

Mrs. Bailey was keen to get started, but Francis Tulp was reluctant. "I haven't unpacked the kit yet . . ." he protested.

"What manner of kit do you have with you, Francis?" Spector asked.

"Oh, the usual," said Tulp modestly. "I have my cameras and trigger-weights—I was planning to set them up overnight—but for the séance I have a few other bits and pieces. Graphite for fingerprints, a vial of quicksilver . . ."

"Quicksilver?" said Imogen.

"Right. I got the idea from Harry Price. What you do is, you pour the quicksilver into a bowl, and then the ripples show you any invisible movements in the atmosphere . . ."

"There will be time for all that later," insisted Madame, dismissing him with a wave of her hand. "To waste a moment longer with inaction could be catastrophic."

Inwardly, Imogen smiled. So far, the old fraud had matched every single beat. She had ascertained just enough information to add verisimilitude to her "vision," she had created atmosphere with her phantom soldier. Imogen would not have been the least bit surprised if she had somehow contrived the incident with the generator, to further set the stage for her performance. And now: pushing ahead with the séance before they had even dined, when they were all tired and agitated and hungry. They would be more receptive, no doubt.

And yet, Imogen noted with some chagrin, Mrs. Bailey's faith did not waver. She simply nodded enthusiastically at everything La Motte said. Francis Tulp, too, was under the woman's spell; that much was obvious from the enthralled expression on his smooth, young face. The Lennoxes traded anxious glances. Fred Powell hovered uncomfortably on the periphery of the conversation. And there was an unmistakable look of disapproval on the face of Joseph Spector. The only one who expressed no particular preference was Walter Judd. He remained in the same armchair into which he had collapsed after returning the fallen mask to Mrs. Bailey. He appeared disturbed and was looking from face to face in confusion.

Clive Lennox turned to his wife, his lips unpleasantly pinched, and said, "Very well. If I might show the other guests to their quarters, Madame, whilst my wife prepares the ballroom? That way, those who do not wish to participate may ready themselves for dinner, which will be served promptly at nine."

This was determined to be a suitable compromise, and Fred Powell breathed an audible sigh of relief.

But before anybody could move, there was another interruption. "If you don't mind," said Mrs. Bailey quietly, "there is something else I ought to mention. Better to do it now than to spring it on you unawares. And since we are all gathered in one room, it seems . . . convenient. It's something of Maurice's, which I have brought with me." She glanced toward Fred Powell. "My black case, Mr. Powell. Would you mind?"

The driver disappeared into the hall and returned with a large leather case, which he placed in the centre of the room. Imogen recalled seeing it loaded into the luggage bay back in the depot, how Mrs. Bailey had watched almost obsessively to ensure it did not receive so much as a tiny knock. Its contents were likely priceless to her, another memento of her dead son.

"It's something which belonged to Maurice," she explained, unbuckling the case. "It meant a great deal to him. I brought it with me because I thought it might assist with the séance."

"Of course, my dear," said Madame La Motte sagely. "That was most astute of you. Something from the war, is it?"

"Actually no," answered Mrs. Bailey, easing open the case and breathing a thin, relieved sigh when she found that the contents were unharmed after the journey. "This was Maurice's *before* the war."

Imogen was unsure what she had been expecting, but it was assuredly not this.

On opening the suitcase, there emerged what appeared at first glance to be a small boy of about five or six years in age. He wore a shabby faded blue sailor suit, knee-high white socks, and black shoes with brass buckles that glinted dimly as Mrs. Bailey propped him upright. It took Imogen a brief moment to determine that this child did not breathe; his chest did not move; his fingers could not clench. Those glassy eyes saw nothing.

The head and hands were wooden, with an off-white china-like finish, skilfully carved and obviously well-maintained at one time or another. Now, though, his jaw hung slackly open, baring two rows of tiny yellow teeth and a painted pink tongue. Initially, Imogen took it for one of those ventriloquist's dummies, save for the fact that its body was obviously as weighty as a living thing. Cradling the object—and it *was* an object, Imogen told herself—as though it were both brittle and priceless, Mrs. Bailey carried it to the centre of the room and placed it very carefully upright. It stood at roughly two and a half feet in height. From the hair protruding beneath its cap to the nails on the ends of its fingers, the utmost attention had been given to enhancing the imitation of life. At a distance, and viewed in the correct lighting, it could almost pass for the real thing.

"What is it?" Imogen heard herself say.

"You mean you don't know?" said Mrs. Bailey with damp eyes and a faintly desperate smile. "But of course, why should you? I imagine this was before you were born, wasn't it? There was a time, my dear, when this little fellow was the talk of London. A darling of the music hall stage. This is 'The Stepney Lad.' Once upon a time, he had it within his power to walk across a stage unsupported, to reach out his hand and wave to the adoring crowds—see how loose and limber his wrists are, so the hands can spin around and around. He could open his mouth and speak, sing, tell jokes and fortunes—see the hinge in his jaw, slightly crooked after all these years. But he was a marvel. And he was built by my son. In some ways, he was the child Maurice never had."

Imogen opened her mouth before she could stop herself. "It must bother you, Mrs. Bailey, that you never got to be a grandmother."

The others ignored her. They were transfixed.

Madame La Motte gently brushed the tips of her fingers against the thing's porcelain face, and said, "Yes, this is wonderful. I can sense that he poured so much of his personality, so much of *himself*, into this glorious creation. With your permission, Mrs. Bailey, I should very much like this wonderful treasure to play a part in our communion. Do I have your permission?"

"Of course," said the unfortunate woman. "That's why I brought him. And that's not all," she continued, reaching farther into the case. She now emerged with a rolled-up theatrical poster, which she unfurled on the nearby sideboard. Imogen craned her neck to see: "The Stepney Lad" was in fact the second on the bill—there was a skilful drawing of a youngish man in a tailcoat with a fresh-faced automaton in his lap. But the upper half of the poster—a different act altogether—caught her eye. There was no illustration, but the space was taken by a cluster of bold letters that spelled: THE SENSATIONAL MISTER SPECTOR.

Madame La Motte's beady eyes snapped from the poster to the man himself. "Spector?" she said.

Spector shrugged affably. "No point in trying to deny it, is there, Madame?" He glanced at Mrs. Bailey, who gave an acquiescent little nod. "Maurice Bailey was a protégé of mine prior to the War. I even had the privilege of sharing a stage with him on occasion."

"So Maurice was a magician too?" said Imogen.

Spector cocked his head thoughtfully. "Automatism is magic by another name, I suppose. They say Hermes Trismegistus bestowed life on statues, turning inanimate forms into moving creatures. And great alchemists like Roger Bacon possessed 'brazen heads' which could speak and predict the future. The Stepney Lad seems like a natural progression."

"He's been in a box since Maurice died," said Mrs. Bailey, eyeing the clockwork boy. "I've had offers, you know, from collectors. All sorts of ludicrous sums. But I've said no every time. The Stepney Lad belongs to Maurice, even now."

While none of the other guests was especially perturbed by this revelation, the challenge it presented to Madame La Motte was palpable. She gazed back at Spector for a moment with a face like granite, and then she said in a sweet, high-toned voice, directing her question at Mrs. Bailey, "My dear, I had thought we agreed there were to be no secrets between us?"

"Yes, I *do* apologise, Madame," said Mrs. Bailey. "But I hope you'll understand why it was necessary. Joseph and I maintain regular correspondence, and when I mentioned to him just how *interested* you were in Maurice . . ."

Spector stepped in. "The suggestion was mine," he said. "I care too much about Maurice to see his mother exploited, if you'll forgive the ugly phrase. I have some experience in dealing with mediums, and it seemed wise to cast a sceptic's eye over proceedings. Mrs. Bailey agreed, that's all. We had no intention to deceive you, Madame. And of course, as a psychic, no doubt you knew already," he added with a smile and a deferential little bow.

Madame La Motte's eyes were narrow, and her lips downturned. "A little candour, Mrs. Bailey. Is that too much to ask?"

Imogen found her interest piqued. This explained why Spector and Mrs. Bailey had gone out of their way to avoid each other, and had not even made eye contact during the journey. Spector was here to debunk Madame La Motte!

"I only came to observe," said Spector benignly. "Surely you don't object?"

La Motte huffed and grumbled. "It is not a matter of objection. It's a matter of disrupting the harmony of the spirits. It can utterly *destroy* our chances of making meaningful contact . . ."

Mrs. Bailey gave Spector an anxious glance, but he seemed to dispel her concerns with his calm, open-palmed posture. "You have already glimpsed him once this evening, Madame. I'm sure he is positively *desperate* to get in touch with his loving mother. I doubt my presence will make an iota of difference one way or the other. But if it helps, I can assure you that Maurice and I had the utmost respect for one another—a respect which I continue to maintain."

Grudgingly, Madame La Motte conceded, although it was plain to all that she was furious about what she considered to be Spector's duplicity. Imogen found the whole thing hilarious—though she dared not let it show on her face—and Tulp was looking at Spector with quiet admiration, as though everything now made sense. Perhaps it did.

"Very well," said Madame, though it was clear that it pained her. "However, I must say, Mrs. Bailey, that I am disappointed that you felt the need to *conceal* your acquaintance with this . . . person."

"We've concealed nothing," said Spector, smiling. "But if we *have* deceived you, I take full responsibility."

Madame La Motte was evidently furious. "Very well," she said finally, "the séance will go ahead. But perhaps we ought to wait until after dinner."

"Really?" said a mock-incredulous Spector. "I had thought there wasn't a moment to waste . . . ?"

With this, Mrs. Lennox swept back into the room. "Everything is in readiness," she said.

———

It was agreed that Madame La Motte would now proceed (albeit somewhat grudgingly) with the séance. The participants were Madame herself, Mrs. Bailey, Francis Tulp, Imogen, and Joseph Spector. While this was taking place, Clive Lennox would carry the luggage up to the guests' respective rooms, and Mrs. Lennox would see to dinner. Fred Powell would refill the petrol tank of the coach. The only one unaccounted for was Walter Judd. When Spector asked him whether he planned to join in with the séance, all he said was, "No, I have other things to be getting on with."

"I'll show you to your room, Mr. Judd," said Clive Lennox. "Let me just fetch your bags."

"I don't have any," he said. "Only this." It was the small travelling case.

"Very well," Mr. Lennox answered, "if you'd like to follow me."

Mrs. Lennox escorted the others through a set of double doors into a large room. "This is the dayroom," she announced. "By which I mean, the *ballroom.*"

"Very good," said Madame La Motte. She oversaw the dimming of the lights. Certain articles were laid out in readiness; these included a slate and a piece of chalk, a notepad and pencil, a Ouija board and planchette, and a candle.

"Mr. Spector," La Motte said, "perhaps you would be kind enough to light the candle?"

Spector did.

"And Mr. Tulp, if you would please take that piece of chalk and trace a circle of roughly six feet in diameter around the table?"

Tulp did this, drawing a thin white line on the bare boards. Then he replaced the chalk on the table.

Before the séance could begin, Madame La Motte had to prepare herself. This needed to be done in private, away from the prying eyes of onlookers. Even Imogen was not permitted to observe, so she simply sat with the others in the ballroom, where the large round table was set, circled with high-backed dining chairs. Finally, the double doors flew open and Madame La Motte reappeared. She was now veiled and swept into the room in spectral silence before assuming her place at the table. She waited as The Stepney Lad was propped up in his own seat.

"Whilst we are in communion with Sergeant Bailey," the medium explained, "it is of vital importance that we do not venture outside the confines of that chalk circle. Now: sit, if you please."

They did as instructed, with Tulp the last of them. He was the one to turn out the overhead lamp, so that the candle was the sole means of illumination. Imogen Drabble sat to the medium's right, looking expectantly around the room, as though Maurice might spring up from behind the furniture. Beside her sat Mrs. Bailey, and to *her* right sat Spector, who went along with every instruction in quiet obedience, but who nonetheless scanned his surroundings with the utmost attentiveness. To Spector's right sat

The Stepney Lad; he gripped its little wooden hand. To the right of the automaton sat Francis Tulp. The circle was complete.

With a defiant air, Madame La Motte spoke into the darkness. "The afterlife is a splendid place," she declared. "I visit it often. A place of wonders, where the old become young again, where the young may grow old and experience the adventures and delights the earthly realm denied them. Where the ground is soft with fresh grass, and the air alive with glorious music. Where the abiding emotion is *love*, purest love. Where every experience is richer, every sensation more powerful. You might say the realm of heaven is more *real* than our world. It is a place where we may know and understand our truest selves."

Her voice was soft and curiously singsong; she always spoke like this when "communing," though Imogen was not sure why. Perhaps the old medium intended to convey a sense of childlike eeriness.

"We are gathered here for a single purpose," she said. "We are gathered here to speak with the soul formerly known as Maurice Bailey. Maurice, can you hear us? Are you present?"

Slowly at first, the table began to sway left and right, slapping the thighs of the assembled participants. Before long it was rocking wildly, leaping from leg to leg as though it had come to life and were now fighting to escape.

"Remain where you are," instructed Madame La Motte. "Whatever you do, for the love of God, do not break the circle."

Tears were already streaming down Mrs. Bailey's face.

All at once, the table was still. The Ouija board in its centre was neatly illuminated by the single candle, which had remained alight despite the disruption. Though the table was now motionless, the planchette in the centre of the board began suddenly to glide. It did so without benefit of a single finger upon its surface. It settled on a word: YES.

Mrs. Bailey let out a sob. Imogen looked over at Spector, who was observing keenly.

"Thank you, Maurice," said Madame La Motte. "Now, I would like to invite you—if you are willing—to speak through me. I shall be your vessel. We have here several physical items which were yours in life. If you care to claim them, please do so."

Imogen's attention was caught by the sinister, expressionless face of the automaton, seated opposite the medium. By the glow of that single candle, it looked positively demonic. Why was it here? What maniacal intelligence had contrived it?

"We are close now," said Madame. "We proceed toward the gates of New Jerusalem, where the purity of the spheres offers only harmony of the spirit. Our great work is begun."

Then, she began to writhe in her seat, gripping Imogen's hand tightly and (Imogen assumed) Tulp's as well. Finally, she fell still; her chin slumped on her chest.

"Maurice? Darling boy, is that you?" It was Mrs. Bailey who spoke, her voice quivering with emotion.

Not looking up, La Motte began to speak in a low, growling voice; an approximation of a masculine tenor. "It is, Mother."

"Oh, Maurice, how I've missed you."

"And I have missed you, Mother. That is why I have come back. To visit with you again."

"It was you, wasn't it, that I saw outside the town house?"

"It was."

"What is it that you want? Do you have a message for me?"

Madame La Motte opened her mouth to answer, then froze. Suddenly, she wrenched free from the grip of those on either side of her, throwing her arms skyward in a dramatic gesture. All at once, the candle was extinguished and the room was in darkness.

"Quickly," said Imogen, "grab her hands."

There was a moment's fumbling in the darkness before Imogen gripped Madame La Motte tightly by the wrist. "Mr. Tulp—do you have her other hand?"

"Yes," came the response.

"Are you holding on tight?"

"I am."

At once, the room was lit by a sudden glow—a floating orb. It was a bodyless face. "I am here, Mother," it whispered. "Your son is returned to you . . ."

Mrs. Bailey let fly a piercing shriek, the connecting doors between the drawing room and the ballroom were flung open, and a silhouetted figure entered. In an instant the light switch had been flicked and the room was fully illuminated, revealing the flustered form of Clive Lennox. The face was gone. "Dear me," he was saying, "dear me, whatever was that noise?"

Everybody looked to Madame La Motte, who was doing her best to regain control of the situation. "He is gone now," she said. She turned to Mrs. Bailey. "I'm sorry, my dear. We must try again another time. But I *did* warn you that the presence of your friend might cause problems . . ."

"Hey!" cried Tulp. "Good God, look up there!" He was pointing at the ceiling, and all eyes immediately followed his gaze toward a message spelt out in quivery grey letters: I AM HERE.

"That wasn't there when we started," said Imogen.

"How can you be sure?" asked Spector. "Did you examine the ceiling?"

"Well . . . no. But I'll bet *you* did, didn't you?"

"As it happens, I did. And you're correct, the message was not in evidence. But . . ."

"Success!" cried Madame. "Success. A manifestation. I hope you are satisfied, dear Mrs. Bailey?"

But Mrs. Bailey was too shaken to answer. Instead, she kept saying, "I saw him. I heard him. I smelled his cologne . . ."

The group returned to the drawing room just as Fred Powell and Mrs. Lennox entered from the hall. "Whatever was that dreadful noise?" said Powell.

"A visitation," said Spector, "or so it would seem."

"Oh, my heart," moaned Mrs. Bailey. "I'm afraid I must sit down for a moment . . ."

"Let me get you a whisky," said Tulp, going over to the drinks cabinet. "Ideal for the nerves."

"Rum," put in Mrs. Lennox. "It thins the blood. Good for palpitations."

Tulp nodded and poured the rum.

Mrs. Lennox looked panicked, but did not say another word. She and her husband exchanged a glance, and Mr. Lennox opened his mouth to speak. He was cut off, however, by the sudden chime of the Pinchbeck clock on the mantelpiece. It was half-past eight.

"Ah," he said, his cheeks flushing pink, "just in time. I was about to say that it is nearly time for dinner. When you have gathered yourselves, my wife and I will show you to your rooms."

———

Side by side, scarcely falling out of step for a moment, the Lennoxes led their guests upstairs and along the west corridor. The first room was the largest and fitted out as a twin. Absurdly, Imogen had let herself be talked into sharing with Madame La Motte—a lapse in judgement she knew she would come to regret. Next door to this room was Joseph Spector's. Opposite was Mrs. Bailey's, and next to *that* was Francis Tulp's. Opposite Francis were the Lennoxes. Finally, at the end of the corridor was Walter Judd's. This room was opposite the bathroom.

Lingering in the open doorway of the room she would be sharing with Madame La Motte, as though she were a child being called in for supper by a hated nanny, Imogen watched the other guests vanish into their respective rooms. It felt like the beginning of a chess match, watching the pawns line up.

"Help me with this," said Madame La Motte.

Imogen turned and saw that the aged medium was struggling to reach back and unclasp her girdle. With a soft sigh, Imogen ambled over to assist, shutting the door behind her so that the two women might change for dinner in privacy.

———

To Imogen's immense surprise, at about five minutes to nine there came the clatter of a gong from the bottom of the stairs. Quaint enough to be charming, and yet, accompanied by the drumming, unrelenting rain, it carried the clangour of ancient menace.

"Shall we?" said Madame La Motte.

They descended, and there was the gong on an old wooden trolley Imogen pictured Clive Lennox wheeling into position. It was an image of bizarre traditionalism that might even have seemed comical. But it was commensurate with the surroundings. It was as if the house itself existed outside conventional notions of time.

Joseph Spector was already at the bottom of the stairs. He gave Imogen a cadaverous smile.

"Shall we?" he said, ushering them toward the dining room. The long dining table was laid for a feast. The Lennoxes stood at opposite sides, like curiously asymmetrical bookends: the mannish, statuesque Justine and the portly, overfed Clive. As the ladies were taking their seats, Mrs. Bailey joined them. She had changed into a fresh cardigan—still black. She sat on Imogen's left. A moment later, Francis Tulp came bounding in.

"Sorry to keep you waiting," he said.

"You're not the last," Madame La Motte informed him sepulchrally.

Tulp looked around. "Ah yes, Mr. Judd. I wonder where he's got to?"

"Don't forget Mr. Powell," put in Imogen.

"Mr. Powell is dining in the kitchen," said Clive Lennox. "Mrs. Lennox," he instructed his wife, "if you'd care to pour the wine."

She did, and Imogen noticed that her hand was trembling ever so slightly, but with a fierce effort she maintained her self-control and did not spill a drop.

"It feels so absurd," said Francis Tulp, "to serve dinner in such a civilised fashion, after everything that's happened this evening." His expression was gaunt, and it was clear he meant what he said—the séance had left him truly exhilarated.

Mrs. Bailey, however, was now in a state of bliss. She said, "I never would have thought it possible. And that it should be *here* of all places that I should find my boy again . . ."

Madame La Motte surveyed this, the scene of her latest triumph, with quiet pride. She had faced up to Joseph Spector's challenge and come through it with aplomb.

"And what about you, Mr. Spector?" Imogen asked. "Were *you* impressed by Madame's performance?"

"Certainly," Spector answered.

"Of course, you must have visited Maurice here as well?"

"To my regret, no. Hospital authorities at the time only permitted close relatives to visit patients. And, bearing in mind the extent of Corporal Bailey's injuries . . ."

Imogen frowned. "That seems rather draconian."

"Far from it," Mrs. Bailey announced in a drab monotone, as though the pain of having her innermost self laid bare during the séance had numbed her to other earthly concerns. "They were worried about security, after that business with the nurse."

"Yes," said Spector. "Nurse Lister, I believe the name was. She had an affair with a shell-shocked patient named Private McGinn. A very murky business." Off the puzzled looks he received, he explained, "I spent some time reading up on the place before the trip."

"McGinn?" said Francis Tulp. "I've heard that name somewhere before, haven't I? I could swear I have . . ."

"On the coach," Imogen informed him, "when Mr. Judd boarded at the depot. There was another name on the passenger list."

"And it was McGinn? Goodness, do you think it was the same fellow? It would be an absurd coincidence, wouldn't it?"

"It would," said Joseph Spector. "But absurd coincidences *have* been known to occur."

"There was indeed a Mr. McGinn on the guest list," said Clive Lennox, "but we heard nothing from him. As far as my wife and I were aware, he ought to have been on the coach with everybody else. However, if, as you say, it was this same McGinn who was caught up in such a dreadful scandal, I doubt he'd wish to show his face here again, even after so many years . . ."

"Why, Mr. Lennox," said Imogen, "I had no idea you were such a puritan. Samuel Draycott reborn!"

Mr. Lennox erupted in gales of forced laughter. "How right you are, Miss Drabble! How positively *antediluvian* of me. And so close to the dawning of a new decade."

"A new decade?" said Mrs. Bailey bemusedly, as though the concept were alien to her. Then, on consideration, "Yes, I suppose so. A new decade."

"But the fact remains," Mr. Lennox persisted, "a nurse engaging in an affair with a patient is certainly not to be encouraged . . ."

"There ought to have been so much more," said Mrs. Bailey. When her meaning was not immediately apparent, she explained:

"More questions about what happened to Maurice. How was it possible? How was it *permitted*? But they were much too concerned with saving their own skins, those high-ups. They were desperate to keep Nurse Lister's impropriety under wraps. She was of course removed. But by then it was too late for my son."

"I wonder what happened to McGinn afterward?" said Imogen.

"Maurice knew him," put in Mrs. Bailey.

Spector's eyes snapped toward her. "Oh yes?"

She nodded. "They were at Fleurrière together, when that wretched shell hit."

"Who told you that?" said Imogen.

"Oh, it was no secret, you know. Even Maurice himself managed to tell me about it when I came to visit him. I'll never forget it. It was the last time I saw Maurice. I approached his room, and there were two brutish orderlies coming out. One of them was talking about Will McGinn and Nurse Lister. They spoke so loudly, and in such uncouth tones—they had no idea I was there. But it's a good thing I was, otherwise my last conversation with Maurice would have made no sense. I'd probably still be puzzling over it to this day."

"A conversation?" said Spector. "I don't believe you've ever mentioned this to me before."

"I haven't," she answered, "because it's personal. But I suppose now there can be no harm. Particularly as we are discussing Will McGinn. Maurice was unable to speak, of course, and he was mostly blind. But his hearing had begun to come back. I brought him a pad and pencil, and he was able to write messages. He was able to respond to questions the doctors asked of him, indicating a particular discomfort, for instance."

"And that last conversation?" Spector prompted.

"Yes. I entered his room, and there he sat in his wheelchair by the window, tweed blanket over his knees, mask in place. I might almost have convinced myself those synthetic eyes could see me. But he was evidently distressed. He was making a guttural sort of sound in his throat—it was all he could manage by way of speech. And he was feeling around for something—I deduced it to be the pad and pencil, so I helped his hand toward them. He immediately wrote the name: WILL MCGINN. I tore it from the pad and asked him what it was that he wanted to tell me, but . . ." her eyes grew damp. "He wasn't able to tell me."

This brought about a heavy, uncomfortable silence. The guests waited. The Pinchbeck clock ticked noisily, and apart from the rain that was the only sound for several minutes. Finally, Spector suggested, "Perhaps one of us ought to check on Mr. Judd . . . ?"

"I'll go," Tulp volunteered. "What with us being neighbours and all." He bounded out of the room once again, and they heard his footsteps pounding on the staircase. Then silence.

Finally, Tulp reappeared, looking a little sheepish. "Mr. Spector?" he said. Spector was immediately on his feet and loping catlike toward the ghost hunter.

"What is it?"

"And . . . um . . . Mr. Lennox?"

Irritated at being left out, Imogen got up and followed them into the hall.

Tulp spoke in a whisper: "I'm afraid I can't get any answer from Mr. Judd. His door is locked. I wondered if perhaps . . . ?"

"Perhaps what?" said Imogen. But Spector simply nodded and they all made their way upstairs.

Imogen paused on the landing looking down the corridor toward Judd's room and felt as if she were trapped in a Rubens painting: the low light, the crimson curtains, the door itself, framed by a glow from within—only a piece of wood and three metal hinges between them and whatever lay inside.

They converged outside Judd's room, where Tulp resumed a heavy, frantic knocking on the oak panels. "I can't get any answer," he said over the din.

Clive Lennox tried the door handle; naturally, it did not yield. Spector watched with disquieting stillness. It was as if some terrible prophecy were coming to pass in front of him; as though he had been expecting this all along.

When Tulp gave up knocking, Spector said softly, "I'm afraid we're too late."

"What do you mean?" demanded Imogen. "Mr. Spector, what do you mean?"

Tulp was backing up, squaring his shoulders, readying for a run-up. Lowering his head like a rampant bull, he thundered toward the door, slamming into it with a messy, painful impact. He groaned, then backed up again.

"Are there no other keys?" Spector asked Clive Lennox. He just shook his head.

Tulp shouldered the door again—and again.

Eventually it gave way and the young man spilled into the room. Spector followed him in, but Lennox and Imogen remained in the corridor, peering through the doorway. Their collective gaze was met, incongruously, by a pair of mud-caked boots at head height. From the boots protruded a pair of legs, swinging pendulously, and, out of view above the doorframe, what remained of Walter Judd.

They entered the room, transfixed by the hanging body. Lennox eased the door shut behind him, as though afraid a passerby might see.

"Dear God. Oh, Christ," said Tulp. "The damned fool's killed himself."

This was undeniably the case, thought Imogen. Swinging from the light fixture with a rope knotted about his neck in a makeshift noose, Judd's face was yellowish grey beneath the unforgiving lamplight, his eyes half-open so the damp whites were visible. His chin had a patina of charcoal stubble, and between his cracked, chapped lips protruded a pitiful pink slug of a tongue, laced with foam. It was an ugly chiaroscuro death tableau, with the pasty flesh about the corpse's throat bruised a livid, melancholy blue. Matters were not helped by the fact that the air cloyed with the chemical-laced scent of varnish, or perhaps white spirit.

"Get him down," commanded Spector.

"He's dead . . ." Tulp said vaguely.

"Tulp! Snap out of it. The rope is tied to the bureau beside you. Undo that knot."

"But . . . ," Clive Lennox put in cautiously, "oughtn't we to wait? For the police, I mean? I'm afraid they shall have to be called."

"You have a telephone here?"

FLOOR PLAN:
WALTER JUDD'S ROOM,
DEVIL'S NECK

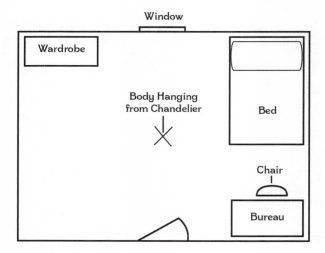

"Well, no, but come the morning the floods will have died down . . ."

Spector shook his head. "We've a whole night to get through before that. Now please, Mr. Tulp: the rope."

There was a rapid exchange of troubled glances among the other men, but Imogen continued to watch Spector who, in turn, had his eyes fixed on the gently swaying body of Walter Judd. It was interesting (to Imogen, at least) how swiftly and adeptly Joseph Spector had taken control of the situation. She reflected now on Tulp's description of the old conjuror; of his strange brain and his knack for unravelling things. All the same, she struggled to see the sense in tampering with the corpse.

"Mr. Spector," she ventured, "I think the police will prefer it if the room is left untouched . . ."

He cut a truly fearsome figure when he whirled round on her, a flash of sudden wickedness in his pale eyes. She recalled the name which had briefly crossed her mind when she first laid eyes on him: Mephistopheles. "Miss Drabble," he said, "it is as I feared. There are certain forces at work in this house. And if I have it in my power to prevent further bloodshed, then by God I shall do it."

"Hold on a moment," said Clive Lennox. "Are you trying to tell me this isn't a suicide?"

Spector did not answer. Instead, he strode over to the dressing table and began to untie the knotted rope himself. When this was done, and with surprising strength for such a spindly framed man, he slowly lowered the body to the ground.

On the rug, spread-eagled on his back, Walter Judd looked even more pathetic. So stark, with his head lolling back and his face as white as alabaster beneath the murky stubble. Spector immediately dropped to his haunches beside the body and began to riffle the pockets. He emerged with a wallet and a crumpled bus ticket. Next he turned his attention to that dead face, gently placing his gloved thumb on the chin so he could move the head from side to side. "I thought as much," he said.

"What?" asked Tulp.

"This man was unconscious when he was hanged."

"How can you say that?"

"The bruising here, behind his right ear. It's slightly darker than the rest. I cannot say for sure, but it looks like an injection site. I think he was drugged."

"This is ludicrous," said a flustered Clive Lennox.

Now Spector began pacing slowly about the room, examining each corner as though a killer might be lurking there. But the room was otherwise undisturbed. Judd had brought no luggage with him, save for a small travelling case containing only fresh clothes. The raincoat he had worn was hanging from the back of a wooden chair by the window, and his jacket was tossed onto the foot of the bed. With a gloved hand, Spector picked it up and began to search the pockets. He emerged empty-handed. "If there was anything else to be found, I'm afraid the killer took it away with him."

"Or her," suggested Imogen.

Meanwhile, Tulp was looking around the room. "I don't know," he said, "it makes sense to *me*. He rigged up the noose, then stood on the bed frame . . ."

"Surely it's the only explanation," said Lennox.

"I'm curious, Mr. Spector," said Imogen. "Why are *you* so convinced it's not a simple case of suicide?"

"For one very simple reason, Miss Drabble," said Spector, brandishing the wallet. "Walter Judd was not an ordinary guest or thrill-seeker, I'm afraid. He was a detective."

CHAPTER EIGHT

ABSTRACTIONS OF THE SLEEPING MIND

What is common in all these dreams is obvious.

—Sigmund Freud, *The Interpretation of Dreams*

August 31, 1939. 6 P.M.

T he rainswept streets of Dollis Hill, streaked with rivers of reflected lamplight, were unchanged since the first time George Flint visited them. That was three years earlier, when a doctor named Rees was murdered in somewhat unusual circumstances.*
Now, Rees's daughter, Lidia—who was herself a psychiatrist—had resumed her late father's practice.

With an icy hand, Flint drew his collar tight about his throat and pressed the bell push. The rain was stippling from the brim of his bowler when the door opened slightly, its progress impeded by

---

* *See* Death and the Conjuror

a chain, and the suspicious face of Olive, the housekeeper, peered out. "Who's that?" she demanded.

"George Flint," he told her. "I'm sorry to be calling after hours."

"George Flint? Inspector Flint? Oh goodness, what's this about?"

"Nothing to concern yourself with. But I should like to see Dr. Rees, if she's in."

"Is it police business?"

"I'm afraid so."

Without another word, Olive fumblingly removed the chain and admitted him to the town house. It had changed little—no doubt out of deference to the memory of Anselm Rees. As Olive led him along the corridor to the doctor's study, Flint was suddenly assailed by flickering memories of his time there three years ago, on a similarly rainy night, when a similarly shaken Olive had led him to the study, where a bloody corpse lay in an armchair.

Olive knocked on the door and informed her mistress of the visitor's identity. Somewhat grudgingly, Lidia consented to see him.

If the rest of the house was a kind of mausoleum to Rees's memory, the study had at least undergone substantial changes. Gone were the bloodstained rugs and the mahogany desk. Now, the décor was distinctly art deco, a reflection of the personality of its present occupant: Lidia Rees.

"Inspector," she said when he was seated in front of her, "long time, no see."

"Yes, and I'm sorry to be bothering you this evening, Doctor. Only it's one of your patients, I'm afraid."

"Which?"

"A chap named Rodney Edgecomb."

She did not seem especially surprised. "And what is the nature of the trouble? As you know, I cannot discuss anything pertaining to a patient without his permission."

"You'd struggle to get that, I'm afraid," said Flint mordantly. "He's dead."

Regarding Flint silently for a moment or two, she finally said, "I see. I am sorry to hear it." She did not sound especially sorry. Her voice was cool and crisp, with only the merest hint of a Viennese accent. Lidia Rees was still young, only in her early thirties, in fact, but she carried a sense of innate authority, and gave the impression that she was in absolute and total control of any situation. "A suicide?"

"The investigation is ongoing."

"Well, I should not be surprised if it turned out that he had taken his own life. I worked very hard with him, but I'm afraid it was a losing battle."

"He mentioned suicide before, then?"

"No. But he did not need to. I can read the signals." She opened a drawer in the filing cabinet beside her desk and emerged with a manila folder. "When did he die?"

"This afternoon."

"And how?"

"A bullet in the brain."

She nodded. "Yes. It fits. He was a soldier, you know. A captain in the War. I believe he suffered badly with shell shock. And there were certain other matters in his past."

"I'm aware of the circumstances. In fact, I believe there may be rather more to it than we first thought."

She twitched a curved black eyebrow. "Well, I'll help in any way I can, Inspector. No need to trouble yourself with a warrant."

"Good. So, when did Edgecomb first come to see you?"

"Last year. He was bothered by his dreams. They were very vivid and very terrifying. He was, in his own words, 'going mad.'"

"All right." Flint nodded. "What about these dreams?"

She referred to the notes. "There were certain recurring images. Candles. A clock. A doll. I have a couple transcripts here." She passed him a few leaves of paper and Flint read:

> *LR: How does it begin?*
>
> *RE: Well, in the dream I'm sleeping. If you see what I mean. That is, in my dream I'm in bed. But there's this knocking on the door. The door to my bedroom. And it's this insistent, heavy knocking, almost like a battering ram. And next thing, I'm sitting up in bed. I'm terrified. Because I know who it is on the other side of the door.*
>
> *LR: And who is it?*
>
> *RE: I don't know. But in the dream, I do know. I get out of bed—I can feel the cold lino under my feet—and I run to the door, I try the handle, but . . . it won't budge. The door is locked. I'm trapped in that room, and there's something outside that's desperate to get in, to get me. To kill me, I assume. I don't know what to do, but I know that I need to find the key. If I'm going to have any chance of getting away, I need to find the key to that door. So I'm looking*

everywhere. I'm ransacking the room. I'm tearing the sheets and the pillows apart. The room is a blur of feathers. I am wrenching the books from the shelves, tearing the pages out. But there is no key anywhere.

LR: And then?

RE: Then . . . well, then everything stops. The hammering on the door stops. There's this deathly silence, which in a way is more terrifying than the knocking. I look round, and I see that the key is in the lock now. All that mess, and the key was in the lock the entire time. And it starts to turn, as though an invisible hand is gripping it tight. And the door is unlocked. And the handle turns, and the door begins to open.

LR: And then?

RE: That's the end of the dream.

Flint looked up from the papers. "So there was nothing specific? No names?"

"During our sessions and the various therapies, the patient's dreams began to take on a more tangible shape. Certain other images presented themselves. Here." She handed him another paper. "This was a more recent session."

Flint read on:

RE: There's a knocking at the door again. Same as always. But the room is slightly different now. There's more of it. More to see, I mean. I'm not sure it is my bedroom at all. I rather think it's somewhere I've been before, though.

LR: Can you describe the room?

RE: Well, there are candles, for one thing. I detest candles, but the room is full of them. All fully lit, like it's a funeral. And with the candles, of course, I can see the walls. There are no pictures, but there are . . . markings. There is a clock on the mantelpiece. I can see the time very clearly. It is seventeen minutes past two. Every night, the same. Seventeen minutes past two.

LR: Does that time have any significance for you?

RE: No. It means nothing. But it's always the same.

LR: And what happens then?

RE: I get up and start to look for the key, just like before. But then I see that the door has something different about it. Now, there's a mirror. And I'm looking at myself. Only it's not quite me. Or rather, I'm not quite myself. And then I see something moving behind me. Something on the bed. I turn back, and it's there.

LR: What's there?

RE: The doll. There is a doll on the bed. A large, Victorian thing with a china head. And it's staring right at me with its glass eyes. The knocking on the door stops. And the doll begins to move.

"This is gibberish," said Flint. "What's it supposed to mean?"

Lidia Rees permitted herself a thin smile. "I think if your colleague Mr. Spector were here, he would perhaps be more receptive to the hypnotic abstractions of the sleeping mind."

"Yes," Flint huffed, "but he's *not* here. Can you explain it, Doctor?"

She looked amused. "Your pipe, Inspector Flint. I note that you spend a great deal of your time chewing upon it, unlit. You demonstrate a certain oral fixation. I wonder if anyone has told you that before?"

Flint felt himself blushing crimson. "If we could get to the matter at hand, Doctor," he said. All the same, while she was searching her filing cabinet for more documents, he took the opportunity to remove the pipe from between his lips and to slip it discreetly into his pocket.

"My father was a pioneer when it came to matters of sleep study and dream interpretation. He was among the first to examine the saccadic activity behind sleeping eyelids," she commenced. "Apart from Freud, no one could touch him. But the oneiric brain still has much to tell us. For instance, the commingling of the literal and the lateral. A dream mirror could be just that: a mirror. But it could also be a symbol of self-realisation. An icon of personal revelation. Personally, in this instance I am inclined toward the latter. The fact that the locked door has now transmogrified into a mirror—that Edgecomb is confronted by his own reflection staring back at him—seems to me an indicator of an unresolved conflict of identity."

"A case of identity," said Flint. "Have you read Conan Doyle, Dr. Rees?"

"Of course. The Holmes stories were one of the few examples of popular literature that my father approved of. He tended to view *them* as symbols too."

"All right—what about the doll?"

"Dolls are symbols of childhood. Perhaps an image of the past, returning. I found it significant that the doll was looming behind him in the mirror, that he saw its reflection before he saw the thing itself. A buried secret? Then, there is the fact that the doll began to move—seemingly without the involvement of any human agency. I am inclined to interpret that as a loss of control. Edgecomb was frightened of something from his past which was beyond his control. Perhaps something that had power over him . . .

"There are other details which are telling precisely because they are so specific. The clock, for instance, and the time upon it. Before we delve into the murky pseudoscience of numerology, the time shown on the clock could be just that. The time. Perhaps a train or a bus? Or an appointment? It is obviously a moment of significance, because Edgecomb's dream self was perpetually trapped in that moment. As to any significance beyond that—I couldn't say."

"What did Edgecomb tell you when you asked him about it?"

"Very little. He served in the War, so the number may refer to a unit, or a code of some kind?"

"Could be."

"The function of the candles was rather obvious, I thought. Illumination. Again, this seems to indicate the cusp of a revelation."

"What revelation?"

She gave him a remarkably white-toothed smile. "We have neglected one of the primary attributes of a mirror, Inspector Flint. Reflection. *Reversal.* The supplanting of an image by its opposite. In the study of tarot, a card viewed upside down bears the opposite meaning to its upright counterpart. Perhaps Captain Edgecomb's reflection was an indicator that he was not all he believed himself to be?"

"So that was the only reason he came to see you, was it? His dreams?"

She stood and wandered over to the French windows, her hands behind her back as she gazed out onto the twilit garden, now awash with mud. "Not quite. There was something else that was rather more perturbing. He had been experiencing instances of what he called 'lost time.'"

"Blackouts?"

"Yes. Periods of up to an hour during which he could not account for his behaviour. He was afraid because—perhaps understandably—he did not know what he was capable of during these fugues."

Flint nodded. This chimed neatly with the allusive passages in the diary. "And what happened during his fugues? Presumably it wasn't just a question of taking a nap in an armchair."

"The first time it happened, he 'came to' on the Tube. The District Line."

"Not the 2:17, I suppose?"

"Unfortunately not. He was passing through Whitechapel, I can tell you that much. The next time, he was on a bus. Again, not the 217. He had paid for his ticket without even regaining consciousness."

Flint got out his pipe and began to chew on it ruminatively. "Where was he heading?"

"Bethnal Green."

"Not too far from Whitechapel. What are the odds, do you suppose, that he was heading to the same place?"

"Very good, I should have thought. He seems to have used public transport in both instances as a kind of muscle memory, lapsing into a previously learned behaviour. Rather like a homing pigeon."

Flint nodded. "All right. Were those the only incidents?"

"Far from it. They were getting worse. More frequent. I tried everything: hypnotism, regression therapy. Nothing seemed to take. Events almost came to a head when he found himself running one night, out of breath. He was on the railway tracks. He was very nearly killed by a locomotive."

"And where was he this time?"

"Close to Cudworth Street, he said. Running away from something, it seemed."

"From what?"

She turned back to face him. "Running from whomever was knocking on his bedroom door."

Flint had stopped making notes now. Their whole conversation had taken on the tenor of a ghost story rather than the testimony of an expert witness. A chill ran through him. He tried not to let Lidia Rees see him shudder. "And what was it that triggered these blackouts in the first place? There must have been something."

"Quite so," answered Dr. Rees. "There is always an inciting incident. It took some considerable rooting around in Mr. Edgecomb's unconscious, but I believe we were able to isolate the event which provoked that first blackout. It was a seemingly innocuous incident—he was walking through Soho and happened to step from the pavement just as a delivery van rounded a corner, almost colliding with him. The sun was in his eyes, he said, and the van seemed to appear from thin air. It came shrieking to a halt and for an instant Edgecomb was face-to-face with the driver through the windscreen glass. Apparently this incident greatly disturbed him, and when he 'came to'—his words—he was on a bus that he did not remember boarding, heading toward a part of London he had never visited before."

Flint was perplexed. "And that's it? That's all you had to go on?"

Dr. Rees cocked her head. "It is considerably more than most patients present."

"Was there anybody else in his life? Did he mention any friends or associates? Maybe a woman?"

"No."

"Did he ever mention Walter Judd?"

"No."

"Or Harold Aitken?"

"No."

"Or Will McGinn?"

"He was a very insular man, Inspector Flint. The only person of any interest to Captain Edgecomb was Captain Edgecomb."

"Did he ever talk about the past? His life before the War, maybe?"

"You seem to have something specific in mind."

"Did he ever mention the Aitken inheritance?"

Lidia Rees's eyes gleamed with animated intrigue. "Never. What is it? Would you care to tell the story?"

"My turn to play the Oracle, Dr. Rees? In that case . . ." He retrieved his pipe from his pocket and began to fill it. "I hope you won't mind if I smoke."

"Not at all. I would encourage it. I find that tobacco helps to put my patients at ease. You'd be surprised how loquacious they can become."

Flint began a brief summation of the Aitken imbroglio—the disappearance of Dominic Edgecomb on the *Titanic*, the death of Harold Aitken, and the legacy that fell into the hands of twenty-two-year-old Rodney Edgecomb.

"Edgecomb was an inveterate gambler. Did he ever mention that to you?"

"Never. Not even once. Which I find rather unusual."

"Well, he soon set about losing the entirety of the vast fortune left to him by his uncle. And that was when *Dominic Edgecomb* made his reappearance."

"He survived the *Titanic*?"

"He did. But he was virtually unrecognisable. He had lost a lot of weight, and his beard, so even his closest friends found it difficult to say one way or the other whether he really was the rightful legatee."

"An awkward situation for Rodney."

"Not for long. You see, it came down to a legal battle between the brothers. But with conflicting assertions about Dominic Edge-comb's identity, the 'deciding vote'—so to speak—lay with Rodney. And he swore under oath that the man who presented himself as Dominic Edgecomb was an impostor."

"Messy," said Lidia Rees, lighting her own cigarette.

"You haven't heard the rest of the story. You see, it wasn't long afterward that the Dominic Edgecomb impostor died. Shot himself in his room at the Hotel Maurienne. Whispers began to circulate, just as they did when Harold Aitken died. Murmurings of a young man seen stalking the hotel corridors the night Dominic blew his brains out: a man whose description corresponded with that of Rodney Edgecomb. But nobody came forward to make a statement on the record—not then, anyway. War broke out, and the whole thing was more or less forgotten."

Sensing Flint's personal attachment to the case, Dr. Rees asked him, "Were you on the force at the time, Inspector?"

He shook his head. "I joined in 1918, straight out of the army. And one of my very first assignments was to take the statement of a man named Barnaby Osgood. He was a diamond merchant from South Africa, who claimed that he saw the phantom bellhop on the night Dominic Edgecomb died."

"What took him so long?"

"Who's to say? The War? The difficulty in getting hold of English papers on the veldt? He first went to Scotland Yard in 1917, but I doubt anyone took him seriously."

"You did, however."

"I did."

"And could he identify the bellhop?"

"He was so convinced. He had a vivid memory of that night four years earlier and was able to describe it moment by moment. I really thought it was a break in the case. My naivety, of course. You see, none of the staff at the Maurienne would admit to entering Edgecomb's room that night, but they wouldn't entertain the notion of an impostor pilfering the key either. It would have made them look like fools. Their negligence would have been a factor in Edgecomb's death, and so everyone kept their mouths shut. And yet, here was an independent witness who was willing to dispute the official version of events. He had nothing to gain—indeed, he came forward at the risk of considerable personal inconvenience.

I had every reason to believe him. And *if*, against all the odds, he was able to identify Rodney Edgecomb as the bellhop who took the master key and entered Dominic's room that night, we could well have been looking at a murder charge."

"So, what was the outcome?"

"None to speak of. I remember Osgood well—he was old, but a dependable sort. And he was utterly unswerving in his statement: 'He had a bellhop's uniform on, but he was no bellhop.'"

"So," said Lidia, "your theory is that Rodney Edgecomb lied in court, and that the 'impostor' really was his brother?"

"I didn't say that. I'm not even sure I believe it. But if this second 'Dominic' really *was* an impostor, nobody's ever managed to explain where he came from, who he really was, or how he came to believe that he was Dominic Edgecomb. But it's a quandary. I mean, if Barnaby Osgood's statement was accurate, then it heavily implies that Dominic was murdered. And Rodney had no motive to murder an impostor. But if the man who died really *was* Dominic . . ."

"Then murder becomes much more likely," said Lidia, finishing Flint's thought. "So what happened then? Presumably you arrested Rodney?"

An unpleasant, glassy expression crossed Flint's face. He took a moment, and then seemed to return to the matter at hand. "I went with Osgood to pay Rodney Edgecomb a visit. Edgecomb was back in London by then, you see—he'd spent a few months in hospital after the War, thanks to a nasty head injury. But his hair had grown back fully, he was more or less back to normal. And I was so convinced we were onto something."

"But presumably this Osgood was no longer quite so confident?"

"That's where you're wrong, Doctor. He was as certain as ever. 'It wasn't *him*,' he told me. 'It wasn't *him*. But it was someone.' For all the good that did."

"So Mr. Edgecomb was in the clear?"

Flint simply grunted. The case had troubled him deeply at the time. But years had gone by. Flint was promoted. Barnaby Osgood died—natural causes; he was unimaginably ancient to young Flint, so this came as no surprise.

And since there was nobody left to accuse him, Rodney Edgecomb had simply faded from view.

"I might almost have forgotten about Rodney Edgecomb, and Dominic Edgecomb, and Barnaby Osgood, and Harold Aitken. I think perhaps I *had* forgotten them. But then, of course, we had this incident today."

"Well, Inspector," said Lidia, "I can tell you for a fact that Rodney Edgecomb mentioned *nothing* whatsoever about this unfortunate episode in any of our sessions. And since he did not mention it, it would not be germane for me to comment upon it."

"Quite right," Flint commented. "All the same . . . I feel as though the very fact that he *didn't* discuss it with you might be meaningful in itself."

The doctor finally stubbed out the remains of her cigarette. "Have you consulted Joseph Spector?"

Flint shook his head. "I can't get hold of him. But I know he'd have this mess untangled in about five minutes flat. It's incredibly frustrating."

Lidia Rees sighed. "Well, I may not be a substitute for Joseph Spector, but I can at least tell you what I know. And while there are many things which it seems Rodney Edgecomb did *not* discuss with me, there are certain things which he did.

"For instance, he occasionally mentioned a place. At first I thought it was imaginary; the name was rather outlandish. But I subsequently established that it was indeed real—a military hospital where he was treated during and immediately after the War. Presumably he had just come from there when he returned to London."

"What was this place called?"

"Devil's Neck."

Edging forward in his seat, Flint asked, "And what did he tell you about Devil's Neck?"

"He said it was a haunted house, on an island, where wounded soldiers were taken and treated. He had certain very specific memories of the treatments there. I would call them almost *cinematic*, as though he had witnessed them closely, but not experienced them himself."

"Almost like a dream," said Flint quietly.

———

After his interview with Dr. Rees, Flint asked if he could use her telephone. She consented, though Olive seemed none too sure. Regardless, she escorted Flint out into the hall, to a small alcove where a telephone stood on a wooden table. Then she hovered nearby, conspicuously within earshot as he made a call.

He gave the operator a number, that of Joseph Spector's home in Jubilee Court, Putney. When there was no answer, he gave another number—this time of Sergeant Hook's desk at the Yard.

"Hook! Glad I caught you. How was your meeting with Walter Judd?"

"He wasn't around, sir, so I spoke with his secretary."

"And?"

"She told me he'd been hired by Rodney Edgecomb to investigate two men: Will McGinn and Maurice Bailey."

"Who's Maurice Bailey?"

"A soldier who served alongside Edgecomb and McGinn in the War. The three of them were invalided back to Blighty together."

"So what became of Bailey?"

"Committed suicide in 1919. It seems as though they were in a field hospital on the Western Front which was destroyed by a stray shell in 1918. Bailey received terrible, life-changing facial injuries. Edgecomb had a bad head wound, which I'm sure you already know about."

"And McGinn?"

"Shell shock."

Flint exhaled deeply, and thoughtfully. "So the three of them were invalided back to Devil's Neck together?"

"For a short time, yes. Will McGinn was discharged—that was in summer 1919. There was some sort of a scandal."

"Really? Do tell."

"Fraternising with one of the nurses, I understand. When he was discharged, he left the country, and doesn't seem to have been back since."

"Until now," said Flint quietly. "And what about Bailey? You said he committed suicide?"

"Drowned himself. This was after a year of treatment and surgeries to rebuild his ruined face. It seems he simply couldn't take it anymore."

Flint had heard many similar stories in his time. "Then *why*," he posed rhetorically, "was Edgecomb so interested in a man who killed himself twenty years ago? And why in the hell did he leave the Aitken inheritance to Will McGinn, only to write him out again? What hold did McGinn have over him?"

Something from the War? he wondered. Or something from *after* the War? Perhaps he and McGinn had become embroiled in some form of criminal activity? Perhaps it was blackmail?

But, if that were the case, why bring the deceased Maurice Bailey into it at all?

Flint was hopelessly, dizzyingly confused. His conversation with Lidia Rees had only compounded the inexplicable nature of so many aspects of this case. At that moment, his mind latched unaccountably onto a detail which he had let pass when he first heard it. "Hook, you said that the three soldiers were in a field hospital on the Western Front. And it was destroyed by a stray shell. Correct?"

"Yes, sir."

"What was the name of that field hospital? I'm sure it crops up in Walter Judd's notes . . ."

"As a matter of fact it does, sir. I made a note of it, although I wasn't sure how relevant it would be."

Flint closed his eyes. "What was the name?"

"It was . . ." there came the sound of flipping pages in the sergeant's notebook. "Fleurrière. An old monastery."

Flint nodded to himself. "Of course. And those three men were all there when Fleurrière was blown to bits by a German shell?"

"Yes, sir," said Hook, becoming a little discomfited. Why was his superior making him repeat this seemingly useless detail?

"I see," said Flint, endeavouring to keep the emotion out of his voice. "Hook, there's one other thing I need you to do for me. Remember the bus ticket Miss Rainsford bought for Edgecomb? I need you to telephone the bus depot and see if they have a list of the other passengers on that bus. I need to know who else is out there at Devil's Neck tonight."

CHAPTER NINE

"EXIT ADALINE!"

Good night, ladies; good night, sweet ladies;
good night, good night.

—*Hamlet*, Act IV, Scene 5

August 31, 1939. 9:45 P.M.

T he remaining guests—the survivors, as they would come to think of themselves—made a poor showing at dinner. Fred Powell was invited to join them, which he did, albeit with little enthusiasm. He was a man who valued his own company, Imogen supposed, and eschewing the empty kitchen for a dining room filled with frightened people was an unwelcome proposition.

They sat around the long banquet table and picked at the gristly stew Mrs. Lennox had prepared. It seemed inappropriate to be eating at all, but Spector (who had effectively taken charge of the situation) assured them they would need their strength, and that it was vital they should choke down at least *some* of the repast. But nobody feasted with much gusto. They were all thinking of the dead man upstairs.

"It's very *sad*, sir," said Clive Lennox sheepishly, "but is a suicide really as uncommon as all that? Particularly if the gentleman came here during the War. I imagine the return visit brought out all kinds of memories. If he was of a less-than-stable disposition, it could surely have made him think of ending it all. Maybe he came here with the purpose of doing just that."

"Such sadness," said Madame La Motte, "there was such sadness in him."

Spector would not be swayed. "Sadness or no, the man was murdered."

"But how can you say that?" asked Tulp. "I know you're always eager for material evidence. And surely everything here points to the conclusion that Judd did himself in?"

Spector had retained the business card from the dead man's wallet. He began to explain, "According to this, Mr. Judd was in fact a private investigator. Which sheds rather a different light on the circumstances of his death."

"When he first boarded the coach . . ." said Imogen, "he wasn't on your passenger list, was he Mr. Powell?"

"No," said Powell, "he wasn't. Not as Judd. But he said the reservation had been made under the name 'Edgecomb.' Which *was* on the list."

"First name?" prompted Spector.

"Rodney."

"Rodney Edgecomb," Spector repeated thoughtfully. "Now there's a name from the past. Caused quite a scandal, back in the day. The case was a press sensation around 1914. It was the sort of story Victorian novelists used to write about. But, like so many other things, it fell from the public consciousness when war broke out.

"For some reason," he continued, "Judd came out here on Rodney Edgecomb's ticket."

"Forgive me for being dense, Mr. Spector," Imogen interjected, "but I still don't see how all of this adds up to murder."

Spector did not answer. Instead, he got up and walked over to the window, which was still being pelted with rain. With his hands behind his back, he peered out.

"We have no means," he said contemplatively, "of contacting the outside world."

"No telephone," said Justine Lennox, her voice little more than a whisper. "We're completely alone out here. Sir—"

"And the causeway's cut off as well," said Mr. Lennox, interrupting his wife.

"You sure about that?" said Powell. "That old bus has pretty sturdy wheels. She holds the road nicely. I reckon I could get her through shallow water."

Mr. Lennox cocked his head incredulously. "You're welcome to try . . ."

Before another minute had passed, Powell was back in his rain slicker and hat and ready by the front door. "Wish me luck," he said.

"Godspeed, Mr. Powell," said Spector.

Powell gave a sharp nod, then, lowering his chin to his chest, he plunged out into the storm.

Within two minutes, he was back in the house, shivering and soaked. "Impossible," he said, "can't be done. No visibility, and the causeway's completely underwater."

"As I suspected," sighed Spector.

The house at Devil's Neck was now an island; scarcely that, in fact; more of an eyot adrift in unforgiving waters.

Powell headed into the dining room in defeat. Mrs. Lennox took his rain slicker from him and spread it in front of the fire to dry.

"For now," said Spector, "we must operate under the assumption that Walter Judd was murdered. And if that's the case, the number of suspects is strictly limited. Indeed, to borrow a cliché, the murderer must be in this very room. This brings us to the question of alibis. Mr. Judd was shown to his room at approximately ten past eight. He was heard locking the door behind him. At some point between ten past eight and ten past nine—just before we broke down the door—an unidentified guest entered the room, strangled Judd, strung him up, and created the cursory impression of a suicide. Then he left, somehow locking the door behind him whilst leaving the key on the inside. It *is* the only key, isn't that so Mr. and Mrs. Lennox?"

"It is," said Mr. Lennox. His wife just nodded.

Spector paced up and down in front of the fireplace. "I cannot help but think," he said at length, "that the answer may be staring me in the face. But regrettably, I did not pay as much attention to Mr. Judd as I ought to have. Did anybody here have a conversation with him?"

"I did," said Clive Lennox, "while I was showing him to his room. But it amounted to nothing more than pleasantries. He complimented my wife and me on the work we had done to make the place habitable after all these years. He enquired what was on the menu for dinner."

"He was planning to join us, then," said Spector. "A man with suicide on his mind would be unlikely to ask that kind of question. What about you, Mrs. Bailey? I noticed he came over to speak with you in the drawing room before the séance."

"Me? Oh, yes. It was the mask, you see. After I tripped like a silly fool and Maurice's mask fell out of my bag. A few minutes after he returned it to me, Mr. Judd came over to ask me about it."

"What did he say?"

"He wanted to know about Maurice."

"What, specifically?"

"He wanted to know if I carried a photograph of him."

"And you said . . . ?"

"I told him of course I do. What mother wouldn't?"

"Did you show him the photograph?"

"Certainly." She began to rummage in her canvas bag. Her face went white. "Good God!" she cried. "It's gone! They're *both* gone! The mask and the picture! It was there! I had it! Somebody's taken it . . ." She peered suspiciously into the faces of each of the guests.

"Sleight of hand," said Spector, "can be the clever criminal's greatest ally. Presumably he—or she—took advantage of Mr. Powell's abortive departure to slip them out of the bag while you were distracted."

"But why?" said Mrs. Bailey.

"That," said Spector, "is a question I cannot yet answer."

"Well," said Francis Tulp decisively, "why don't we search?"

"The thief has had plenty of time to stow them somewhere," answered Spector, "and not necessarily about their person. A search would be a waste of time."

"You really think it's somebody in this room?" said Imogen.

"I have no doubt. And yet the *motive* for the theft eludes me."

Mrs. Bailey dabbed at her eyes with a lace handkerchief. "I knew I should not have come here," she moaned. "I *knew* it would all end badly."

This was punctuated by a sudden blackout. The room was plunged into darkness, and a woman screamed—Imogen could not be sure, but she thought it was Mrs. Lennox. Her eyes struggled to adjust to the sharply obtenebrated room.

"Everybody remain calm," said Clive Lennox. "Just the generator again, that's all it is. Mr. Powell? Do you have the torch to hand?"

"I do." He clicked it on, shining its beam up into his own face.

"Give it to me," said Clive Lennox. "I'll go."

"You oughtn't go alone," said Spector.

"Then I'll come too," said Fred Powell.

"And leave the rest of us in the dark?" protested Madame La Motte. "I'll not stand for it."

"Well, what would you have us do?" said Mr. Lennox, who now held the torch. He shone its beam into Madame's face, illuminating the pasty flesh, mapped with creases, in a dreary corpse light.

"Enough," said Spector, his voice cutting sharply through the rising tension among the group. "We will *all* go. Together."

They marched in procession into the hallway, Lennox still carrying the torch. The darkness was absolute, and thick as the ancient stone walls. That was the only explanation Imogen could come up with for what happened next.

With a sudden, piercing cry, Clive Lennox dropped to his knees. The torch fell from his hand, skidding across the floor and sending mad wheels of light as it spun.

"What is it?" yelled Francis Tulp. "Mr. Lennox, what's the matter?"

"Somebody tripped me!" he cried. They heard him groaning as he clambered to his feet. But somebody had beaten him to the torch and stooped to grab it. It was Madame La Motte—Imogen had no idea how the old medium had moved so quickly, but moved she had. She shone the torch beam into her face to show her look of quiet triumph.

In an instant her expression changed, transmogrifying into a sudden grimace of horror. "There," she said, pointing. "At the bottom of the stairs . . ."

She aimed the torch beam, and they all saw it—a dark shape. The torch beam followed it up the staircase, and to the landing, where it disappeared from view.

"After him!" yelled Tulp, before following his own instruction and bolting for the staircase. Madame La Motte pursued him, torch in hand, closely followed by Spector. Imogen, unwilling to miss a moment of the action, also darted up the stairs as quickly as she could. The going was treacherous in the dark; the wooden steps were warped in places, and uneven, so it was almost impossible to gauge the depth from step to step. It would be easy to trip, to fall, to crack one's skull against the wood, or against the stone wall . . .

"Which way did he go?" said Spector.

"To the right," said Tulp. "I saw him go running off. The torch caught the shape of him as he went round the corner."

Tulp led the way, running along the upstairs corridor until he reached its end. "Where did he go?" he said. "I saw him come round this way. I did."

That's when the lights came back on. It was so abrupt, it made them all jump—all except Joseph Spector. He, Tulp, Clive Lennox, Imogen, and Madame La Motte were all looking bemusedly about the landing, while Mrs. Bailey and Fred Powell remained at the bottom of the stairs.

The front door flew open and Mrs. Lennox stepped back into the house. "It was turned off," she said. "The generator, I mean." She was now out of breath and windswept. Her hair glistened with rain. "Somebody turned it off."

There was a meditative expression on Spector's lined old face. "Whilst we were all—conspicuously—in the dining room," he noted.

"There's somebody else in the house!" said a panicked Mrs. Bailey.

"There's nobody else in the house," said Mr. Lennox with what Imogen perceived as undue sharpness.

"What are you talking about?" This was Tulp, slightly manic in the face of the spectral manifestation. "You *saw* it, didn't you? We all saw it!"

They found themselves on an entirely empty landing. "Show me which way the man went," said Spector. Again, Tulp led the way, followed by Madame La Motte, who clicked off the torch and handed it back to Lennox.

They reached the mouth of another corridor. "He went down there. I saw him."

"No, he didn't," replied Spector.

"What do you mean? I saw him with my own eyes! Madame La Motte shone the torch right at him."

"Mr. Tulp, there's no way the man could have headed down that corridor. Look. The floor."

They all looked. A fine layer of grey dust stretched evenly along the full length of the bare wooden floorboards, all the way to the very end of that long passage.

"But I *saw* him," Tulp repeated, sounding less convinced than before.

Imogen stepped in. "I saw him too," she affirmed.

"And I," Mr. Lennox admitted. "But I can't understand it . . ."

"What did he look like? Did any of you observe a mask or a uniform?"

"He was facing away from us, so we couldn't have seen his face," said Imogen. "And he was just a silhouette in the torchlight. But surely that's immaterial, Mr. Spector. The point is that we all *saw* him. And this is the way he went."

Spector frowned. Slowly, he knelt and examined the floor. With the tip of his index finger he lightly touched one of the boards and then examined his finger. The creases and whorls were darkly peppered with dust motes.

Clive Lennox cleared his throat. "That wing of the house is closed, Mr. Spector. You're wondering about the floor, no doubt. Well, since none of the guests are staying in that part of the house . . . and since it's just my wife and I out here . . ."

"Not at all, Mr. Lennox." Spector got to his feet. "If anything, the dust is most instructive."

Madame La Motte spoke with authority. "Dust is merely the detritus of the earthly flesh. What I saw—what *we* saw—was no creature of flesh."

"Of course it was," said Imogen, surprising even herself with her sharpness. "It had to be."

"There are two options," said Spector, "and neither is especially palatable, I'm afraid. Either the vision we all saw was the ghost of Maurice Bailey, or else—and this is my favoured outcome—it is another guest. An unanticipated presence here, a living one. An intruder in the house."

Spector led the way back downstairs, and the household reconvened in a panicked huddle in the hall. Imogen watched Clive Lennox sidle up to Spector and whisper something to him. After a moment's thought, Spector nodded. Taking this as a signal, Lennox cleared his throat loudly and began to address the group. "Ladies. Gentlemen. I am afraid there is nothing more to be done this evening. The storm is worsening, which means there is no means of returning to the mainland at least until the morning. So I would personally like to suggest that we take to our beds, and try to get some rest. It's been a remarkably trying few hours, and sleep seems to be the order of the day."

"You want us to *sleep* after all this?" said Mrs. Bailey in a state of high agitation.

"Sleep or not," put in Spector, "but taking to our rooms seems an advisable course of action. We must keep our doors locked, of course."

"No," said Mrs. Lennox. "That is to say, we should stick together, surely." She looked from Imogen to Spector, and there was something manic in her eyes.

"You and your husband will be quite safe," Spector assured her. "After all, we have certain means of guarding our safety here which the typical country house does not contain. I'm talking about your ghost-hunting kit, Mr. Tulp. If we rig the upstairs hallway with your bells, strings, and other alarums, no one will be able to leave their room without alerting at least one of their neighbours."

Imogen had to admit it wasn't a bad idea.

And so they set about it, carting spools of thread, jangling bells, and all the other accoutrements of Tulp's morbid trade up the stairs to the mouth of the corridor. Imogen's inquisitive reporter's eyes paid close attention throughout the following minutes—she felt as though she were being tested somehow, as though somebody were making a conscious effort to sneak something past her. But for the life of her, she could not spot it. There was no shortage of unusual incidents, however. It was their *significance* that was lost on Imogen.

First, and most notable, Fred Powell remained downstairs. He would not be sleeping in that first-floor corridor, but instead in a room adjacent to the kitchen. Why?

Second, there were the bells. Five handbells, which Tulp strung together between the banisters at the top of the staircase.

Madame La Motte, who had been uncharacteristically quiet for a little while, now said, "The camera."

In an instant, all eyes were on her. "The tripod," she explained. "It would be wise to consider setting that up as well. In case this house were to be beset with any more . . . phenomena."

Tulp readily agreed, handing the spool of thread to Clive Lennox and thundering down the stairs once again to fetch it.

He rigged up the camera at the mouth of the corridor, facing down it so that its viewfinder took in every door. Then he set up a "trigger-weight," as he called it, which swung pendulously from the tripod and was connected to a series of rubber-looking floor tiles that he arranged along the corridor, slipping them beneath the rugs as though he were shuffling a deck of cards. "If anybody steps on one of these pads," he explained, "the trigger-weight will be deployed and the individual will be caught on camera." There were not enough to cover every inch of the floor, and so he was forced to arrange them in an alternating tessellation, rather like a chessboard. But it meant nonetheless that traversing the corridor required wide, loping footsteps.

Next came the business of the doors. They started with Mrs. Bailey, whose room was closest to the landing. She bade them all good night and disappeared inside. They all heard her lock the door. Clive Lennox, who still held the spool of thread, passed one end to Tulp and, following Tulp's instructions, began to unfurl it slowly. Tulp looped the thread around the door handle and followed Mr. Lennox to the next door. They continued this punctilious procedure until every door was connected by this single thread, looped around each door handle in a bizarre cat's cradle.

"There," said Tulp with satisfaction. "I used the same arrangement at Borley. Ought to do the trick, oughtn't it?" He looked at Spector, who nodded wordlessly.

"What about this end?" said Mr. Lennox, holding the remains of the thread.

"Pass it to me," said Tulp. "I'll tie it to the handbells. That way, if any of these doors is opened in the night, the rest of us will hear it." He did so, and then demonstrated by pushing open the door to Imogen's room. The bells jangled. "You see?" he grinned.

"Very clever, Mr. Tulp," said Spector. "Thank you. And, if I may, I'd also like to suggest that everyone lock their doors as well. With all these security measures in place, we may yet have a fighting chance."

They all took to their rooms in a cacophony of bells, which eventually stilled into silence. The only doors along that passage that were not secured in this elaborate fashion were the bathroom and the room containing Walter Judd's body. The rest were both locked on the inside *and* secured externally.

Imogen listened as the bells fell silent. The house was still.

"And so to bed," Madame La Motte declaimed, a satisfied little smile creasing her lips.

The callous old vampire, thought Imogen as she gave the key a mighty twist in the lock. Satisfied that she and the old medium were sealed in tight, Imogen filled a glass with water from the basin in the corner, then turned her back on Madame La Motte while the two women undressed. It was futile, she thought as she scrambled beneath the covers and drew the cretonne quilt up to her chin. Her mind was awhirl. Her body was incapable of sleep. Madame La Motte turned out the light with one final, cheery good night, and Imogen rolled onto her back and commenced what she predicted to be a lengthy session of staring at the black ceiling, watching imaginary shapes assume sly, dancing forms as she waited for her ideas to coalesce—to coagulate, she supposed, like drying blood.

FLOOR PLAN:
WEST WING, FIRST FLOOR,
DEVIL'S NECK

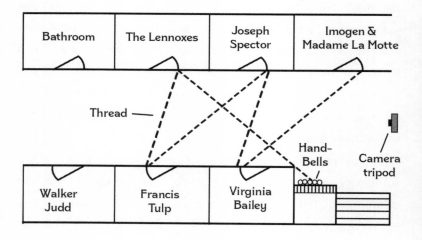

Bathroom | The Lennoxes | Joseph Spector | Imogen & Madame La Motte

Thread —

Hand-Bells

Camera tripod

Walker Judd | Francis Tulp | Virginia Bailey

Where to begin?

The dead man: Walter Judd. A mere cipher—a hollowed-out shell. What was to be said of him? He was an enigma.

No; that was not quite true. He had obviously come to Devil's Neck because he had been paid to do so; to find something out. To watch them all. Evidently, he had troubled another member of the party during the journey, or upon their arrival. And yet, sifting through her usually reliable memory, her abiding image of him was of that sullen, watchful expression. There was nothing else, was there?

There was.

She replayed that moment in her mind, a few minutes after their arrival at the house. Mrs. Bailey tripped on the edge of the carpet and spilled the contents of her handbag. That was when they had got their first glimpse of the mask, as it went skidding across the floor. And yet . . . the expression on Judd's face underwent a perceptible change as he stooped to pick it up. Who had seen that look cross his face? Any of them, in theory. But what could that look have meant?

She turned her attention to the others. Like a cast of players at a triumphant curtain call, they assembled before her in a row and stepped forward one by one to take their bows.

Francis Tulp. Young, handsome Francis. Boyish and a little silly, she thought, though that may simply be a front. And yet: there was the equipment, and the obvious earnestness of his belief in spirits. There was also the matter of his prior acquaintance with Joseph Spector.

Which brought her neatly to Spector.

He was an old ham, but he had a keen eye—after all, he was the one who had sussed out the fact that the suicide was not a suicide. In fact, Spector carried himself with a certain authority—almost like a detective, she thought.

The spectral Spector took his bow and retreated from view.

Next was Mrs. Bailey, whose son killed himself all those years ago. Was there a motive? None that could be discerned.

Exit, Mrs. Bailey.

And now, the Lennoxes. Clive the blowhard, who talked a little too much, and seemed afraid of what the silences of Devil's Neck might hold. All the same, she liked him. Was it liking, or merely pitying? He seemed fit to be pitied, with that strange, fearsome wife of his. Justine Lennox. Obliging, yet ice-cold. There were secrets behind that inscrutable visage. And there was one more guest at Devil's Neck who had not yet received the lens of her attention . . .

Before she could focus in too closely on Fred Powell (the outlier, the only one who was not snared in the web of strings and bells), she noticed this parade of imaginary faces had begun to merge; to blend. Soon they had become a single face, which stared back at her from the darkness with uncanny malevolence: the mask of Maurice Bailey. It was the last thing Imogen saw before a heavy, unanticipated slumber descended, and all around her was darkness.

―――

Her sleep was heavy and dreamless, but it was ultimately short-lived. Her eyes came open with difficulty, slow and creaky as a rusty shop shutter. The room was still in darkness. She had no idea what the time might be, and no way of finding out without disturbing Madame La Motte—which she was loath to do. Frustratingly, the clock at her bedside was just out of sight. She could practically feel the presence of its smooth white face, but she could not make out its hands. The gentle metronomic tick was the only sound, apart from her own shallow breathing.

She listened for a moment, and her weary brain began to compute the strangeness of her surroundings. The room was in darkness, and utterly silent, yet something had woken her. What was it? Certainly not Madame La Motte, who slept like the dead. Had there been some other movement in the closeness of this shared bedroom?

Blinking slowly and feeling as though her corneas were peppered with sand, Imogen shifted beneath the covers, propping herself up on her elbows to try and get a look around.

She knew then that she and the medium were not alone in the room. This was no mere hypnopompic hallucination; no vestige of sleep. There was a third figure, another presence, hovering in the shadows. Biting on her lower lip, Imogen eased herself farther upright, pressing her back against the bedstead. Her breathing was heavier now; louder and more erratic. Bizarrely, the room was spinning. She felt as if she were hungover, though she had only sipped a glass or two of wine at dinner. She had not even let herself enjoy it. Now she felt as though a balloon were slowly inflating behind her eyes.

Had she, perhaps, been drugged?

This was a troubling thought for numerous reasons, not least of which that she had no idea who might have been responsible.

Then, she recalled the glass of water at her bedside, and how she had turned her back on Madame La Motte when she was undressing. Had the medium slipped something into the glass? And why?

Energised by her sudden realisation, Imogen lunged for the bedside lamp and switched it on. What she saw—the hideous Penny Dreadful tableau—made her do something she had not done since she was a little girl: she screamed.

The sight that met her foggy, sleep-clouded eyes was the product of a nightmare imagination. In the bed against the opposite wall lay Madame La Motte; Imogen recognised the distinctive arc of her body beneath the covers. But the covers themselves were a tattered, crimson ruin, shredded by a blade and soaked in blood. The old medium's head was turned toward the wall so that Imogen could not make out the expression. Somehow this was worse, for she could only imagine the look of horror on the dead face.

In a way, though, the sight of the murdered old woman in the bed on the far side of the room was not even the worst part. There was a yet more monstrous piece of the puzzle. In the centre of the room, equidistant between the two beds, stood The Stepney Lad. The automaton, too, was covered in blood, its face unblinking and contemplative as it stared at the door. Its right hand was upraised—poised to strike, Imogen thought—and in its palm it clutched the wooden handle of a kitchen knife. The blade itself was keen, and obviously the murder weapon. It ought to have shone in the lamplight, but every inch of its silvery steel surface was soaked in the old woman's blood.

Still drowsy, Imogen kicked aside the bedclothes and tumbled out onto the floor. In her panic, she almost knocked over The Stepney Lad. She drew in another heavy breath and screamed once more; she would hate herself for it later and wish that she had conducted herself with more decorum. But the panic was like a living creature about her shoulders, tightening its grip on her throat.

She lunged toward the door, halting for the minutest instant to note that the key was still protruding from the lock. She gave it a quick twist and then grabbed the handle, pulling the door inward.

Francis Tulp was the first to emerge from his room in a cacophony of bells. He came out into the corridor without fear, striding over the webwork of strings, carelessly traipsing over to her across the pads, and when he saw the look on Imogen's face he halted. "Dear God, what is it? What's happened?"

Next came Joseph Spector. He was also still fully dressed, and if he had slept at all he did not show it; there was no hint of bleariness about him. Striding out, cane in hand, he navigated the tangle of threads across the floor with positively feline agility. But he did not take his eyes from Imogen.

"Miss Drabble, are you all right?"

The others, too, began to emerge. Mrs. Bailey peeked through a crack in her door, calling out, "What's happened?"

Clive Lennox was next. He came out of his room in ill-fitting pyjamas, and his wife followed, fully dressed. Some were sharp and quick in the way they navigated the threads, while others were lumbering and graceless, as though they had been sleeping very heavily indeed. The expression on every face was one of dread commingled with utter bewilderment.

"It's . . . Madame La Motte," said Imogen, gulping for air as though she had just surfaced from a deep-sea dive. "Somebody's killed her."

CHAPTER TEN

A LIST OF NAMES

. . . the neurotic is very often psychic, and the psychic is very often neurotic.

—Dion Fortune, *Psychic Self-Defence*

August 31, 1939. 7 P.M.

Abbaye Notre-Dame de l'Annonciation du Fleurrière was a small Benedictine monastery erected in approximately 1140, and for over seven hundred fifty years a bastion of contemplative solitude in the Belgian countryside. In May 1915, however, its immaculate serenity—as well as its ancient stone walls—were obliterated by German shells. What remained—essentially a single stone bulwark of around thirty feet in height and a few hundred yards in length, along with assorted nubs of brick jutting from the ground like broken teeth—was swiftly appropriated by Allied Forces, and in the shadow of that single crumbling wall a shantytown of tents was constructed and the site was renamed the Fleurrière Casualty Clearing Station, or CCS.

It was a field hospital, known affectionately as "the abattoir." Its proximity to the Western Front gave it a fearsome reputation among staff of the Royal Army Medical Corps. No nurse or doctor lingered there long. It was a small but necessary entity, so close to the front lines in a region where medical provisions were scarce, and disease and gruesome injury commonplace. As with any other CCS, the aim was to restore the injured to active duty as soon as possible—though of course this was not always practical. In many cases (and bearing in mind the limited resources at their disposal) often the best they could manage was a simple patch-up job for an unfortunate patient who would then be transported to a better-established field hospital (with, at least in theory, a functioning roof) some miles behind the line. Whether the patient was alive when they got there is a matter best left undiscussed.

The fact is, Fleurrière was a desperate place peopled by desperate individuals: soldiers maddened by war, and medicos maddened by a paucity of equipment with which to ply their trade. CCSs such as this were also incredibly vulnerable—they were, after all, mere flaps of fabric shielding the dead and dying from enemy artillery. In theory, such places were protected by international law. In fact, however, the fog of war was thicker here than perhaps anywhere else in Europe. With tragic inevitability, a stray shell struck the dead centre of the Fleurrière site, annihilating it completely. Whether the attack was intentional, nobody knew or particularly cared. This happened in spring of 1918, by which point pervasive battle fatigue had rendered the air soupy, every step a lumbering trudge, and every unfortunate soul sadder and haunted.

Top brass, in one of their habitual abrogations of moral responsibility, chose to take the incident as evidence of the efficiency of their strategists, who had after all warned them of precisely this outcome. Sitting ducks they were said to be, and sitting ducks they were. Of the hundred-odd residents of the Fleurrière CCS, only a handful survived. Three of these were swiftly shipped back to England, and to Devil's Neck; these three were Rodney Edgecomb, Maurice Bailey, and Will McGinn.

"Fleurrière," said Flint thoughtfully. "I might have guessed."

"You know it, sir?"

"Know it? Hook, my dreams take me back there most nights. I sometimes wonder if I'll ever be free of it." Off his sergeant's disconcerted expression, he expounded, "I spent three days and three nights there in the summer of 1917. By then it was a foetid hellhole, with tattered tents, knee-high mud, and a stench of death in the air. To this day, that stench clings to my nostrils. I remember hearing of the shelling and how the place was obliterated in early 1918. Rather than mourning those lost, my first thought was an unaccountably callous one. 'Good,' I thought. 'Such a place as that should never be allowed to exist on God's earth.'"

The two men had regrouped at Scotland Yard, in Flint's office, where Hook presented the results of his questioning of Judd's secretary, as well as the passenger list he had obtained from the bus depot.

"You'll never guess whose name is on that list, sir," he said.

"I've a feeling I might, you know."

"Joseph Spector."

Despite his overall fatigue and dissatisfaction with the investigation, Flint could not help but smile a little. "This case has got Spector written all over it," he commented. "All it's been missing is the man himself."

"Makes you wonder, though, doesn't it, sir? If *he* might know something about what's going on?"

"Oh, I'm sure he's got the whole thing sussed out by now. All over bar the shouting, I'll wager. Still, might as well show our faces, eh?" His words were sardonic, but Flint was nonetheless greatly comforted by the revelation that Spector—who seemed to have perpetrated one of his fabled disappearing acts—had in fact been in on the investigation all along. "All roads lead to Devil's Neck, it seems. Better fire up the car, Hook, before the storm gets any worse." Fist-like raindrops pummelled the windows. Hook wondered how it could possibly be any worse. Regardless, he did as instructed and without complaint.

Meanwhile, Flint spent a moment or two gathering his thoughts, gazing out at the grey, lumbering Thames, his pipe clenched tight between his teeth. He was close. He knew it. Cases like this, that seemed illogical, seldom were. It was merely that their logic was subtler, and better concealed, than the casual observer might anticipate. But it was always there. Spector had taught him that.

The locked-room murder in Crook O'Lune Street was a neat bit of business, but Flint had to concede that it wasn't the work of a genius or a criminal mastermind. After all, he, Flint, had seen through it in a short space of time. Spector would likely have taken seconds. No, the murder of Rodney Edgecomb was a hastily contrived affair. An act of sudden desperation. And it made no logical sense—killing Edgecomb meant killing the only means of accessing the inheritance, after all.

"Car's ready, sir," said Hook.

"Good," answered Flint. "Well, we'd better get on the road. There's a killer waiting to be caught."

Since it was such a trek, Flint and Hook opted to share the drive out to Devil's Neck. Flint took the wheel first. He knew that Hook was the more skilful driver, and thus better equipped to traverse the swampy marshland as they came nearer to the house. But even the roads near London were waterlogged, and the going was hazardous. Flint needed to focus his mind.

After pulling up at a small petrol station en route (the same petrol station, in fact, where the coach had stopped some hours earlier, though Flint had no way of knowing this), they set off again.

"Hook—the passenger list for the coach journey. Read me some of the names."

Hook scrambled for the slip of paper in his pocket. With his other hand he ignited his cigarette lighter, so that he might read the names by its amber glow. "Imogen Drabble," he commenced. "She's a secretary, sir. Used to work at the *Chronicle*, now employed by an agency."

"What happened at the *Chronicle*?"

"Word has it the editor made an unwelcome pass, so she blacked his eye for him and left him on crutches for a month or two."

"Ha!" Flint barked happily. He could quite imagine one of his daughters doing the same thing. "What age is she?"

"Twenty-three."

"A little young for the Aitken affair. Go on."

"Virginia Bailey."

"*Bailey*? Any relation to Maurice?"

"Stands to reason, I'd say. Spector we know. Judd we know. Next on the list is Adaline La Motte."

"The medium?"

"You've heard of her then, sir?"

"My wife developed a fascination with mediumship a year or two ago. Madame La Motte was one she took an interest in. Went to see her a couple times at the Egyptian Theatre." What Flint had neglected to mention was that it was not his wife who had taken an interest in spiritualism but Flint himself, and that it actually dated back six or seven years, around the time that his mother died. But of course the roots of this interest lay even deeper in the past. This was despite his friend Spector's avowed dedication to logic, rationality, and the debunking of frauds, not to mention Flint's own experience and observation of the many tricks and gimmicks used in the creation of seemingly uncanny phenomena. To him, Madame La Motte was just about as convincing as any of them—though this was not saying much, he conceded.

"I'll bet Spector knows her," Hook observed.

"I'd be astonished if he didn't," said Flint. "Who's next?"

"Francis Tulp."

"Male or female?"

"Male."

"Any other information?"

"Only his age: twenty-six."

"Again, that makes him too young for the Aitken business. Anybody else?"

"Just one more name, sir. Will McGinn."

"Will McGinn's out there too? Well, well."

"No, sir, it says here he didn't actually board the coach."

"Even more interesting! Is that it?"

"For passengers, yes."

"The driver?"

"Not listed on the manifest, but the secretary told me his name is Frederick Powell. He was originally supposed to stay at a bed-and-breakfast on the mainland, but what with the weather as it is I reckon he'll be staying at Devil's Neck too. The causeway must be impassable."

Flint grunted affirmatively. "Did he give you any other information about Powell?"

"Not much, sir. Didn't seem to know him well, and was keen to point out that Powell was a quiet sort who kept himself to himself."

"That could mean anything," said Flint glumly. He went on, "You do realise, Hook, that we may be required to get our feet a little wet?"

"The thought had occurred to me, sir."

"You know how to operate a boat?"

"Only from little jaunts on the duck pond when I was a lad. Couldn't claim to have my sea legs, sir."

"Well," Flint offered, "sounds as though you've a damned sight more experience than me."

They pressed on into the dark, toward the house at Devil's Neck.

PART THREE

EXPIATION

If there is anything to Spiritualism then the world should know it. If there is nothing to it, if it is, as it appears, built on a flimsy framework of misdirection, then too the universe must be told.

—Harry Houdini,
A Magician Among the Spirits

Whether these séances are the result of a living or a physically dead mind at work is a question with which some of the best minds continue to wrestle.

—John Mulholland,
Beware Familiar Spirits

CHAPTER ELEVEN

CAMERA OBSCURA

Some more details of it will have to be given,
though I cannot hope to put before you the look of
the picture as clearly as it is present to my own eye.

—M. R. James, "The Mezzotint"

September 1, 1939. 3:15 A.M.

*T*ime.

The thought ran through Imogen's mind. In her panic, she had not looked at her bedside clock. "What time is it?" she asked Tulp.

He took out his pocket watch. "About a quarter past three," he told her. He was sleep addled and sluggish, but still fully dressed. He must have collapsed into bed without even removing his jacket.

Four hours, then. The murder had been committed between eleven and three—roughly. A large enough expanse of hours for all manner of chicanery to be perpetrated.

The entire household was now awake: the Lennoxes had gone downstairs to alert Fred Powell. Clive Lennox now wore a dressing gown in kidney-coloured silk (more of a smoking jacket, Imogen thought, though she had not seen him smoke a single puff throughout their brief acquaintance), which seemed faintly absurd, clownish, a pure affectation. He seemed keen to keep his wife by his side at all times. Francis Tulp and Mrs. Bailey loitered on the landing, stealing occasional glances into the murder room. Mrs. Bailey wore a long, unflattering nightdress rather like Madame La Motte's. Imogen hovered by the open bedroom door, watching Joseph Spector explore the room. The old conjuror was fully dressed and wide awake. He took slow, cautious steps, as though he might hit upon a fatal trapdoor and plunge to his doom at any moment. Imogen realised (her sluggish brain was coming back to life) that he was testing the floorboards for creaks. He stopped by the window. "Has this been opened at all?"

"Not by me," she answered honestly.

Spector dropped to his haunches, just as he had beside Walter Judd's body. With the tips of his fingers he gently brushed the carpet. "Rainwater," he said. Then he got up and, in a sudden, sweeping motion, threw open the window. Gusts of rain-spattered air drenched both him and the carpet, but he leaned out and peered down into the darkness. When he was finally satisfied, he pulled shut the window again. "Yes, this was definitely opened at some point," he said.

"Could anyone have clambered in that way?" asked Tulp.

"In theory," Spector answered. "It's a sheer drop down to the water, but there's a drainpipe—a steel one. If the killer were especially agile, he *might* have clambered up . . ."

"Well, there you have it," said Imogen, perhaps a little too eagerly. "It could only be one person."

"Oh yes? And who is that?"

"Well, isn't it obvious? Fred Powell! His room's directly below this one, isn't it? All he had to do was open his window, climb up, and climb in."

"Why?"

"What do you mean?"

"Well, what motive does he have? I'm not aware of any."

"Does it matter?"

"There's always a motive, Miss Drabble. Besides, as you pointed out, Mr. Powell's room downstairs is the only one that *wasn't* secured by the strings of Mr. Tulp's trap. So there was nothing to prevent him from leaving his room via the door. Not to mention the automaton—I very much doubt *anyone* could have climbed up a drainpipe with The Stepney Lad slung over his shoulder. No, I'm inclined to believe that Mr. Powell is innocent on this occasion."

"How can you say that? Surely you can't dismiss him out of hand?"

"I assure you, Miss Drabble, that I'm not dismissing anyone. But I believe there's another explanation. The automaton must have been brought up the stairs—we can agree on that, can't we? And it must have been brought into the room via the door."

Reluctantly, Imogen gave a nod.

Spector crept over to the door, his shoulders slightly hunched, looking like a caricature of Nosferatu's silhouette from the Murnau film. He got down on his knees and examined the lock. "Doesn't appear to have been tampered with," he said. "And yet the door was definitely locked on the inside?"

Imogen nodded.

Spector turned to Tulp. "Francis, I believe you were the first one to enter the room when Miss Drabble screamed?"

"Yes, I was."

"Do you happen to remember if the string around the door handle had been disturbed?"

"I . . . now that you mention it, yes—the string was on the floor!"

Spector got to his feet again. "So the door could have been opened without disturbing the bells. Opened from inside, that is. And yet, I can't see anything to indicate the lock was disturbed. No scratches or burn marks. It would *seem* to the casual observer that the killer could *only* have entered via the door, because he—or she—carried the automaton, and could *only* have exited via the window because the door was locked on the inside. Does that seem a fair summation?"

"More or less," said Tulp.

"Then there's only one suspect: Fred Powell," Imogen reiterated.

Spector shook his head. "No. That's incorrect."

"Why?"

Spector ran his hands over the pair of old door hinges then examined his fingers. They came away clean.

"Why?" Imogen repeated.

Next, Spector turned his attention to The Stepney Lad, which stood upright amid a gruesome mess in the centre of the room, the knife still upraised, the blank expression now tinged with mania as the murky brown blood had begun to dry. He had not yet devoted any significant attention to the body on the bed; instead, he

FLOOR PLAN:
ADALINE LA MOTTE AND
IMOGEN DRABBLE'S ROOM,
DEVIL'S NECK

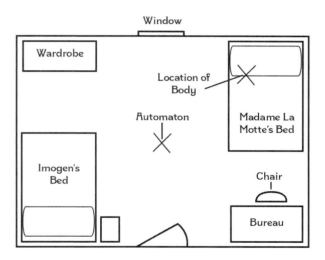

Window

Wardrobe

Location of
Body

Automaton

Madame La
Motte's Bed

Imogen's
Bed

Chair

Bureau

focused on the knife in the automaton's hand. He did not touch it. It occurred to Imogen that the other guests were treating Spector as though he really were an officer of the law, instead of simply a performer playing at being a detective for the night. But she didn't say anything.

"I would suggest," he said, "that the murder was committed between one and two o'clock. This is an entirely unscientific estimate, albeit based on two significant factors. First, the blood on the blade has more or less dried. And there is a *lot* of blood. I would therefore say that the murder could not have been committed less than an hour ago. The other factor is Miss Drabble, who appears to have been drugged. Assuming the drug in question to be laudanum—and going by the specks of sediment in the bottom of the water glass on the bedside table, that seems to be the case—I suggest that it would have taken until at least one o'clock for Miss Drabble to have descended into a sleep deep enough that she would not be disturbed by the frenzy of violence which took place."

"How did you know I was drugged?" she asked him.

"Your speech," said Spector. "You may not have perceived it yourself, but your words are somewhat slurred. I think, however, that it was a largely harmless sedative which was administered to you in your water. Knockout drops, you might say. I imagine their effects will wear off fairly soon." At last, he turned his attention to the corpse. "And it appears that your assailant will not be repeating the offence."

"It was *her*?" said Tulp, indicating the body of Madame La Motte.

"I don't see who else it could have been. You did not take any sleeping pills yourself, did you?"

Imogen shook her head, then immediately regretted it, for her headache came roaring back.

"And presumably you filled the glass yourself, from the sink in the corner?"

"Yes."

"At what time was that?"

"I don't know. Whenever it was that we came to bed."

Spector nodded slowly and thoughtfully. "Then I assume the late Madame La Motte took advantage of a brief lapse in your attention to slip something into your drink. Evidence may yet remain within the room, though I think it more likely that the murderer has disposed of it."

He leaned over the dead body, angling himself so he could examine the dead woman's face, which was turned toward the wall. "A monstrous, ugly death," he said. "She was a schemer and a confidence trickster, but she didn't deserve this. Nobody does."

"Have you any idea *who* . . . ?" asked Mrs. Bailey.

"I have plenty of ideas," Spector said. "Too many to count. Now, it becomes a matter of sifting through them for flaws."

"There's somebody else in this house," said Mrs. Bailey. "There has to be. It simply couldn't have been one of *us* who did this. What about the man we saw on the stairs—the man in the mask? Couldn't he be hiding somewhere?"

"Mr. Spector," Imogen commenced, "this whole thing is impossible. Walter Judd died in a locked room, and now *this*.

The killer was in the room with me, maybe mere *inches* from my bed. How did he get in? And how did he get out again?"

Spector stood upright. "The matter of getting in is perhaps not as complicated as it might appear. In fact, I'd go so far as to say it's horribly simple. The killer was admitted to the room by his victim. Whether this was a prearranged rendezvous or not, and whether it was the reason behind your doping, Miss Drabble, I cannot yet tell. But it's the simplest and therefore likeliest explanation. It also, I'm afraid, supports the notion that the killer is a member of our party. Someone known to Madame La Motte."

"How come?" said Tulp. "I mean, I knotted that string round each door handle myself. Nobody could open their door from inside without rattling those bells loud enough to wake the dead."

"The window?" offered Imogen. "Could someone have opened their window and shimmied along to this one, perhaps? Is there a ledge?"

Spector shook his head. "No ledge."

"Then it's the soldier. It has to be. The soldier we saw on the stairs. He must be hiding somewhere in this house, picking us off one by one . . ."

"The man who left no footprints in the dust," said Spector thoughtfully. "Well, whoever it was, I would suggest that the killer came to the room with a plan to kill. However, it seems that the method was more or less impromptu. This was no calculated faux suicide. It was a swift and bloody murder, judging by the state of the body. I'm almost tempted to call it a crime of passion; the repeated stabbings bespeak of sudden fury, not shrewd calculation. And yet we know our killer is a clever planner. It seems to be an interesting paradox—perhaps the very unplanned nature of the crime was actually *part* of the plan?"

"The knife . . ." said Francis Tulp. "Where did it come from?"

"A good question," answered Spector. "I've checked with the Lennoxes, and they confirm that it was *not* pilfered from the kitchen. At a guess, I would say it belonged to Madame La Motte."

"How come?"

"I believe she brought it with her, and concealed it about her person—perhaps in a pocket within the lining of her dress."

"Why?"

Spector smiled mordantly, but did not answer. Instead, he turned to Imogen. "Don't think too harshly of Madame La Motte, Imogen. I believe the fact that she drugged you was the very thing that saved your life. Had you woken, I've no doubt whatsoever that you, too, would have been killed. As it was, the killer either deduced that you had been doped—or perhaps Madame La Motte told him."

Imogen felt sick. She must have looked dreadfully pale, for Mrs. Bailey put a consoling hand on her arm. "Why?" she said. "And why the automaton?"

"I do not yet know," said Spector. "But I'm quite sure that the automaton was highly significant. After all, the killer went to the considerable effort of heading downstairs to retrieve it, and then of arranging it so carefully. Needless to say, he did all of this while you slept, Miss Drabble."

"I've been thinking about that automaton," said Tulp. "As ludicrous as it seems, I can't help but wonder if perhaps there *is* some mechanism—a quirk in the mechanics—which could be exploited somehow . . ."

"You think Madame La Motte was killed by The Stepney Lad?"

Tulp shook his head, dismissing the idea. "No, of course it's foolish. The stuff of boy's own fiction . . ."

Imogen's instinctual urge was to concur with Tulp's assessment of his own theory. And yet, she did not. Because the fact remained that she had been in that room—*alone* in that room—with Madame La Motte. The door was locked on the inside. How could Imogen be sure? Because Imogen had locked it herself. As simple as that. She therefore *knew* the room was inaccessible. Sealed. A locked room.

"Perhaps," she suggested, "The Stepney Lad was already in the room when I locked it. Hidden somewhere."

"I'm afraid that will not hold water," Spector asseverated. "I checked the ballroom before we came upstairs. I *saw* The Stepney Lad in precisely the position that we left it: sitting at the table. There can be little doubt that—regardless of how it was achieved—The Stepney Lad was brought up to the room by the killer."

"But why?"

"Why," repeated Spector. "Of all the questions, *that* seems to me the most apropos. I've encountered many unusual and apparently impossible tableaux in my time, and many murders arranged like a theatrical mise-en-scène. Perhaps none has been quite so incongruous as the two we've encountered here at Devil's Neck. For, make no mistake, these are two murders, albeit very different. The starkness of the staged suicide, and the lurid grotesquerie of this latest abomination. And the automaton . . . *Why the automaton?* It's always significant when a killer goes to seemingly unnecessary lengths. The retrieval of The Stepney Lad would seem to be an entirely unnecessary extravagance. Unless, of course, the very absence of a reason is the reason itself."

"Meaning what?" said Imogen.

"Meaning that the obvious and intrusive presence of the automaton may serve a less tangible purpose. May, in fact, solely have been intended to cloud our reason . . ."

"A red herring."

"Just so."

"But that implies there's something else to be found in the room," said Imogen. "And there isn't anything. Is there?"

"I can think of one thing," said Tulp.

"What's that?"

"You."

"And what the hell is *that* supposed to mean?"

"A psychological trick," said Tulp, evidently proud of his deduction. "The introduction of something from *outside* the room to distract us from the fact that the real killer was already inside . . ."

Imogen's face was white with fury. "Is that a serious accusation, Mr. Tulp?" she said through gritted teeth.

"Now, now," said the young man patronisingly, "no need to fly off the handle. Because, you know, you *may* have managed to commit the dreadful crime without even realising it . . ."

"Please explain."

"Well, there are such things as hypnotic trances. Assuming control of another person's will. Taking over their mind, making them do things, turning them into—"

"An automaton," said Joseph Spector.

Imogen was about to centre her anger on him, but his expression silenced her.

"It's an appealing theory, Mr. Tulp. Suitably Grand Guignol. But wrong. Utterly wrong."

"How can you be so certain?" Tulp said. "You know well enough that there are many, many cases of the human will being . . . *subsumed* by that of another. No doubt you're familiar with the Thompson-Gifford case?"

"Yes, I know it," said Spector. "A wonderful story." For the benefit of Imogen, he explained: "Robert Swain Gifford was a landscape painter of some renown, who died in New England in 1905. Around six months later, a goldsmith named Frederic Thompson began to experience visions, to hear voices, and eventually claimed to be possessed by the spirit of the dead painter. He sketched and painted landscapes, as Gifford had. The works he produced were considered by art critics to be the stylistic equal of Gifford's. Thompson claimed that Gifford's spirit spoke to him, and dictated what he should paint and how he ought to go about it."

"You're forgetting something." Tulp folded his arms triumphantly. "Thompson was able to paint scenes which he himself had never visited, but which Gifford had. This was all down to the descriptions conveyed to him by Gifford's ghost."

Imogen was too horrified to comment. It was not that she believed the story, but rather the matter-of-fact manner in which it was posited.

"Indeed," said Spector, smiling back, "a good story, certainly, but not without holes. First, how may we *know* that Thompson had not visited those scenes before? One cannot prove a negative.

Furthermore, how may we know for certain that Thompson *did* paint those pictures? Pictures which, to the untrained eye, were the product of the late Robert Swain Gifford? And I think *you* are forgetting something, Mr. Tulp. You are forgetting that Thompson and Gifford *had* met before, on at least two occasions. While they weren't friends, they were certainly aware of one another's existence. Which means that Thompson knew of Gifford's work."

"You think it was a scam, then?" Tulp seemed affronted. Imogen, however, was relieved.

"I find it hard to conclude otherwise."

"And the motive?"

"The oldest there is! *Money*. The death of an artist increases the value of his work considerably, that much is true. But which do you think would be more likely to yield a fortune? The paintings left behind by a deceased yet middling artist, or fresh paintings produced by the artist's *phantom*? The right sort of collector would pay top dollar for the latter. And it would serve as a handy explanation for Thompson's possession of the paintings, of course, if he had in fact come by them via insalubrious means. Where a positive cannot be proven, a negative must be assumed."

"That sounds like something out of Sherlock Holmes," said Imogen. She meant it as a compliment.

"You think so? I doubt Conan Doyle would approve of my empty theorising. In fact, I'm positive he would have been taken in by every single trick up Madame La Motte's voluminous sleeves."

"Tricks, Joseph?" said Mrs. Bailey.

"I'm afraid so, Virginia. I'll explain fully in due course, but here's a little aperitif." He leaned over beside the open suitcase at the foot of Madame La Motte's bed and retrieved a small metallic item from within. It looked rather like a pen: thin and dull, perhaps five inches in length. With a flick of the wrist the object doubled, tripled, quadrupled in length, extending telescopically like a pointer. "Maskelyne caught out the Davenport brothers using just such a device as this in one of *their* 'séances.'" He held it out, tip upraised. "They would often attach bells or tambourines to one end. But all it takes is the addition of a stick of graphite to produce the rather sinister message we saw on the ceiling."

"As simple as that?" said Imogen.

"Easy enough to conceal, and even if you *had* spotted it, would you have known what you were looking at?"

She shook her head. "I would probably just have thought it was a pen."

"As would any untrained observer," said Spector. "Likely Madame was counting on that. Let's go downstairs, shall we? I imagine Mrs. Lennox will be making tea."

"Wait a moment," said Tulp. "So you don't believe the Thompson-Gifford story. All right. But that doesn't disprove the hypnotism theory. If it wasn't Imogen who did it, then how was it done?"

"You know," said Spector, "we could argue the toss when it comes to hypnotic possession. What *cannot* be argued is the practical side of things. See, Miss Drabble's white nightdress is entirely unmarked by even the tiniest speck of blood. If she had stabbed Madame La Motte, she would be positively drenched."

"She could have changed her nightdress before raising the alarm."

"Why? If she were under hypnosis there would be no need. And if she committed the murder herself, under her own volition, why create the fallacy of a locked room with herself as the only suspect?"

This silenced Tulp.

Spector returned his attention to the exploration of the room, focusing particularly on the murder weapon. With a silk crimson handkerchief, he slipped the blade from between the tight, insensate fingers of the automaton. He did not focus on the sharp end, but on the handle. "I would be immensely surprised if the killer had left so obvious a trace. Nonetheless it would be remiss to neglect the possibility altogether."

Francis Tulp's ghost-hunting kit included a small pouch of powdered graphite, which Spector now applied to the knife handle in search of fingerprints. But there were none. He did not seem perturbed by this; in fact he looked positively relieved. It was as though the presence of a trace left by the killer would shatter the chain of logic that he had begun slowly and methodically to develop.

Next, he turned his attention to the keyhole and, more precisely, the key. It was an ordinary-looking brass key, quite old, and with a hasp the size of Imogen's thumbnail. It fitted snugly into the lock and turned with a satisfying click. Imogen knew this—she had turned it herself. And yet, through that locked door a killer had walked. The window offered only a sheer drop down to the ocean. Spector traced a slow circuit of his surroundings, cane in hand, occasionally tapping the wall. Imogen watched as he reached the wardrobe and spent a good five minutes combing its exterior. It was polished oak, gleaming with dried varnish. He knelt by its keyhole and peeked through, but there was nothing to see. Then, absurdly, he sniffed the wooden surface. Finally, he eased open one of the doors. Madame La Motte had assiduously hung her things from the steel rod therein, creating a parade of heavy black dresses with occasional ribbons of white lace.

Spector's search was an exact duplication of his investigation of Walter Judd's room. Indeed, save for the twin beds, both rooms were essentially the same. The same wardrobes, the same bureaus, the same rugs.

"The automaton," he said suddenly. "Why use the automaton at all? The killer was obliged to descend the staircase once again in order to fetch it. And it is heavy; it would take considerable effort and concentration to bring it through Mr. Tulp's traps and into the room. So, why? Just a macabre joke? Or was there a more practical purpose?"

"Do you *know* the answers to any of these questions?" asked Imogen.

"Alas, no. But I sometimes find that exercises in free association can be productive. They establish connections where none previously existed. Sigmund Freud wrote extensively on the uncanniness of dolls, of their capacity to evince feelings of fear through their *familiarity*, the very fact that they look like us, and yet they are *not* 'us.' An automaton compounds this uncanny feeling, because it not only *looks* human, it moves like a human. Sometimes it speaks. Sometimes, as with The Stepney Lad, it walks. In a way, I suppose our killer may be likened to the automaton. He—or she—has the outer appearance of humanity. And yet, underneath, what is there?

Only the clockwork mechanics of an unreal entity. An imitation of life. Perhaps the killer knows this. *Perhaps* the killer is possessed of such self-awareness that he—or she—perceives a certain kinship with The Stepney Lad. Maybe *that* is why the automaton was important. Maybe its very presence is a cryptic message . . ."

"Mr. Spector!" Tulp called out. Spector emerged from the bedroom and found the young ghost hunter cradling the large camera, which he had just removed from its tripod.

"What's the matter?"

"The trigger-weight—I hadn't noticed before, but the trigger-weight's been deployed."

"Could it have happened when the Lennoxes went downstairs?"

"No, I would have noticed. It must have happened before we came out onto the landing." His eyes were wide and manic. "Maybe the killer set it off . . ."

"Do you think it will have caught a photograph of the killer?" asked Imogen.

"I don't know," said Tulp, disentangling the elaborate webwork of strings and retrieving the camera, "but I know how to find out. I'll need a darkroom."

"Let us head downstairs," Spector suggested. "Imogen, you look as though you could do with a drink. I rather think we all could."

Spector pulled shut the bedroom door, and the four remaining guests at Devil's Neck descended to rejoin their hosts. The kitchen, at the back of the house, was a small room for seven people, but they made do. The room was comfortably warmed by a fire. Fred Powell was sitting at the spartan wooden table looking vexed. Imogen was rather bemused that no attention had been paid to the driver so far. Spector seemed to view Powell as an outlier; the odd one out in this eclectic house party. She wanted to know why.

Sidling up to the driver, she began, "Mr. Powell."

"Yes, miss?"

"There is a drainpipe outside the window to my room. It leads down past your room, which is directly below. Is that right?"

"So I understand, yes."

"Well, did you see anything unusual? Anyone climbing up the drainpipe? Or maybe you climbed it yourself?"

"Afraid not, miss," he said genially. "I slept like a baby until Mr. Lennox came and knocked on my door a short while ago."

"So you didn't even hear Miss Drabble scream?" Spector interjected.

"Nope."

Spector seemed satisfied with this, which troubled Imogen all the more. She sat down at the table in uneasy silence.

Mrs. Lennox was pouring tea with a shaky hand, while her husband stood by the window, his back to the group. What was he looking at?

Tulp approached Mrs. Lennox, camera in hand. "Mrs. Lennox," he said, "is there somewhere I could use as a darkroom? I need to develop this film."

"You mean you caught him on camera?" She looked stunned.

"The pantry," said Mr. Lennox, turning to indicate a door on the other side of the kitchen. "Through there."

Powell and Lennox helped him to rig the windowless pantry as a makeshift photography studio, carting through the equipment that had been heaped in the hall. Spector, meanwhile, assumed Mr. Lennox's spot by the window, peering out at nothing.

The film took around thirty minutes to develop. During this time, an uneasy silence pervaded the group. Even Imogen, who was itching to ask so many questions, held her tongue in a kind of deference to the late Madame La Motte. Eventually, Spector's patience ebbed and he went to join Tulp in the pantry, slipping through the door with spidery swiftness so that only the briefest insinuation of light went with him.

He found Francis Tulp hunched over a tin tray brimming with developing fluid. The young man was concentrating furiously, and did not seem to notice that the conjuror had appeared. Spector was content to leave him to his work.

At last, Tulp lifted the photograph delicately from the tray with a pair of steel tongs and held it up to the dim light bulb, which he had wrapped in cotton to dampen its light. Spector watched as the image developed, growing bolder and more sharply defined. "There," Tulp said, more to himself than to Spector. With a wooden peg he attached it to a clothesline and the two men stood side by side to watch it come into focus.

Tulp suddenly shivered. "Do you feel that, Mr. Spector? An ungodly chill. A 'cold spot.'"

Spector nodded wordlessly: he had felt it too.

Neither man took his eyes off the photograph in front of them. They recognised the familiar symmetry of the upstairs hallway, with the row of doors on either side. But it was the figure framed in the dead centre of the image that shocked them into silence.

A tall, broad-shouldered figure. And on its face was the mask of Maurice Bailey.

CHAPTER TWELVE

"IT ALL FITS"

There watched I for the Dead; but no ghost woke.
—Wilfred Owen, "The Unreturning"

One hour earlier.

*F*lint *blinked, and found himself back at Fleurrière again, surrounded by the screams of the dying. Tents flapped like ragged
strips of skin, all frayed and torn. Mud gripped his ankles like clawing
hands from under the earth. He was rooted to the spot. He looked left
and right, and out of that terrible blood-and-smoke-streaked mist
figures started to emerge. The denizens of Fleurrière. These ill-formed
shadows came slowly out to greet him, their hollow eyes and bone-white
flesh ravaged by time and the merciless elements. He saw soldiers; boys
like him. He saw cynical, battle-numbed medicos. And he saw nurses.
He saw a nurse.*

*Back then, naive, unworldly Flint had taken a shine to Nurse Emily
Hancock; he still recalled her name all these years later, though he'd spent*

only two days in her company. She had seemed to him a sliver of paradise amid all that hell. He wanted to marry her and give her children (this was before he knew Julia, of course). And when he left Fleurrière shortly afterward, he carried that smile of hers with him.

Now, here she was again, as though not a second had passed. There was that same smile, the one he had dreamt about all this time. But then, the smile began to change. Flint remembered well the effort he had gone to in tracking her down after the War. And how suddenly, cruelly bereft he felt when he discovered she was one of the casualties in the shelling of Fleurrière. He prayed there had been some mix-up. Such errors were commonplace, after all. But it was wishful thinking. She was of course quite dead, and whatever puerile fantasies he had entertained were obliterated.

Even years later, when he met and married Julia, the love of his life, he found himself occasionally biting his tongue to stop himself from calling her Emily. And then, when Julia had their first child, a girl, and Flint asked her what name she had chosen and she said Emily, he nearly fainted dead away on the spot. Here, lurching from the dark recesses of his unconscious, was the real Emily, wearing the same smile with which she had bade him farewell.

A shadow fell across that smile.

Flint looked up and saw the shell, inching toward earth at a crawling pace. They should have been scattering pell-mell, all those soldiers and nurses. They ought to be diving for cover. But they were all staring at him. They stood like a parade of china dolls. Flint opened his mouth to bellow a warning, but nothing came out. Not even at the last moment, when the shell touched ground like a falling meteor, and everything went white, then black.

—ⵡ—

Sergeant Hook hit a bump in the road, and Flint was awake with a jolt.

"I think I understand," he said with perfect crispness; there was not a hint of fatigue in his voice.

"What's that, sir?" Hook did not take his eyes from the road. He was hunched over the wheel, gripping it tight, wresting control of the car from malevolent elements.

"I said: I understand *why* Edgecomb was so desperate to acquire Devil's Neck. It was there in his dreams like some kind of cryptic crossword. He spent decades running from it, Hook, but those dreams were a lesson. The past always, always comes back. And I know about the secret he shared with Will McGinn."

"Go on, sir!"

"Yes—I understand it perfectly. Keep your eyes on the road, Hook, but listen well. Rodney Edgecomb wasn't Rodney Edgecomb at all. He was Will McGinn. The two men traded identities. It must have happened in the War—either at Fleurrière or Devil's Neck. And it was all a scheme to keep the Aitken inheritance."

"So the dead man in Crook O'Lune Street is . . ."

"Will McGinn. He was Will McGinn all along. You see, Hook"—Flint puffed out his chest, approximating Joseph Spector's demeanour when he solved a case—"Rodney Edgecomb knew that if he was identified as the one who murdered Dominic in 1914, he'd lose the money and receive an unwelcome date with the hangman. But if *another man* became Rodney Edgecomb, then he couldn't be identified as the phantom bellhop. Because he *wasn't* the phantom bellhop! And if he wasn't identified, the Aitken inheritance was safe. So . . . I reckon he got McGinn to take his place, and *he* became McGinn."

"Why McGinn, of all people?" asked Hook.

"Just a stroke of luck. They were both being treated at Fleurrière—the difference was that McGinn had a head wound that gave him amnesia. Remember the scar on the dead man's head? Anyway, trading papers and uniforms would be the work of minutes. And McGinn was vulnerable. Obviously he believed whatever Edgecomb told him. So Edgecomb groomed him to take his place. And it fooled everyone. Everyone!" Flint slapped the dashboard with the palm of his hand. By everyone he was referring to himself.

"So you reckon Edgecomb really *did* murder his brother all those years ago?"

Flint nodded enthusiastically. "Lucky for him, the War intervened before he could face justice. There was so much blood and death, even a man like Edgecomb found himself promoted to captain before too long. It also allowed him to seize the chance of a lifetime, and steal another man's identity."

Hook winced as he swung the wheel. The previous year he had suffered a stab wound,* and the cold weather still caused it to act up. The police doctor had warned him that this would likely be the case from now on. He would be subject to the vicissitudes of the weather.

While Hook drove through the hammering rain, he said, "And the dreams, sir? And Walter Judd?"

---

* *See* Cabaret Macabre

"It all fits," Flint assured him. "See, the problems started when McGinn's memory started to come back. It began with the dreams and the blackouts. He went to Lidia Rees to try and unlock the other memories. And he hired Walter Judd to do some digging. All unbeknown to the real Rodney Edgecomb, who must have been horrified when he found out. No doubt *he* was quite comfortable on the continent, pocketing chunks of the Aitken inheritance, living a life of leisure."

"So how did Edgecomb—the real Edgecomb—convince McGinn to keep handing over the money? Surely McGinn could simply have cut off the payments, and there'd be nothing Edgecomb could do about it?"

"I've no doubt Edgecomb is a credible liar. He probably convinced McGinn he had some sort of evidence that he really *had* killed Dominic Edgecomb back in 1914."

Hook risked raising a hand from the wheel to rub his forehead. "But he wasn't really Edgecomb . . ."

"He *thought* he was Edgecomb! That's what matters. And if he could be convinced that he was Rodney Edgecomb, then he could be convinced he was a murderer. So the real Edgecomb blackmailed him."

"It seems a complicated way to lay your hands on an inheritance." Hook observed.

"But it was the only possible way! Edgecomb must have heard about Barnaby Osgood. He knew the game would be up when he returned to England. The imposture was the only way of making sure he wasn't identified as the phantom bellhop from the Hotel Maurienne. And it was also a way for him to escape his creditors.

It gave him a puppet he could control from his new home on the continent. I imagine he thought it was worth it. Besides, it never stopped him from laying his hands on the money, did it? McGinn never missed a payment. That is, until his memory started to come back. Edgecomb must have coerced him into making out that will. And when McGinn began to realise the true nature of his situation, he changed the will. He left Edgecomb with nothing."

"So Edgecomb killed him?"

"Presumably Edgecomb didn't *know* he'd been written out of the will. I bet he thought he was ridding himself of a nuisance and simply cashing in the payment that was rightfully his. And then, after twenty-five years, he'd finally be scot-free."

"But Will McGinn had the last laugh on him, eh sir?"

"True enough. Well? What do you reckon, Hook? Have I beaten Spector at his own game this time?"

"Certainly seems like it, sir," admitted Hook grudgingly. "But there's just one thing, sir."

"Hmm? What's that?"

"Devil's Neck, sir. What's Devil's Neck got to do with any of this? Why are we heading out there at all?"

Flint opened his mouth to answer, but found that he couldn't. He folded his arms and sat in silence for a while as the car coursed through curtains of rain.

CHAPTER THIRTEEN

SOIREE FANTASTIQUE

What the seer observes is not only what is projected from self, but that which has been conveyed there by other minds.

—James Coates, *Photographing the Invisible: Practical Studies in Spirit Photography, Spirit Portraiture, and Other Rare but Allied Phenomena*

T he photograph sent a stir of silent horror through the house. The guests left the kitchen for the drawing room, where the fire was stoked and the lamps lit. The photograph remained on the kitchen table; none but Spector could bring themselves to look at it as they filed out of the room. It was proof positive that they were not the only ones at Devil's Neck.

After a long, thoughtful silence, during which he smoked a trio of rancid-smelling cigarillos, Joseph Spector got to his feet. "I must take another look at Madame La Motte's room," he said. "There is something I've missed."

Imogen followed him out into the hall. "I'll come with you if you don't mind. There's something I'd like to discuss with you."

He shrugged. "As you wish."

When they reached the bedroom, Imogen paused on the threshold, unsure whether she was quite ready to see it again. Spector, however, plunged straight in. To her surprise he did not head for the corpse, or even the automaton. Instead he made for the wardrobe. Pressing his palms flat against it, he began to run his hands along the smooth surface of the wood.

Imogen watched from the doorway for a few moments, then said, "Mr. Spector, I need to ask you something."

"Please do," he said, still with his back to her.

"It's about Fred Powell."

"Yes?"

"I want to know why you haven't questioned him. He's the obvious suspect. It's true that any of us might have gone to Walter Judd's room and killed him. But he's the only one who could have brought the automaton up the stairs. He was the only one whose room wasn't secured by Tulp's traps."

Finally, Spector looked at her. "What makes you think that?" he asked her evenly.

"Why haven't you at least *questioned* him about what happened?"

"Come with me," he said, breezing past her, out of the room and then tracing a diagonal path across the corridor to the room that had been Walter Judd's. He tried the door handle and stepped inside.

Judd's body lay where it had fallen, now covered by a large blanket. Again, Spector ignored it and made for the wardrobe.

As he did, he spoke. "Have you considered, Miss Drabble, that I have not questioned Mr. Powell precisely *because* he appears to be the likeliest suspect?"

"Is that the truth?"

"Not in the slightest. I refute your thesis that Fred Powell is the likeliest suspect because his room is not on this corridor. Sadly it becomes apparent that all of Mr. Tulp's efforts were in vain. You see, Miss Drabble, the likeliest suspect is *you*."

"Are you serious?"

"As the devil. You were, after all, sealed in a room with the victim, were you not? And, as you so rightly said, any of us might have killed Walter Judd—provided we were able to orchestrate the locked-room trick. To kill Madame La Motte you would not *need* a locked-room trick." He stopped and sniffed the air. "Do you smell that? Wood varnish. The wardrobes in both rooms have been recently varnished. But only *this* room retains the smell . . ."

"Stick to the subject, Mr. Spector. You really think *I'm* the most likely suspect?"

"Without a doubt. You have been keeping certain secrets of your own, haven't you?"

"What do you mean?"

He looked at her and smiled. "You cannot trick a trickster, Miss Drabble. You came here with an entirely different purpose than to serve as Madame La Motte's dogsbody. In fact, you came here because you are the late Maurice Bailey's daughter."

She gaped at him. "How . . . how did you . . . ?"

"You gave yourself away early on, I'm afraid. You knew just a little too much about Maurice Bailey. You called him corporal, his proper rank,* whereas Madame La Motte mistakenly referred to him as sergeant,† thus you had not gained your knowledge from her. And you had a rather curious reaction when Mrs. Bailey made her claim that The Stepney Lad was 'the child Maurice never had.'‡ It occurred to me then that you were mocking her. Because you knew something she didn't.

"Your mother was Maude, wasn't she? And you are Maurice's child. A war baby. You were conceived while he was on leave—that must have been around 1915, is that so? And your poor mother kept you a secret. Did Maurice know he had a daughter, I wonder?"

"I doubt it," Imogen said sharply. "Not if that woman had anything to say about it."

"You mean Mrs. Bailey?"

"That's who I mean. That story she told, about how Maude abandoned Maurice when he was injured . . . it's a lie. Maude was desperate to see him. *Desperate.* And the old witch wouldn't let her. She told my dad that mum had abandoned him. She condemned the both of them to an early grave, with grief and sorrow. And I hope the guilt tortures her."

Spector shook his head sadly. "I am quite sure it does. My condolences, Imogen."

"I'd appreciate it, Mr. Spector, if you'd keep this information to yourself. I don't want the others to know."

"Of course. You may rely on me. But I'm curious, Miss Drabble. How did your presence here *really* come about?"

---

*   *See Page 94*
†   *See Page 105*
‡   *See Page 100*

"Simple enough." She smiled. "I really *am* Madame La Motte's secretary. But I was the one who put her in touch with my grandmother. I let them both think the other had initiated the correspondence. Simple enough to do, when one of them thinks she's psychic. And then I planted the idea of this whole trip, séance and all."

"That was very clever of you," said Spector. He had now positioned himself by the window. Framed by the rain-spattered glass, Imogen thought of the photograph downstairs—the man in the mask, framed in the centre of the corridor. The masked man, who was somewhere in this house.

"But I had no motive," she said. "I really didn't. You can't honestly think *I'm* the one behind all this?"

Again, the smile: Mephistopheles.

"Miss Drabble, I don't believe that's what I said. I simply said that you're the likeliest suspect. Which is precisely why I *don't* suspect you."

Imogen blinked a few times.

Spector was standing eerily still by the window, staring out toward the mainland. What did those pale eyes see? To Imogen, there was nothing out there but blackness, but something in the dark had plainly snagged his attention. He could not look away.

"Imogen," he said, not even glancing in her direction. "I think we ought to head downstairs. To congregate in the drawing room, in the grand tradition. There is one final task I must perform, and then we can lay these unquiet spirits to rest."

"What is it?" she said, anxiety filling her heart.

"Go downstairs," was his only answer. "Go and wait with the others. I need to prepare myself."

She inched reluctantly toward the door, periodically glancing back at the old conjuror. But he did not move.

When she reached the drawing room, the conversation of the others came to an abrupt stop. She got the impression that they had been talking about her. Virginia Bailey was the only one among them who looked at her sympathetically, and she gave the empty seat beside her a welcoming pat. Imogen went over to join her, suddenly feeling the need to talk with someone—anyone.

"He'll be down shortly," she said. "He has to prepare."

"I know," Mrs. Bailey commented. "This is the way he does things. He can't resist making a show of it. And he has here a captive audience, quite literally."

"You've known him a long time?"

Mrs. Bailey nodded. "And I trust him implicitly. You should too."

"I think there's been too much trickery here tonight."

"You may be right," said Mrs. Bailey inscrutably, "or you may not be. I've often found it unwise to try and fathom the workings of Spector's mind."

Imogen glanced sideways at the old woman. "Do you really think he has what it takes to put an end to this horrible mess? It feels as though ever since we've been here, up is down and black is white."

Mrs. Bailey spoke soothingly; serenely. "I don't know. I'm not sure it matters. He's here, and that gives us a better chance than we might otherwise have had. But there's certainly something in this house. Something *else*."

An image flashed in Imogen's mind: the automaton. She shuddered. It was still in the bedroom where Madame La Motte died, still smeared with the old medium's blood. The arm upraised; the hand clutching. And at the feet of The Stepney Lad lay the blade, where Spector had placed it.

"Imogen," said a voice. There was something gentle in its quietly boyish tone. She whirled round, all set to rail on Francis Tulp. But his contrite expression stilled her. "I want to apologise. I'm sorry for that nonsense about hypnotism earlier. I never really believed it, you know."

Imogen opened her mouth to say something sharp, then surprised herself by commenting, "It wasn't an *entirely* ludicrous theory. In fact I've heard of such things myself, though I'm loath to admit it under these circumstances. But it didn't happen."

"No," said Tulp, "I'm quite certain of that now. Does this mean my unreserved apology is accepted?"

She nodded, and he seemed genuinely relieved, breaking into a smile and puffing out his chest a little with renewed confidence. "It's a foolish foible of mine," he said. "Had it ever since I was a tot. This obsession with the supernatural. The otherworldly. I suppose there's a part of me that thinks *this* world is not quite enough."

"Hmm," said Imogen thoughtfully, unwilling to admit (though she was unsure why) that there were times when she felt the same thing. Unlike the gullible (was that too harsh a word? Was *credulous* perhaps kinder?), she could not coax herself to put her faith in the unseen.

Joseph Spector appeared in the doorway. He wore his cloak and homburg hat, and carried that cane, topped with its silver skull.

"Ladies and gentlemen," he said, "everything we have seen and heard here this evening has been part of a performance. The question is: whose?

"Initially, I had thought it was entirely Madame La Motte's. But as the evening progressed, it dawned on me that her séance and other assorted trickery was really just a piece of a more substantial puzzle, orchestrated by an ingenious and malevolent brain."

All eyes were on him as he reached the centre of the room.

"The dark can hide a multitude of sins. To allay suspicion, a true séance ought to take place beneath blazing lights. Lights such as these." He glanced heavenward, toward the brilliant crystal chandelier. "In fact, now seems an opportune moment for an experiment. Spiritualist mediums frequently induce their spectral assistants to prove themselves by rattling some inanimate object, do they not? Something akin to a tambourine?" From the folds of his cloak, there emerged a tambourine, which he placed on a wooden stool. "Or a bell?" This, he also produced—an old brass bell with a wooden handle—and placed it beside the tambourine. "It is common for a medium, then, to utilise a spirit cabinet, some sort of box, in which the objects are sealed from view. Then, by calling on the spirits, the sound of the instruments is heard."

He slipped a pair of white evening gloves over his fingers and cracked his knuckles noisily. He stepped behind the chaise longue and gripped its antimacassar with both hands, whipping it away in a single, studied motion. Then he returned to the wooden stool and positioned himself behind it, dangling the thin sheet in front of it like a makeshift stage curtain, shielding the objects from view. "Yes," he said, "the spirits are with us. I can feel them now. And soon, you shall hear them . . ."

His eyes fluttered shut, and there emerged from behind the antimacassar a sudden jangle of tambourine and bell. Mrs. Bailey squeaked with fright.

"Goodness," Spector continued, "they are strong indeed. Perhaps a little too strong. In fact, I fear I may be losing control . . ." From behind the sheet, the tambourine came whirling over the heads of the audience, clattering against the wall at the back of the room and eliciting further consternation.

"A simple enough trick," Spector explained, "which relies on a single deception. Namely, the illusion that both of my hands were visible at all times."

"But they *were*," said Francis Tulp. "You were holding the sheet, weren't you?"

"Yes," said Spector, "with *this* hand." He held up his left. "Alas, *this* hand"—his right—"was the one I used to manipulate the objects, and to fling the tambourine in a bold coup de théâtre. You see, when I stepped behind the chaise longue and whipped away the antimacassar, I actually switched it for a duplicate cloth, identical in pattern, but with a white glove stitched to it. The glove was filled with padding to simulate my right hand. Stowing the glove up my right sleeve was a mere moment's work, and holding the other end of the sheet with my left hand created the illusion. But with my *real* right hand concealed from view, I was able to bring the spirits to life to my heart's content. And of course, the hurling of the tambourine was to control your attention, so that you did not see the sheet *and* glove drop to the ground, nor the swift concealment of the padded glove beneath my shoe." He lifted his right foot, revealing the padded glove. "A cheat," he expounded.

"And an especially infuriating one, for it is designed to evince not only belief but *fear*. A conjuration of angry ghosts.

"Consider this an educative demonstration. The skilled illusionist does not misdirect the eye, but the mind.

"There can of course be no doubt that Madame La Motte *was* a highly skilled illusionist. But she was no more than that. She was no criminal mastermind—only a confidence trickster. As soon as she set foot in this house, the performance began. She took advantage of that first blackout to invent an encounter with a phantom soldier in a mask. It was obviously based on her limited knowledge of Maurice Bailey. It was nonetheless an efficacious prologue to her main performance: the séance."

He let the silence hang in the air for a moment or two. That was when Imogen knew she was in the presence of a true master performer, whose controlled silences could be more eloquent than speech.

"If you would like to know," he finally continued, "I am now in a position to tell you how she performed her tricks. Those that were not entirely performance based (unlike the husky, masculine voice, and the common spiel about spirits beyond the veil) required minimal preparation. First, the table tilting. It's easy enough to achieve, even with one's hands flat on the surface of the table. There are various methods which have been passed down the centuries, but I think the one used this evening involved a long, flat object concealed in Madame's sleeve, strapped to her wrist. She was dexterous enough to slide the object *under* the edge of the table, while her hands remained visible on the surface. Thus, the table was gripped in a kind of makeshift clamp, and she could move the table without appearing to do so. Incidentally, the 'object' in question was likely the same knife that killed her. A smooth, flat blade could be slid discreetly beneath the table with ease. Before long, the rest of us were simply playing along, either consciously or unconsciously. The act of raising her arms dramatically caused the knife to slide back up her sleeve and out of sight, to be removed later.

"Second, the Ouija board. We saw the planchette moving unaided, didn't we? No, we did not. Because, even with Madame's hands restrained, she was free to move her feet as much as she liked. The underside of the planchette is steel, therefore, with a piece of magnetised metal concealed in one of her shoes, she could make it move as much as necessary to spell out her message."

"Very clever, Joseph," said Mrs. Bailey, "but you cannot explain what I saw and heard. I spoke with my *son*."

"Suggestion," he said sympathetically. "That's all it was. The scent of his cologne—our sense of memory is closely linked to our sense of smell. It's true, is it not, that the scent of a certain flower or a certain perfume can bring us immediately back in time to a very specific moment. Proust's genius lies in his perception of that simple fact. Likewise, the evocation of spirits can be accomplished via scent. This was actually the simplest aspect of the whole performance. All she had to do was swap the candle for a preprepared duplicate with a certain fragrance soaked into the wax. Then, as it burned, the scent was released and the presence of the spirit effectively evoked.

"You remember how adamant she was that the circle remain unbroken? And yet it was she herself who broke it with a sudden, spasmodic movement—creating, incidentally, a sudden current of air which extinguished the candle and plunged the room into darkness."

"But Mr. Spector," said Imogen, "the circle was only broken for a second. We grabbed her hands again immediately."

Spector, smiling, inclined his head. "You had hold of her wrist very tightly, didn't you Imogen?"

Imogen nodded.

"And you, Francis, had hold of her hand; your fingers were intertwined, I believe?"

"That's right."

"In the darkness, you would presumably have been unable to tell whether the two of you were in fact holding on to *the same hand*?"

Tulp and Imogen looked at each other. Spector continued: "The intertwining of fingers could be done with either the left or right hand, you would have been none the wiser. And likewise, Imogen, one wrist feels very like another. I would hazard a guess that when you both lunged in the darkness, Madame La Motte made sure you both grabbed her left hand. This kept her right entirely free."

"And what about the ghostly face?"

"Her own. You probably wondered why she wore the veil? No? Well, it was not mere costume. It served a practical purpose; namely, it concealed the phosphorescent makeup that glowed eerily in the dark. Again, it was just a matter of lifting the veil with her free hand, and we would experience the sudden materialisation of a phantom face, floating in midair. That leaves the writing on the ceiling, which I have already explained."

He looked at the sea of frightened faces. "You see now how easy it was? These are tricks which have been in use for thousands of years. Individually they are unimpressive, but their cumulative effect on a willing audience is undeniable.

"Her whole persona was a fictional creation, and not even an original one. The notion of heaven as more 'real'* than earth is lifted directly from the writings of Emanuel Swedenborg. So is the idea of the spirit as an effigy of man's earthly love.[†]

"The phony levitation is right out of the Eusapia Palladino playbook. Nothing particularly impressive there. And the jiggery pokery with the hands and wrists is one of Eusapia's too. Sometimes the 'spirit rapping' will be brought about via more elaborate means, such as a mechanical device specially constructed for this purpose by a clockmaker. There was no need for that here; all she had to do was to use her feet, which were not monitored in any fashion. I thought that rather remiss of you, Francis. After all, some investigators have been known to bind the medium's limbs before a séance in order to mitigate such circumstances."

"I believed her," said Francis with a faintly sad lilt to his voice. "More fool me."

"Not at all," Spector said. "She is a professional. Making fools out of people is her stock-in-trade. It used to be mine, though we went about it in rather different ways."

"But wait a moment!" Tulp suddenly cried. "There's somebody else in the house! Of *course* there is! We all saw him on the stairs, didn't we? And then he vanished into thin air!"

"You're correct about one thing, Mr. Tulp. We are not alone in this house." Another pause, during which Spector's amiable gaze passed evenly over the faces of his audience. "We all wear masks,"

---

* *See Page 106*

† *See Page 96*

he said in a voice that was soft yet impossible to ignore. "Every single one of us. And for different reasons. Some, to conceal. Others, to deceive. But masks are funny things. The very presence of a mask tells us there is something behind it. And so the very act of deception is itself a revelation.

"The man who built this house, Adolphus Latimer, understood that. So, too, does the one who killed Walter Judd and Madame La Motte. Therefore, the most effective masks are those which hide behind another mask. Or, better yet, those which do not resemble masks at all. Listen," he suddenly hissed. "Can you hear it?"

They listened. Imogen, especially, screwed up her eyes, concentrating. At first, she could discern no external sound, but then she heard it. A heavy, echoing thump, and then another. By the third, it was apparent that these were footsteps out in the hall, and that they were approaching at an agonising pace. All eyes were fixed on the door as it slowly—very slowly—began to ease open. Nobody said a word. Scarcely a breath left their lips.

In the dark, Imogen could discern the outline of a wide, hulking figure. Square shouldered and masculine. As it inched into the room, she made out gleams of reflected light in the rivulets of dripping water. The creature was soaked. It looked to be wearing some sort of heavy cloak and traipsed painfully, as though it had only just risen from the depths of its watery grave.

How ludicrous it would be, Imogen thought, if I were to scream. Like the stuff of bad fiction. And yet the urge remained at the back of her mind as she gritted her teeth and watched the creature enter the room.

CHAPTER FOURTEEN

THE MAN IN THE TUNNEL

The quickness of even a highly skilled hand cannot
deceive an attentive eye.

—Nevil Maskelyne,
"The Theory of Magic," *Our Magic*

One hour earlier.

The rain was now heavier than ever, and the roads impassable
torrents of swampy water. Eventually, Hook had no choice
but to bring the car to a halt.

"We can't go any further, sir."

"What are you talking about? We've got to get out to Devil's
Neck."

"Then we'll need a boat or something, sir. The car won't make
it across the causeway."

Flint thought for a moment, then said: "Come on, Hook. I hope
you brought your waders. We'd better go on foot."

The two men wrapped themselves in hooded slickers and braved the hellish weather. Grabbing torches, they pressed on a little way, the water reaching halfway up their shins. Flint could just about discern the outline of the house in the distance; perhaps three-quarters of a mile from his present position. But between himself and Devil's Neck there lay nothing but dark, murky water. The causeway was indeed completely submerged. With the rain still coming down, the water would only continue to rise.

"This is ludicrous," Flint yelled. "We need a *boat*."

Hook pointed toward the house. "Sir! Look! The light!"

Flint looked and saw what had so captivated his sergeant. One of the upper windows of the distant building was aglow with yellow lamplight: nothing unusual about that. But what *was* striking about it was the manner in which the light appeared to be flicking on and off with surprising regularity. "My God," he said, "Morse code. That must be Spector—I'll bet he spotted the headlamps."

"What's he saying, sir?"

Flint watched for a moment. The light continued to flick on and off in methodical fashion.

MURDER.

Flint leaned into the driver's side of the car and used the head-lamps to spell out a reply: WHO.

Then he waited while Spector responded: JUDD.

"Judd's dead," said Flint. "Murdered, says Spector."

"Ask him how we get out there, sir. The road's completely impassable."

But Spector—if indeed it *was* Spector—was already onto the next stage of his missive: T-U-N-N-E-L.

"Tunnel? What's that supposed to mean? There's no tunnel here."

"Maybe there *is* a tunnel somewhere along the coastline. A tunnel between the mainland and Devil's Neck."

"But how are we supposed to find it, sir? It could be anywhere . . ."

Patiently, diligently, Flint spelt out: WHERE.

Then came Spector's answer: CAR.

And with that, the light went out. Either Spector had reached the end of his message, or else something had come along to disturb him. "Car," said Flint. "It's somewhere near the car."

They scouted around their vehicle, torch beams alighting on tree stumps and hillocks and the relics of drystone walls. But there was no sign of a tunnel, or even the trace of a tunnel.

Finally, Flint caught sight of it by the water: a grey Alvis, half submerged, that looked to be abandoned. Flint cupped his hands around his eyes and pressed his forehead against the glass window while Hook shone his torch through the windscreen. The light showed only the empty front seats, without even so much as a folded road map. Stepping back from the car, his boots sloshing in the shallow water, Flint peered around.

That's when he saw the tuft of earth, overgrown with grass and weeds. It was a hillock, swelling from the water like a carbuncle a few yards away. He strode around to its far side and realised what Spector had been trying to tell him.

"Here!" he yelled. Embedded in the hillock was a square, grey stone that looked to have been simply abandoned. In fact, the stone was very carefully placed, covering a deep embrasure in the earth, and a set of ancient stone steps leading down into a dark tunnel. Hauling the stone aside, Flint breathed, "Well, I'll be damned."

Slowly, cautiously, the two men began their descent.

Down in the tunnel, the pounding rainfall was little more than a susurrous hiss. Overhead, the sweeping arched ceiling looked to be carved from the very earth itself. Flint was reminded of the escape tunnels in certain old houses that had been used by priests to escape marauding agents of the Crown.

They pressed on, their footsteps echoing hollowly, the glow of their torches puncturing the heavy darkness ahead of them like a pair of pins.

Hook stopped. "Sir! Look!"

Flint did. His sergeant had spied the shape of a figure in their path—a body blocking the tunnel. They approached gingerly.

It was a man. There were chains about his wrists tethering him to a sticking place in the ground. Gently, Flint turned him over. He had been badly beaten about the face; one of his eyes was swollen shut, and his nose was broken. His mouth oozed blood between split lips.

"He's alive," said Flint.

"Who is he?"

Flint felt in the fellow's pockets, but they were empty. "I don't know. You stay here with him, Hook."

"Yes, sir." Hook dropped to his knees beside the unconscious man and shone the torch in his face. It was impossible to determine anything other than purely surface details, but the man seemed to be about fifty years of age. His clothes had once been of decent quality, but were now hopelessly ragged and tattered. Hook did not care to speculate how long the fellow had been down here, or how he had come to be in this wretched state. He pressed his ear against the man's unconscious chest and detected the faintest ripple of a heartbeat. He slapped the man's face to try and rouse him; this produced only a brief fluttering of the eyelids, and then he was lost again to a heavy deliquium. Hook glanced up just in time to see the silhouette of George Flint traipsing farther along the tunnel, into the darkness, until he finally disappeared from view.

—⁓—

The creature, which had seemed for an instant to be the very spectre of death itself as it crept into the quiet drawing room, lowered its hood to reveal a bemused face with a very damp moustache.

"Spector, what's going on here?" said George Flint.

Spector was on his feet in an instant, dashing over to turn on the light. "My dear fellow," he said with undisguised joy. "I'm delighted that you understood my message. It's been a long time since I've used Morse code. I had to do so once when the padlock warped on a water tank from which I was trying to escape. I was afraid I might have lost the knack."

Flint turned from Spector to take in the sea of stunned faces. "You said there'd been a murder."

"As a matter of fact," Spector informed him, "there have been two. Most recently, a psychic medium by the name of Madame La Motte. And before her, a private enquiry agent named Walter Judd—he was, however, travelling on Rodney Edgecomb's ticket. Both bodies are upstairs."

"Good Lord. That's at least twice Rodney Edgecomb has been murdered, then," said Flint. "He was shot dead in London this afternoon. The killer made it look like a suicide. And there's a man back there in the tunnel, beaten to a pulp . . ."

"Alive?" said Spector sharply.

"Only just. Hook's looking after him."

"Thank God," Spector exhaled.

"Who the hell is this?" It was the taciturn Fred Powell who had finally spoken.

Spector turned to the other horrified guests. "Please forgive me," he said. "I must introduce another unexpected guest. This is Inspector George Flint of Scotland Yard."

"How did you get here?" said Imogen. "Boat, or something?"

"An underground tunnel," Flint explained.

"Running parallel to the causeway," added Spector.

"You knew that was there all along?" Tulp was irritable.

"No, not all along," said Spector, with the closest he ever came to modesty in his voice. "But it became clear to me that it was the only explanation for certain features of this case—and this house. It was the pantry, wasn't it, Flint?"

"The *pantry?*" repeated Francis Tulp. "You mean the place I used as a darkroom? How in the hell did you work *that* out? You were only in there a couple minutes."

"A second was all it took. You yourself were the first to perceive what you described as a 'cold spot,' Francis. A seemingly impossible occurrence, since the pantry is windowless* and the kitchen was warmed by a fire.† Therefore, the draft of cold air was coming

---

*   *See Page 188*

†   *See Page 187*

from elsewhere—between the floorboards or, more likely, from a concealed trapdoor.

"Ladies and gentlemen, I thank you for your patience. I believe it is now going to be rewarded. My friend Flint's arrival was the last piece of the puzzle. I knew he wouldn't let me down. Now, if you can bear to wait a moment or two longer," he grinned darkly, "all will be revealed."

WHEREIN THE READER'S ATTENTION IS RESPECTFULLY REQUESTED

Once upon a time, this would be the point in the narrative where a challenge is issued to the reader. "This lethal web has been woven by a lone criminal mind," I would say, "and the pages are littered with clues to the murderer's identity. The question is: Did you spot them?"

Nowadays such practices are antiquated and rather passé. But who am I to stand in the way of a reader's fun? If there are any would-be sleuths among you, now is the time to make yourselves known. There is no prize, material or otherwise, save the quiet glory of having triumphed at what a wise man once termed "the grandest game in the world."

CHAPTER FIFTEEN

HOW FEAR DEPARTED
FROM THE LONG GALLERY

I have sought the ghost long enough; if he has anything to say, he must now seek me.

—Catherine Crowe, *The Night-Side of Nature*

T he houseguests were growing restless. It was now ten minutes since Flint and Spector had stepped into the adjoining
ballroom to confer.

It occurred to Imogen that they were now in Spector's domain.
This house belonged to him as surely as if he had built it with his
own two hands, as it had belonged to Adolphus Latimer.

On cue, Spector swept into the room. "My apologies," he said,
resuming his spot centre stage. "I hope you have been amusing
yourselves? My friend Inspector Flint and I had one or two things
to discuss. Flint, where are you? Don't be shy now."

Sheepishly, Flint came into the room.

"Thank you all for your patience," Spector said urbanely. For a moment, he might actually have been the benevolent host welcoming guests to his abode. "I think it is high time we brought this charade to its end. This house has witnessed two deaths tonight. God forbid there should be any more."

"Mr. Spector," Imogen ventured, "we've all been inhumanly patient. Are you going to put us out of our misery?"

There was a sudden clamour. "How about it, Spector?" said Flint.

Spector looked thoughtfully into the fireplace; the firelight was mirrored in his pale eyes, giving each a luciferous gleam.

"I've tackled many clever killers in my time," he began with a hint of nostalgic wistfulness, "but I doubt any were as cynical as this. Killers are not to be pitied, though they may sometimes—in spite of our better nature—be understood. That is not the case here. Here, we are faced with a killer who has entirely absented himself from reconcilable humanity. On the outside, a man or a woman. But on the inside, only a shadow.

"By rights, the solution ought to have been obvious. In some ways, it was. We were simply deprived of the requisite perspective from which to view it. Thankfully, Flint and I have now put that to rights. Combining the fruits of our respective labours, the truth becomes apparent. Its roots may be traced back over twenty-five years."

With that, he gave a swift précis of the Aitken inheritance and associated scandals, culminating in the 1914 murder of Dominic Edgecomb. "Some of you no doubt recall the story," he said, glancing at Mrs. Bailey, then the Lennoxes. "What you *won't* recall is the rather anticlimactic events of 1918. Rodney Edgecomb, freshly returned to London following a protracted stay here at

Devil's Neck, was interviewed by a young constable named George Flint. A diamond merchant from South Africa had come forward, claiming to have witnessed certain suspicious events at the Hotel Maurienne the night Dominic Edgecomb died. Specifically, he saw a bellhop exiting Dominic's room at around the time of the murder. This 'bellhop' was not a member of hotel staff and therefore, presumably, an impostor.

"The significance of what this witness saw did not become apparent until after the fact, and the witness himself was unaware of the mystery and ensuing investigation because he lived in South Africa, and international news was of course cluttered with details of the ensuing War.

"If he was able to identify Rodney as the one he saw that night, it would indicate that the young heir was in fact a murderer. In any event, the witness did not return to England until 1917, by which time the case was long forgotten. Indeed, it took him a considerable time to convince Scotland Yard of the significance of what he had seen. That this phantom bellhop was a killer, and that the Aitken inheritance should be called into question once again. Grudgingly, Scotland Yard began to take an interest once more. Twenty-five thousand pounds is, after all, a great deal of money. And it was worth even more in those days, of course. But the reopened investigation proved to be an embarrassing nonstarter. When the witness was presented with a confused Rodney Edgecomb in 1918, he was *not* able to identify him as the phantom bellhop after all. Thus, Rodney was exonerated, and the mystery remained.

"However, certain facts which have come to light now indicate that the real problem—the *true* problem—was the inverse of its original appearance. Officials concluded that the man seen at the Hotel Maurienne in 1914 could not have been Rodney, since the unimpeachable testimony of a sworn eyewitness—a jeweller, no less, and therefore possessed of an especially keen eye for detail—confirmed that the phantom bellhop and Rodney Edgecomb were two different people. But what if the man who presented himself as Rodney Edgecomb in 1918 was not Rodney at all? What if, during the course of the War, a switch had taken place? A brilliant deception orchestrated by the real Rodney, who is, I am convinced, a ruthless killer?"

The guests looked at one another in perplexity.

"During the War, at a hospital in France, Rodney assumed a false identity: 'Will McGinn.' He kept that name for twenty years. And with it, he kept his very own 'automaton': the *real* Will McGinn. McGinn was an amnesiac and, during the early days of their acquaintance at least, a vulnerable, suggestible individual. At that time, Rodney needed a buffer between himself and the Aitken inheritance, to ward off suspicion. And, thanks to a potent cocktail of intimidation and blackmail, Rodney kept McGinn in his power. That is, until a month or two ago. Walking through Soho, something happened which restored a heretofore broken connection in Will McGinn's mind. He started to become 'himself' again. His past began to reassert itself, and the true nature of his situation became apparent. He realised he was merely a pawn in another man's game. And so, he devised a plan to seize the reins of his own destiny once more.

"It was a multifaceted plan which required a suitable backdrop; hence the acquisition of Devil's Neck."

Spector grinned at the general bewilderment of the assembled company. "You didn't know that, did you? The anonymous buyer of Devil's Neck was none other than Will McGinn. Of course, the purchase was made in Rodney Edgecomb's name, and used up a substantial portion of the Aitken inheritance. But he went out of his way to keep that fact a secret.

"McGinn knew that if he tried to explain his situation to police he would likely be laughed out of the building, or else condemned as a madman, so he opted instead to rely on a private enquiry agent. But he also wanted an independent eyewitness, someone who knew both Devil's Neck *and* Rodney Edgecomb. Someone who could be relied upon. Hence, the Lennoxes."

"Us?" said Clive. "What about us?"

"Not you," said Spector. "Rather, your wife." He looked at Justine. "I'm right, aren't I, Mrs. Lennox? You were here before, weren't you? During the War? This was before your marriage, of course. In those days you went by a different name: Nurse Lister."

She hung her head. "How did you know?"

"I didn't know; only suspected. You referred to the ballroom as the 'dayroom,' for instance.* Needless to say, that is the sort of parlance a nurse would have used—and a nurse who had worked here when it was a functioning hospital. During the blackout, you went straight to the generator, whereas your husband had previously struggled to find it.† Then there was your knowledge of the

---

*　*See Page 104*
†　*See Pages 69 and 148*

blood-thinning effect of rum,* something which likely came to you during wartime. Each of these might have been coincidental, but in combination, they indicated that you had been a nurse here during or immediately after the War. And if you *had* been a nurse here, why keep quiet about the fact? Only if you had been involved in some sort of embarrassing scandal. Thus, it occurred to me that before you were married you were Nurse Justine Lister.

"And you could not turn down the offer, could you? It was a remarkably generous salary. Enough to lure you back here after all this time.

"But he *needed* you here. He needed you here to identify 'Will McGinn'—the real Rodney Edgecomb. You were, I'm afraid to say, another pawn in his game, just like the unfortunate Walter Judd. He was out to snare a wily prey, and was desperate to remain a step or two ahead of the man who had manipulated him so terribly."

"It wasn't the way it seemed," Mrs. Lennox said quietly.

"What's that?"

"When I was a nurse here all those years ago, he made out that I . . . 'seduced' him. It wasn't that way at all. What really happened was this: I caught him sneaking between the wards one night, and he said that if I breathed a word he'd tell everyone we were having an affair. It would lose me my job, and throw the whole hospital into disrepute. I never told, but he spread the rumour anyway. That's the way it happened, I swear it. Matron despised me, and was only too willing to believe it. But I doubt even she could have predicted the scandal that followed. I had no choice but to leave.

---

*   *See Page 109*

And *he* was long gone from the hospital by then. McGinn, or Edgecomb, or whatever his name really is."

"And the hospital at Devil's Neck was closed down for good less than a year later," concluded Spector. "Rodney Edgecomb is a man who poisons everything he touches. But there was a reason for what he did, Mrs. Lennox. I think you can all see that now, can't you? We may not know this for sure, but I surmise that when you caught him prowling the corridors that night, he was in fact searching for the secret means of egress by which my dear friend Flint arrived mere minutes ago."

"What for?" asked Flint. "Why did he need a secret passage?"

"So that he could return whenever he wished; when the weather was bad and the causeway cut off. That way, he could never be suspected in the death of Patient 217."

"What?" Bailey's mother was on her feet. "Joseph, what are you saying?"

"I'm afraid it's true, Virginia. When you described your final encounter with Maurice, where he went to such drastic lengths to write the name 'Will McGinn'—Maurice most likely knew the real McGinn. And Edgecomb, who had no way of knowing the full extent of Maurice's injuries, didn't like the idea of there being another patient at Devil's Neck who could potentially identify him as an impostor or—worse yet—recognise the real Will McGinn and destroy the elaborate plan he had concocted.

"We have no way of knowing how many nights Edgecomb spent prowling the corridors before he stumbled upon Adolphus Latimer's secret—the concealed passageway in the pantry. But when he found it, his plan was complete. He waited until the weather was suitably bad, when it would seem impossible for an intruder to reach Devil's Neck, and he sneaked back below the causeway and put an end to the utterly defenceless Maurice Bailey."

Mrs. Bailey had begun to weep. "That monster. Dreadful monster . . ."

"You see now what we are up against. And what Will McGinn was up against when he devised his own plan. And hopefully, you also see by now why Devil's Neck was so vital to the scheme. McGinn knew that with Barnaby Osgood long dead, it would be impossible to convict Edgecomb of murdering his brother in 1914. However, if he could expose Edgecomb as the killer of Maurice Bailey . . ."

"But Edgecomb killed him first," said Flint.

"It appears so." Spector shrugged. "And yet, McGinn's plan was already in motion. The excursion was already underway. Mrs. Lennox was already out here, Mr. Judd was on the coach. Edgecomb, as we know, prefers to leave no loose ends behind him. Therefore, even with Will McGinn dead, he came out here."

"Wait a moment," said Imogen. "Surely all this means that you can identify him, Mrs. Lennox? If he's one of the house party, you must have spotted him as soon as he stepped off the coach . . ."

Spector smiled. "You're beginning to catch on, Miss Drabble. But I'm afraid you don't yet see the entire picture. Let us be methodical about this, and take each step chronologically. The pieces were all in place. McGinn himself was dead in Crook O'Lune Street, but the game continued. Edgecomb is here in this house, just as his 'automaton' planned.

"However, he is not a man who responds well to finding himself trapped. That is why, earlier this evening, he murdered Walter Judd and rigged the crime scene to look like a suicide. The charade was not intended to hold up to any major scrutiny—merely to buy some time. And it was easy enough to perpetrate. Poor Judd was even kind enough to isolate himself in his room. And, as diligent an investigator as he was, he did not know what Edgecomb looked like. Mrs. Lennox was, unfortunately, unable to assist him—for reasons that will soon become clear. The killer found it easy to bluff their way into Judd's room, to knock him unconscious with a sedative and to string him up . . ."

"And the locked room?" put in Flint.

"Simple enough to orchestrate. I did not realise until later that the clue had been in my possession all along." With a deft flourish, he produced from thin air a silver coin—the spurious double-header with which he had bewildered Francis Tulp on the coach journey. "Not *this* coin, of course, but one just like it. Easy enough to spot, you might think. But look at the edge. See how *thin* a coin is. How inconspicuous. And thin enough to fit snugly into the space between door and frame."

"We would have noticed," said Francis Tulp. "I mean, we *would* have, wouldn't we? Nobody tampered with the doorframe or the lock."

"Nobody tampered with the lock," said Spector. "At least, not *before* we entered the room and discovered the body. Indeed, the pristine nature of the lock was a clue in itself. The door was not locked at all—it could not have been.

"The clue came when I visited *your* room, Miss Drabble, and investigated the wardrobe. It called to mind a mild anomaly I had perceived at the first crime scene—the scent of varnish. I assumed it was emanating from the wardrobe—but then it occurred to me that the wardrobes in both rooms were identical—yet yours bore no telltale scent. Thus the smell was coming from elsewhere in Judd's room. There was no sign of tampering with the doorframe from within the room. But from *outside*, in the dimly lit corridor . . .

"You see, the third ingredient was crucial as a means of hiding the coin. Ironic, I suppose, that a tool designed to reveal the presence of spirits should be used to conceal a murder . . ."

"What tool?" asked Tulp.

"Three ingredients were required: a penny, a tub of boot polish, and—crucially—a syringe filled with quicksilver, or liquid mercury. We know the killer possessed a syringe, because it was used to administer the sedative to Judd.[*] A penny and a jar of boot polish would be easy enough to come by. And as for the quicksilver, Francis Tulp announced early on that his ghost-hunting kit contained a vial of the stuff.[†] Edgecomb was a trained chemist,[‡] a fact which is oft forgotten in discussions of the Aitken case because it seems at first glance irrelevant. But it's not irrelevant. Edgecomb knew that an ordinary copper coin would produce an interesting reaction with quicksilver, and one that he could use to create the illusion of a locked room. The trick did not involve the lock at all, but the *doorframe.* The killer slipped a copper coin into the very narrow gap between door and frame; it was a snug fit, and about to be even snugger. Then he injected the quicksilver directly above the coin, knowing it would trickle down and onto the copper. The two

---

[*]   *See Page 120*

[†]   *See Page 97*

[‡]   *See Page 20*

metals would thus react, creating what's known as an amalgam. Thus, the coin's overall density increases. The coin, which already fills the gap between the door and frame, *absorbs* the liquid mercury the way a sponge soaks up water, creating a hard alloy that sealed shut the door from outside.

"But, you say, the mercury is bright silver! Even a copper amalgam would be bound to catch the light. That is why," said Spector patiently, "the killer used not varnish but *boot polish* of the sort a traveller might carry. In the dim light, polish more or less matches the shade of the oak. He could have applied it in a matter of seconds with a gloved hand, covering any trace of the trick—except, of course, for the distinctive scent."

"And that's all there was to it?" said Francis Tulp.

"The most effective tricks tend to be the simplest," shrugged Spector. "Although, the same cannot be said of Madame La Motte's murder, which was positively dazzling in its complexity."

"Why was she killed, Mr. Spector?" asked Imogen.

"The why must wait. For the moment, let us concentrate on the how. We know the circumstances of Madame's death: she admitted her killer to the room, he stole her knife—the one she used in the table-tilting trick—and proceeded to butcher her most savagely. This left him in a room with two bodies—one dead, one drugged with laudanum.

"And this is where the automaton comes into play. You know, one of the great Robert-Houdin's most famous illusions relied entirely on automation: His 'Orange Tree Trick,' in which he borrowed a handkerchief from an audience member, concealed it inside an egg, which he then concealed inside an orange, which then burst into flame, only to sprout anew from the top of a beautiful orange tree in the centre of the stage. Finally, the orange split into quarters and from its heart two beautiful, mechanical butterflies emerged, clutching between them the borrowed handkerchief, ready for the illusionist to retrieve it. The audience was bamboozled by the sheer *magnitude* of the illusion. Not the scale, you understand, for there are many more grandiose tricks, but the—if you like—*philosophical* magnitude of it. It's a trick which placed considerable demands on an audience's attention, which is of course partly the reason for its success. When the mind is forced to compute a sequence of tricks in swift succession, inevitably it is unable to do so. And for each illusion to follow in such a satisfying sequence from the last is theatrical craft of the highest order. There is also the multifaceted nature of the performance to consider: the sleight of hand which conceals the handkerchief, and the elaborate technical feat which causes the 'orange tree'—really a magnificent clockwork machine—to sprout flowers, then fruit, and of course the fluttering butterflies. Entirely different disciplines, skills, and performance styles, all in service of the same outcome. I suppose one may liken the murder of Madame La Motte to the Orange Tree Trick. It has the appearance of a single, elaborate effect, but in reality it was the result of a sequence of minor illusions which give the impression of a single, unified whole. A grand illusion, composed of little tricks.

"After the murder itself, the assailant came up with a bold plan to frame an innocent—a plan which almost worked on you, Imogen. You see, the fact that Fred Powell was the only one whose sleeping quarters were *not* secured with string suggested Powell as a scapegoat."

"Now hold on . . ." said the man himself, Fred Powell.

Spector raised a conciliatory hand. "Don't fret, Mr. Powell. I am merely describing the killer's thought processes. The presence of the automaton was a psychological trick—because it had been carried from downstairs, it suggested that the killer had come from down there too. But of course, if the killer had devised a method of escaping a room sealed by string, it was perfectly easy to fetch the automaton *after* the murder."

"Then who is it?" demanded Mrs. Bailey.

"I should have thought it obvious by now," said Spector. "But no matter. The creation of the second locked-room illusion was a bold piece of work. Almost admirable, to a deranged sort of brain. Remember the automaton—the automaton is important.

"You see, by its very nature, it created the idea of motion. Of movement. I myself was preoccupied with a theory that the mechanics of The Stepney Lad had played a part in the killing of Madame La Motte. In fact the opposite was the truth. By which I mean, it was The Stepney Lad's *immobility* that was vital to the creation of the locked room. Its position was also carefully calculated. In fact, I shall begin with the positioning. Why was The Stepney Lad arranged in that specific location in the middle of the floor, do you suppose?"

"Equal distance between the beds?" suggested Imogen.

"A clever idea, but the answer is much simpler. The automaton was placed in the centre of the room because this meant that it faced the door.

"Picture the room as it was at that moment. The automaton in the middle of the floor, the two bodies in their respective beds, the key in the lock. Locking the door from outside was in some ways the simplest part of the entire illusion. With the string—let us say perhaps three feet in length—he created a miniature approximation of the webwork in the corridor. With one end of the thread in his left hand and the other in his right, he set to work. He looped one end around the hasp of the key in the lock. Then he looped it around the automaton's upraised thumb, around the blade of the knife—which was, at this point, angled toward the ceiling—and finally out and under the door. Thus, by pulling on the end of the string in his right hand, the string pulled tight around The Stepney Lad's thumb, which in turn pulled tight around the key hasp. The sudden pressure caused the hand to revolve its wrist joint, twisting the key and locking the door. Also, incidentally, giving the automaton the sinister posture in which we found it, as though he were raising his arm to strike a deadly downward blow. Finally, once he heard the lock click into place, the killer pulled the end of the string in his *left* hand. This tightened the loop around the blade itself—this time, the sudden pressure simply severed the string and pulled it free of the automaton and under the door, to be gathered up and destroyed. The killer then deliberately left the string from the door handle to perpetuate the idea that the killer had locked the door on the inside and exited via the window, shinning down the drainpipe."

"Well," said Clive Lennox somewhat awkwardly, "you'll forgive me, but who's to say that *isn't* the way it happened?"

Imogen looked at Powell, expecting to see rage or consternation written on his face. Instead, the driver was smiling. So, too, was

Joseph Spector. "Mr. Powell," the conjuror said politely, "would you care to explain?"

"If you like. You see, there's no way I could go shinning up any drainpipes. Even ordinary stairs are a bit much for me."

He leaned forward and rolled up his left trouser leg, revealing that the limb terminated just below the knee where a well-worn prosthetic was appended.

"A souvenir of the Somme," he explained.

"So you see," Spector resumed, "for all the killer's ingenuity, he chose to try and frame the one person who could not physically have committed the crime. An unfortunate error."

"And you knew about it all along . . ." said Imogen.

"As soon as I boarded the coach." Spector nodded. "There were two details which suggested themselves—first, Mr. Powell can only drive with one hand on the wheel—the other operates the manual levers which, in turn, controls the accelerator pedal.* And second, the badge pinned to Mr. Powell's cap.† The crimson ribbon with the miniature bronze emblem—"

"Bloody hell!" This came from George Flint.

"Yes, Flint. We are in the presence of a recipient of the Victoria Cross. The highest honour a soldier may receive."

Flint strode over and shook Powell by the hand. Powell shifted uncomfortably in his seat. "It was a long time ago," he said. "Dim and distant past. I don't mention it much. The badge speaks for itself."

"Indeed it does," Spector said while he nodded.

---

*   See Page 62

†   See Pages 4 and 63

"My God," said Flint, "if *I* had one of those, you can bet I'd wear it on my chest."

Powell smiled again. "Oh, the medal's long gone, Mr. Flint. I sold it to pay my wife's medical bills."

"I see. I'm very sorry to hear it."

"It's all right. I lost her last spring. I'd trade all the medals in the world to have her back."

"I'm sure you would," said Spector, resuming the narrative. "And I commend you for your strategic silence, Mr. Powell. As a rule I prefer my suspects to be entirely candid. This case, however, is the exception that proves that rule. Your silence, Mr. Powell, has enabled us to trap the killer with his own ingenuity."

"Then where is he?" demanded Francis Tulp, springing to his feet. "He's been leading us a merry dance all night, with the blackouts, the visitations . . ."

"Let us take your points methodically," said Spector. "I can assure you the only ghosts here tonight are those inside our heads. Point one: the blackouts. The first, as I have said, was a genuine accident. But the second was planned, precisely so that the 'visitation' could take place."

"But how?" asked Imogen. "We *saw* a man up there, dressed like a soldier and wearing a mask. He disappeared along the corridor. Who was he? And where did he go?"

"'He'
was nobody, Imogen," Spector answered. "There was no man."

"But we saw him! I saw him."

"What did you see? Truly? An epicene shape, that could by rights have been anyone? A silhouette, darting round the corner?

You said yourself that you could not even be sure what colour his uniform was, let alone whether or not he wore a mask over his face."

"Even so," she protested stubbornly, "a silhouette means there was someone there, and then he vanished."

"What is a silhouette?" Spector inquired rhetorically. "It's a shape; an obstacle between a source of light and the backdrop onto which the light is projected. Nothing more than that.

"You've heard of the 'magic lantern,' I presume. Devised by Christiaan Huygens in the seventeenth century—that ingenious Dutchman who also gave us the pendulum clock. Well, the appearance of the phantom was achieved with a rudimentary iteration of that magnificent, revolutionary device.

"You remember what happened immediately after that blackout?"

"We argued among ourselves for a minute or two," said Tulp. "And then . . ."

"We filed out into the hall," Imogen supplied.

"That's not all. En route, you will recall, Mr. Lennox fell."

"Tripped over something like a blasted fool," said Mr. Lennox, blushing again and shaking his head.

"That 'something,' I suggest, was Madame La Motte's foot. Naturally, the torch fell from your hand and went rattling across the floor, and who was the one to retrieve it?"

"Madame La Motte," said Imogen, catching on.

"Right. A neatly calculated opportunity for her to perform a swift sleight of hand. She'd arranged for the lights to go out using a device common among fraudulent mediums. I mentioned previously that some mediums employ clockmakers to produce materials that simulate knocking and other phantom sounds during a séance, didn't I? Well, Madame La Motte had no need of them, but what she *did* need was a homemade device consisting of a small wooden block and a glob of spirit gum. The block is attached to the 'roof' of the generator box with spirit gum, directly above the switch. Magic shops, incidentally, sell spirit gums of varying strengths, so an illusionist may estimate with considerable accuracy how long it will take to wear off. This can be used to time the dropping of an object. The dropping block caught the switch and turned off the power. She must have rigged this up before the séance, planting the seed for a future manifestation. Of course she had no way of knowing that Judd would be found dead in the meantime, but when the second blackout came, she decided to continue with her plan.

"Then, after tripping Mr. Lennox and snatching the torch, there is the matter of the silhouette. This is as old a trick as I have come across. The so-called phantasmagoria, meaning the use of lanterns to project moving shapes. It's similar in principle to the 'camera obscura,' though in this instance the images are intended to represent supernatural phenomena. Jesuit scholar Athanasius Kircher was one of the most prominent figures to write about the possibilities for mischief that such devices afforded; that was in his work *Ars Magna Lucis et Umbrae*, in 1646. But really, the illusion itself has been around as long as humans have had the means of creating and controlling light—it has simply been a question of refining it throughout the subsequent generations. By the 1770s, Johann Georg Schrepfer of Leipzig was performing séances and necromantic experiments which employed all the splendid wonders of phantasmagoria. He projected the images of ghosts and spirits onto clouds of aromatic smoke. The only problem with Schrepfer's act was that it was so convincing he took in just about everybody around him—including himself. He shot himself in 1774, while surrounded by friends and associates, having promised he would use his wondrous powers to rise from the dead soon after." Spector gave a malicious grin. "I imagine they are still waiting.

"But back to *our* problem. It was simple enough—a child could have done it, and indeed many have. A paper shape, the outline of a man, appended to the torch to create a large humanoid silhouette when the torch was switched on. It was a smoke screen. A red herring. Whatever nomenclature you prefer to use for such a contrivance. Purely a distraction technique. And it worked wonders. Madame made a point of grabbing the torch, shining it on her own face so that we might see its unobstructed light,* and then turning it in the direction in which she had ostensibly seen the soldier. This is a classic sleight-of-hand illusion: as she was rotating the torch, with her free hand she slipped a thin sheet of paper in front of the light—a preprepared cutout of a humanoid shape. With the torch behind it, the long shadow had the appearance of a man-sized figure. This was the ghostly soldier. And so our killer thought there was another person out here, when of course there could not have been. But it brought out all his paranoia, and sent him spiralling toward madness. The disappearance of the mask, which Adaline La Motte concealed in the folds of her dress while the rest of us were hunting for the phantom, might have tipped him over the edge. But he was no fool—he knew that she was the only one who might have taken the mask. And yet he was confused as to her motives.

---

*   *See Page 147*

Knowing little about the practice of illicit mediumship, he was unaware that the mask could be used for the purposes of doctoring a 'spirit' photograph. Instead, I believe he thought Madame La Motte was in league with Will McGinn, perhaps a co-conspirator. And so he had no compunction whatsoever about killing her."

"No, no, no," said Tulp. "I'm sorry, Mr. Spector, but I don't buy it. We didn't just see a paper shape projected on a wall. We saw a *soldier*."

"The first person to make reference to a uniform or a mask was Madame La Motte.* For both you and Imogen, the notion that the figure was a soldier was suggested purely by that—as well as the obvious associations between the house and the War. There was no soldier who vanished into thin air. There was nobody.

"Unfortunately, this same trick sealed Madame La Motte's fate. You see, it convinced the killer that we were not alone in the house—that there was an additional guest, in league with Madame. In that respect, the illusion was too effective for the illusionist's own good."

"So you're saying there *is* nobody else in the house?"

"Come now, Spector," put in Flint. "I think we've waited long enough."

"I couldn't agree more. To trace the roots of this mystery to their source, we must examine three patients who were treated here at Devil's Neck. These three men were together at the Fleurrière field hospital when the infamous shelling occurred. One man lost his face. Another man lost his memory. It is the third man who is our killer. The name he gave when he arrived here in 1918 was

---

* *See Page 68*

'Will McGinn.' But he was not Will McGinn. He was Rodney Edgecomb—the real Rodney Edgecomb—the only Rodney Edgecomb there has ever been."

"Well, for God's sake," cried Flint, "who is he?"

"Do you really want me to say?" a coquettish Spector asked the assembled company. "Or would the gentleman in question like to step forward and make himself known?"

A dreadful silence. Then:

"Yes. All right. I rather think this has gone on long enough."

Striding forward, toward centre stage, and flexing his shoulders, assuming a more upright posture than he had previously employed, came Clive Lennox.

Spector gave a vulpine smile. "Mr. Lennox—or rather, Mr. Edgecomb—has had a remarkably busy day."

"*You?*" said Imogen. "*You're* Edgecomb? And *you,*" she faced Justine Lennox. "Why in the hell didn't you say something? Why didn't you try and warn us?"

The caretaker was struck dumb.

"Mrs. Lennox had a good reason—the best there is," said Spector. "Remember, Edgecomb here is adept at assuming control over others. And he knew something she did not: the location of the secret passage.

"On his way here, Flint found a man being held captive in the tunnel, and who had clearly been there for several hours. He is alive, Mrs. Lennox. Your husband is in safe hands. And so, Rodney Edgecomb loses his last bargaining chip."

"Oh! Oh, thank heaven!" This was the first genuine, unguarded emotion Mrs. Lennox had displayed, and it transformed her. Gone was the austere demeanour. Tears of joy and gratitude seeped down her face and pooled at her chin. She gripped Joseph Spector by the arm, her face finally crumpling with the strain of the damnable stiff-upper-lipped-ness. "Thank you," she said softly, and to no one in particular. Then she resumed her habitually tight expression and looked at the man they had all known as Clive Lennox. "Bastard," she said.

"Bastard. Yes," he said, warming to the description. "I've often wondered quite what I am. I think you've hit upon as good a description as any."

Spector continued to smile. "If you are wondering how I knew it was *he* and nobody else among our party, you must remember two details. First, 'Lennox' was the last one into Judd's room when we broke open the door.* Therefore, he was the only one who could have turned the key while the rest of us were distracted by the body, thus causing it to *appear* that the door had been locked all along, when in fact it was the coin trick that wedged the door shut.

"And second, he was also the one who assisted Francis Tulp in setting up his traps. Specifically, *he* was the one who unspooled the thread while Francis rigged the door handles.† This enabled him to use an old magician's trick—another sleight of hand. He kept a couple loose loops in the palm of his hand, then pulled the remaining string tight, creating the illusion that he was doling out the entirety of the string. Thus, when his *own* room was rigged, six additional inches' worth of string were employed without

---

*   *See Page 117*
†   *See Page 152*

Tulp's knowledge. Plenty of give, in other words, to allow the door to be opened a crack from within and a hand to emerge and untie the string from the door handle, thus freeing the door without disturbing the bells.

"It must have been quite bewildering for you," Spector said to the killer, "to find that you possessed such a gift for killing, when you have failed so utterly in every other aspect of your life."

"Steady on, Mr. Spector." Edgecomb grinned. "You're liable to hurt a chap's feelings."

"If only that were possible," answered the conjuror.

Imogen could not bring herself to look away from Clive Lennox's face—it was undergoing a horrendous transformation. The pleasant, bumbling aspect of his character was gone, and in its stead was . . . something else. Dark, avaricious eyes; pinched, downturned lips; shoulders hunched. Fingertips trembling, itching for violence. This was a killer.

He dropped to his haunches and sprang—not in their direction, but toward the tall window overlooking the driveway. Imogen flinched at the sound of shattering glass. Flint and Tulp bolted toward the dark maw of the empty window frame, through which sheets of water and blasts of stormy air came rushing. Only Spector remained motionless, his cloak flapping about him like a bat's wings, as Rodney Edgecomb vanished into the night.

There was nowhere for him to go, thought Imogen. Taking an instant to catch her breath, she, too, lunged for the window. Bracing herself against the wooden frame, with the heavy damask curtains rippling wildly on either side, she watched the shape of portly, benign "Clive Lennox"—who was really the malevolent

Captain Edgecomb—running through the bosks and thickets, twigs and branches clawing at him as he darted through the darkness. Arms upraised, shielding his face from the brunt of the storm, he slowed to a lumbering pace as he reached the causeway. Fearless, foolish Francis Tulp was running after him at a wide-legged sprint, while Flint trailed behind.

The wind had swept aside the heavy nimbus clouds, revealing the bare face of the moon. By its iridescent light, still streaked with rain, Imogen was able to see quite clearly as Edgecomb paused a moment, glancing back toward the house, and toward his pursuers. She saw the dreadful malevolence on his face, which was broadly gashed and crisscrossed with little cuts, all smeared with blood from the shattered glass. Now, the faintly absurd purple smoking jacket looked like a ceremonial robe. He plunged toward the causeway; a futile move, since the eerie moonlight showed a row of police cars on the mainland, and a lone figure (whom Imogen took to be the fabled Sergeant Hook) waiting, unmoving.

But he pressed on. After all, Edgecomb had escaped justice and the machinery of law too many times to give up now. He had been in tighter spots than this one, and as he ran no doubt multiple escape plans flickered in his head like a zoetrope. With whitecapped waves crashing at either side of the thin spinelike causeway, he slowed his pace slightly, his bare feet skidding on the cobbles (his slippers had come free at some point since the fall from the window) and he found himself trapped.

When Imogen had taken her seat on the coach a scant few hours earlier, she could not have known that the ensuing night would change her life so irrevocably; not only her life but her perception of life. She had been a staunch sceptic; after what happened next, she would never refer to herself as such again. Because in that moment, the tallest and most fearsome wave—an awesome behemoth—rose above the causeway like the clutching hand of a sea god to carry Rodney Edgecomb away. But before it did, Imogen saw something she was never able to explain. Something which would haunt her dreams years later, even during the darkest days of the next war.

A man on horseback, riding full pelt toward Edgecomb. She saw it as clearly as she had seen anything that night. Perhaps clearer. His gaunt face, though young, and his eyes alive with righteous fury. The sudden change in his expression as he saw Edgecomb; uncanny dread echoing across the centuries. The horse rearing on its hind legs, bucking Samuel Draycott into the air. She would replay that vision (hallucination? Waking dream?) countless times in her memory, to the point where she was unable to determine how much was genuine and how much merely the product of her imagination. But it didn't matter. She had seen something; that was enough.

In a second—less than a second, perhaps—the wave broke, and then there was nothing. The causeway was desolate. Rodney Edgecomb was gone, swallowed by the swirling, caliginous waters. All Imogen could make out were the gleaming cobbles, and all she could hear was the pounding rain.

She turned frantically toward Joseph Spector. He stood expressionless, his pale eyes fixed on the causeway. She would never know for sure whether he had seen it too.

She left the house, not via the window but by the front door. Any sense of urgency had dissipated like the great crashing waves.

She walked toward Flint and Francis Tulp, who were standing helplessly at the mouth of the causeway.

"We can't cross!" Flint yelled. "It's too dangerous. And we'd never find him anyway."

However, this was not what had drawn Imogen from the confines of the house. Instead, she approached Francis Tulp (poor, credulous Francis!) and grabbed his hands, staring deep into his bewildered eyes. "Did you see?" she asked him. "You saw it, didn't you?"

But it was evident from his expression that he had no idea what she was talking about.

The hamlet of fishing cottages on the mainland was abuzz with activity; Sergeant Hook had wasted no time in initiating a rescue mission. A fishing boat was dispatched, and the survivors of Devil's Neck were carried away from the accursed island.

As she sat, swathed in blankets, rocking back and forth with the waves, Imogen realised the storm was abating at last. The rain was thinner now, as though the energy of the pitiless elements had finally been sapped. Beside her sat Sergeant Hook, who was conversing intensely with Inspector Flint.

"How's Lennox?" Flint asked.

"He'll live, sir," said Hook. "The doctor thought it might be a case of exposure, what with the damp down there in that tunnel. But he seems to be in better shape than we might have guessed."

"What about the head wound?"

"Concussion, but nothing that'll leave lasting damage."

"His wife wants to see him."

"I'll bet she does, sir. He's conscious now, anyway. Not completely coherent, but I'm sure he could cope with a visit."

Imogen glanced over at Mrs. Lennox, who looked harried yet, paradoxically, rather serene. Free from Rodney Edgecomb's pernicious grip, she was herself again.

Finally, Imogen looked at Spector. He sat in the same position as he had on the coach, with his spindly fingers threaded around the skull handle of his cane.

"He would have killed us all, you know," Spector said, as though answering a question she had not yet asked.

"I'm sure he would. Your friend Flint reached us just in time. How did you know there was a secret tunnel leading to the mainland?"

"I didn't," Spector admitted. "But I had an idea of its existence—after all, it was the only real means of explaining Latimer's disappearing act. What I *did* know was that Edgecomb must have travelled by auto. Since there were no cars at Devil's Neck, it stood to reason that he would have parked up somewhere close to the other end of the passageway."

"And that was all you had to go on?"

"It was enough. Once I worked out that 'Mr. Lennox' was not Mr. Lennox at all, I wondered how on earth he had induced Mrs. Lennox to go along with his charade. Simple—she was doing it to save her husband's life, or so she thought. Of course, if Edgecomb had managed to obtain what he was looking for, I imagine he would have had no qualms at all about murdering her and simply leaving her husband to die in that miserable tunnel. But she wasn't to know that, was she?"

"I don't understand why he felt compelled to impersonate Clive Lennox, and why he intimidated Justine into playing along. Knowing his history, wouldn't it have made more sense to simply kill them both?"

"He was, above all, a lazy man. All of this came about because of his laziness. He was a gambler who lost his money. He wanted more, but he did not wish to obtain it by working, or by any other lawful means—he chose the path of least resistance, at least as he perceived it. He *stole* the money because it was easier. He killed because it came naturally to him. And he knew that there were guests coming out here to Devil's Neck, and that they were expecting to be waited on. He had no intention of playing host, cook, butler, and all the other domestic roles. And he knew that the only way to keep Mrs. Lennox from spilling the beans was with the threat on her husband's life. As long as Clive was alive in that tunnel, she could be relied upon to persist with the imposture. And, to her credit, she did. She is a devoted wife indeed. I'm pleased that her husband is going to recover. He is a lucky man."

"I'll bet he's not feeling too lucky at the moment," said Flint, wryly joining in on their conversation.

"Indeed. But hopefully in time he will come to terms with the fact that he had a genuine brush with death. So many other people who have been obstacles to Rodney Edgecomb's progress have met a much less salubrious fate. Six altogether, I think."

Flint tutted. "Six people dead. And all so he could lay his hands on a bit of money."

"Correct. Though, of course, the irony is that the more people he killed, the further he moved from his objective. By the end, there was no conceivable way he could have obtained the Aitken inheritance, most of which had been frittered away over the decades anyway."

"So the whole thing was pointless. Futile."

"More or less. But with a man like Edgecomb, killing is a compulsion. It has an appeal all its own, which transcends any earthly objective. I doubt this was ever about the money, you know. It was always about the game."

———

A week later, Rodney Edgecomb made his next (and final) surprise appearance. This time, he washed ashore some six miles along the coast from Devil's Neck, spoiling the view for several day-trippers. He was a wretched sight now, lying face up on the wet sand with water sluicing over him as the tide drifted in. The cuts and gashes on his face, which had given him such a demonic aspect on the fateful night one week earlier, might now have been mere pencil lines on the sagging, waxy skin. The half-lidded eyes had a sardonic cast to them, as though even he were unsure if it had all been worth the trouble. They had rolled back in his head, giving them the appearance of pupilless opalescent orbs. His purple dressing gown, which had looked so incongruous in the drawing room at Devil's Neck, and had rippled so impressively on the causeway, was a ragged mess. His body was as green and bloated as a bullfrog's, swathed in seaweed, dead now for the last time.

A considerate onlooker covered him with a beach towel and, when the ambulance finally arrived to collect his remains, it was noted how loosely his head lolled, as though skin were the only thing tethering it to the spine. His neck had snapped completely.

VAPOUR TRAILS

The promised visit from Joseph Spector took place a week after the brutal, bloody events at Devil's Neck. In fact, Sergeant Hook admitted the visitors to Flint's Thameside office at the very same moment Rodney Edgecomb's body was being shoved unceremoniously into the back of the waiting ambulance. To Flint's surprise, Spector had brought a guest: Imogen Drabble.

"How do you do, Miss Drabble?"

"Considerably better than the last time we spoke, Inspector."

"Care to sit down?"

They took their seats, and Sergeant Hook served tea. Flint was gleefully and unashamedly chewing on his pipe as Spector lit up a cigarillo and began to speak. "Thank you for seeing us, Flint."

"How could I refuse?"

"There is some information I would like to share with you, even though it has little bearing on the outcome of the Devil's Neck case. It changes nothing and yet, at the same time, it changes everything. I've already discussed it with Miss Drabble, and she gives me her permission to share the information with you."

"Oddly formal, Spector," said Flint. "But very well. Please go on."

"It's about the man who died in Crook O'Lune Street. It's also about the *way* that man died."

"What about it?"

Spector shifted a little awkwardly in his seat. "I'm afraid your logic was specious at best."

"What do you mean? The dry ice bomb? The key encased in ice? The killer on the roof? It all fits together . . ."

"Yes," said Spector, "and that's precisely the problem. Both murders at Devil's Neck served a practical purpose. The first was designed to mimic a suicide. The second was designed to frame an innocent man. The death in Crook O'Lune Street was not so efficacious."

"What do you mean? It was meant to look like a suicide . . ."

"Superficially, yes. But with so many other clues littered around the place that the suicide angle would never hold up to serious scrutiny. You said it yourself, Flint: you cracked the puzzle in a matter of minutes. Therefore, it was not fit for purpose."

"So what are you saying?"

"What I'm saying, my dear Flint, is that the locked-room puzzle in Crook O'Lune Street was *meant* to be solved. What happened in that room was *disguised* as a locked-room murder."

"Well, if it wasn't a locked-room murder, what was it?"

"Why, a suicide, of course."

"So you're telling me McGinn really *did* shoot himself? Why on earth would he do that? And why did he try and convince us it was a murder? Why bother with the locked room at all?"

"Perfectly valid questions," said Spector. "It might be best if I took you through my thought processes step-by-step. First of all, there's the matter of the killer's identity. If it had been Rodney Edgecomb, as you were supposed to think, then how could he have got out to Devil's Neck?"

"He went by car, didn't he?"

"He did—he drove a grey Alvis, which he left parked on the mainland. And while he *could* have committed the Crook O'Lune Street murder and then driven out to Devil's Neck at such a speed that he reached it before the coach party, that is not what happened. Shall I tell you why? Because of the rain. It began to rain whilst you and Sergeant Hook were outside the house in Crook O'Lune Street, isn't that so? And, by your account, the killer would have needed to be in position on the roof to drop the dry ice bomb into the chimney at the appointed moment. Which would mean he was still there when it started to rain. However, there were no tracks on the dirt road leading to the place where the Alvis was parked.* That tells us it was driven into position *before* the rain began. And, as we know, it was driven by Rodney Edgecomb. Therefore, he could not have been in Crook O'Lune Street to commit the murder *and* driven the Alvis to Devil's Neck. One or the other, Flint, but not both."

"Then he must have done it some other way."

Spector shook his head. "No. He had no motive. Edgecomb could not have known the will had been amended to deprive him of the Aitken inheritance. And besides, his behaviour while he

---

*   *See Page 62*

was at Devil's Neck makes no sense if he knew the man in Crook O'Lune Street was dead."

Flint shook his head in disbelief. "So you're saying Will McGinn set him up?"

Spector nodded thoughtfully. "I think that's what I am saying. I am saying that the final act of the man in Crook O'Lune Street was designed solely to defeat his nemesis, his 'wicked shade,' the real Rodney Edgecomb. What you saw, Inspector Flint, was a suicide disguised as a murder disguised as a suicide. He knew that by killing himself he would rob his enemy of the Aitken inheritance for good. He *also* knew that if he made his suicide look like a murder, he might be able to achieve justice where Scotland Yard had failed. But his ingenuity did not stop there. His investigation of the circumstances surrounding the murder of Dominic Edgecomb in 1914 suggested the notion of re-creating those circumstances, to create a conscious echo of that earlier crime. The connections would be too strong to miss. And, to his immense credit, you followed the trail he set for you."

"I don't believe it," said Flint. "So he shot himself after all?"

"Yes—though not with the weapon found at the scene; as you observed, that had fired only one round—a blank. I rather think that if you search the chimney, you shall find the *actual* weapon. And everything else—the bottle in the fireplace, the dry ice, the pistol at his feet—these were all part of the setup." Spector shook his head slowly with an expression of wistful pride. "Rather ingenious, I'm sure you'll agree."

"How did he do it, then?" Flint asked resignedly.

"He did it with *two* weapons, one held in his right hand and aimed at his temple, the other—the one you found—containing a single blank cartridge, and aimed at the ceiling. As for *how* he got rid of the actual weapon, I think that if you had taken a little more time to examine the details of the room, you would have spotted it for yourself. You had the answer the entire time, you know. When you itemised the corpse's clothing—do you recall what he was wearing?"

"I think so. A suit, shirt, tie, socks, underwear . . ."

"Anything else?"

Flint shook his head.

"Don't you find it strange, Flint, that a man as well-dressed as he was did not possess a belt? Or, indeed, a pair of elasticated braces? He had the braces round his socks, though. And his trousers had buttons on the inner waistband, and were therefore tailored for braces.* It would be bizarre not to have worn them, and a killer would have had no reason to remove them. The only possible reason a pair of braces might be missing is that the victim removed them himself. For what purpose? To dispose of the real weapon, of course. And I know just how he did it.

"I would urge you to investigate the chimney of the house in Crook O'Lune Street. I believe you will find the second weapon, the one that killed your victim, suspended from a pair of elasticated braces, tied at arm's length up the chimney."

"Tied to what?"

Seeming to ignore Flint's question, Spector said, "Mr. Horsepool mentioned a pigeon. Isn't that so?† You were told that was the

---

*   *See Page 76*

†   *See Page 55*

reason for the fireguard, and I believe you were correct. But a more common and effective remedy would be a metal grille in the flue, or even a chimney cap, which could quite easily have been installed at the same time. Tell me, Flint, did you actually examine the *inside* of the chimney when you were surveying the crime scene?"

Flint, who had not, hung his head.

"Well, it will be simple enough to verify. But *if* such a grille exists, I'm afraid it negates your dry ice bomb theory. However, it makes my own theory more plausible. Our man secured the elastic to the grille, then secured the weapon to the elastic and hauled it across the room to the desk, causing said elastic to stretch almost to breaking point. I have studied the floor plan, and estimate a distance of six feet between the fireplace and the desk. Assuming the braces are about five feet in length, and may be stretched to approximately three times that length, it would be quite practicable. Then he took his seat, did the deed, firing the blank at the exact same moment. While the dummy revolver dropped to the ground, the elastic whisked the real weapon from his dead hand and up the chimney. This required it to pass through a four-inch gap between the top of the fireguard and the underside of the lintel, causing the dent in the fireguard and the chipped pieces of brick[*] on its travels."

"Wouldn't the braces have lost their elasticity after all that stretching?"

"No doubt. But the elastic force, not to mention the kickback, would nonetheless have sent the weapon and braces careering back up the chimney. I imagine he tested it a few times to make sure

---

[*] *See Page 56*

that it worked. You see, most chimneys possess a thermal barrier made of brick, called a smoke shelf. Most likely *that* is where you will find the weapon. So there you have my theory, but of course, I'm perfectly happy to be proven wrong."

"I'm not disputing you, Spector," said Flint, "but how in the hell did you work it out?"

"It was simply a question of examining the crime scene photographs, and the detritus from the fireplace. You assumed these were caused by the dry ice bomb; in fact, they were caused by the weapon flying from the dead man's hand, propelled by elastic, and catching both the top of the fireguard and the underside of the lintel as it returned to its position inside the chimney. There was also the rather awkward position of the body, which was perfectly visible in the crime scene photographs. The way the head lolled to the left, but the body was leaning to the right.* The position of the head made sense, bearing in mind the force and trajectory of the bullet as it entered the temple. The sideways position of the body, less so. It suggested a force diametrically opposed to that of the bullet had acted on the body at the very moment the fatal shot was fired. This was the elastic, stretched almost to breaking point, snapping back into position and withdrawing the pistol just as soon as the dead man's fingers slackened. It caused the body to lean to the right while the head lolled left."

There was a silence, save for the quiet clacking of Flint's teeth as he chewed on his pipe. "All right," Flint said finally. "All right, it fits. And we'll know soon enough—I'll send Hook to have

---

*   *See Page 18*

a look in the chimney. But what you're saying doesn't really change anything, does it? Whether McGinn killed himself or not . . ."

"Ah. This brings me neatly to the *second* reason for my visit. Perhaps the main reason for my presence here today—and for that of Miss Drabble."

Imogen, who hadn't said a word throughout the preceding exchange, remained silent and watchful.

Spector stubbed out the remains of his cigarillo in the ashtray and swiftly lit another. "You are familiar with the so-called parallax effect?" Flint shook his head, so Spector explained, "It's a phenomenon of perspective. It refers to the nature of an object in relation to the position of its observer. Put simply, an object's appearance—though unchanging—might *seem* to change because of the position from which it is viewed. The problem at Devil's Neck seems a neat analogy for the effect."

Flint rubbed his eyes, then poured more tea. "Too abstract for this early in the morning, Spector," he said. "Perhaps we can get to the point?"

Spector smiled. "All right. I'll keep it as simple as I can. But the fact that the man in Crook O'Lune Street shot himself raises an unfortunate question. Namely, if Rodney Edgecomb did not know that his living automaton had put an end to himself, then why was he compelled to murder Walter Judd and Madame La Motte?"

"I believe I can answer that question. Both murders were committed for the same purpose. They were committed because of the mask.

"Soon after our arrival at Devil's Neck, a curious incident occurred. Not the blackout, but what happened immediately *after* the blackout. Mrs. Bailey tripped and spilled the contents of her canvas bag onto the floor. This was the first time any of us in the house had seen the mask she carried with her. Walter Judd got a long look at it, and the expression on his face betrayed his recognition. *That* is why Edgecomb had to kill him."

"But why?" said Flint.

"The answer to that question can be readily deduced. And from that deduction, all manner of sinister implications begin to emerge. The mask was meticulously modelled on Maurice Bailey's face as it appeared in photographs from the days before the War. The fact that Walter Judd recognised it indicates—what, exactly?"

This question, clearly, was open to the floor.

"He'd seen one of those photographs?" Flint suggested lamely. "Or he knew Bailey during the War?"

"There is a third answer," said Spector, "and it is most damning indeed. By rights, I ought to have invited Mrs. Bailey here this morning as well. But, for reasons that will soon become clear, I did not. I should not wish for her to hear this. The third answer, my friend, is this: Walter Judd recognised Corporal Bailey's face because he had seen it recently. In the flesh. He therefore knew for an absolute fact that, in spite of his mother's assertion that he had been dead for over two decades, Maurice Bailey was alive. Alive and unscathed. He was not Patient 217."

"You can't seriously be saying that Maurice Bailey is *alive*?" said an incredulous Flint.

"No, I am not saying that," Spector corrected. "Only that he has been alive all these years that he was *believed* dead. Now, regrettably, he is well and truly dead. I broke the news to his daughter this morning." He glanced at Imogen, who was stone-faced and dry-eyed.

"Maurice Bailey shot himself in Crook O'Lune Street, where he had been living under the name Rodney Edgecomb. It was *Maurice Bailey*, and not Will McGinn, who had been Rodney Edgecomb's puppet all these years."

"But how's that possible? Bailey was so horribly injured at Fleurrière . . ."

"No, he was not. *That* was Will McGinn. Even Mrs. Bailey herself was the first to admit she could not have recognised her son after the injuries he had apparently sustained. And he was left both blind and deaf. Unable to communicate, or to perceive the world around him. He spent most of his days swathed in bandages. And when he did not, he wore a mask of Maurice Bailey's face, modelled on pre-War photographs. When we consider the situation from that perspective, it would be a perfectly easy and natural mistake for Mrs. Bailey to make. After all, she had been told that the injured man was her son, and that she might struggle to recognise him. Thus, she was psychologically prepared to accept the unfortunate soul in the hospital bed as her son Maurice. In fact, he was Will McGinn.

"A clue came in Mrs. Bailey's story of the last time she saw her son—his hearing had begun to return, she said. He was beginning to comprehend the world around him once more. And what did he hear? Spurious gossip from orderlies about Nurse Lister and *Will McGinn*. And he began to write a message on a notepad. What did he write? *Will McGinn.** The talk must have shocked him because the name the orderlies were using was *his*. Unlike Maurice Bailey, you see, his memory was perfectly intact. He knew who he was. What he did not know was how he had come to be in his present state, or how those around him had come to spread such pernicious stories.

"Soldiers are trained to withstand interrogation by providing only select pieces of information. Name, rank, serial number. And that is precisely what he was doing. His final message was to state his name—his *real* name. Tragically, no one around him understood that."

"I'm struggling myself," said Flint, rubbing his forehead again.

"Don't you see, Flint? You came so *close* to the truth with your theory of imposture. But you ran out of steam a little too soon. As a matter of fact, the fog of war enabled not one but *two* separate impostures to take place. Rodney Edgecomb did indeed assume the identity of Will McGinn at Fleurrière. But he did so *after* he had already assumed the identity of Maurice Bailey.

"Remember how both Maurice Bailey and Rodney Edgecomb came to be at Fleurrière in the first place? Bailey was a driver, his mother said,† who had been ferrying high-ups around when his vehicle happened to strike a land mine. He had a mild concussion, but his passenger, the 'hotshot young captain,'‡ received more serious injuries. At least, that is the official version of events.

---

*　　*See Page 115*

†　　*See Page 93*

‡　　*See Page 93*

"The truth is actually somewhat different. You see, Rodney Edgecomb and Maurice Bailey were rather alike in appearance. Both well-built. Both gentlemen. And yet Edgecomb, in spite of the scandals in his past, was a product of 'old money.' Toward the end of the War, the immense number of casualties meant that men in their twenties were receiving all kinds of promotions, simply to fill the gaps—I assume that is how a man like Edgecomb ended up as a captain, being chauffeured around by Maurice. And Maurice . . . what was he?" Spector gave Imogen a wistful smile. "He was a performer. Like me. By a quirk of fate, the two young men might easily have traded places. And one day in 1918, just such a quirk of fate occurred. It came in the form of a land mine, which was struck by the front right tyre of the military vehicle driven by Maurice. By rights, both occupants ought to have been killed. But they were not—you see, armoured vehicles bore steel plates on their undersides, designed to protect against just such an incident. Nonetheless, the two passengers would be unlikely to escape injury entirely. And yet, miraculously, one of them *did*. The driver, Maurice, escaped without so much as a scratch on his body. He crawled from the wreckage utterly unscathed. His passenger, Captain Edgecomb, was not quite so lucky. His head was split open; an ugly wound that left a lasting scar. A scar that was still in evidence when his deceased body was found,* isn't that right, Flint?"

Flint nodded.

"At least," Spector continued, "that is what we have been led to believe. But consider carefully: the *front* wheel struck the land

---

*   *See Page 19*

mine, and yet it was the passenger in the *back seat* who sustained an apparently life-threatening injury. Surely it would make more sense for the *driver* to receive the life-threatening wound, while the *passenger* was unscathed?

"And that is exactly what happened. You see, Captain Edgecomb was running out of time. If not for the War, he might already have been condemned and executed for the murder of his brother in 1914. There was only one man who might be able to identify him, though—an old diamond merchant named Barnaby Osgood. Propitiously enough for Captain Edgecomb, the odds had fallen in his favour, though the rest of Europe—and the world—would suffer for it. War broke out, and he escaped justice during that strange and confusing time. And yet, inevitably, the War would one day end. And then he would have no choice but to face recriminations for his actions. All in the name of an inheritance. And so, he decided to turn the horror of the explosion into another triumph. Emerging from the wreckage without a single scratch, he must have pulled the driver out after him. Taking him for dead (a natural conclusion, given the severity of the head wound), he stole the man's identity. Captain Edgecomb *became* Maurice Bailey. It was an impromptu decision, but he knew that if he played his cards right, he might just be able to pull it off.

"As 'Bailey,' he reported the incident, and that 'Captain Edgecomb' had been killed. Medics arrived and, likely still affected by the shock himself, he was quickly invalided out to Fleurrière." Spector's smile, which had not entirely left his face throughout the preceding tale, now widened into a grim rictus. "I can scarcely imagine the horror he must have felt when he was informed that his 'passenger,' Captain Edgecomb, was *not* dead after all, just gravely wounded . . .

"Of course, if Maurice—the real Maurice—was alive, it would mean the scheme had fallen to bits before it was even underway. There could not be two Maurices, could there? But Edgecomb, now in the guise of Maurice, was a gambler. Not a good one; indeed, one who was overly attracted to risk. One who did not know when to fold. And so, again, he gambled. When it transpired that the real Maurice was alive but that his gruesome head wound had robbed him of his memory, Edgecomb realised that all was not lost—not yet.

"Then came the second cataclysm. The field hospital was struck by a stray shell during a barrage of bombing. Many killed, and others gravely injured, but Edgecomb and Maurice emerged without further injury.

"Another man, a *third* soldier, received irreparable facial injuries. That was a man named Private Will McGinn. Sensing once again that fate had given him an opportunity, he traded papers with the unfortunate young man whose face was ripped from him by flying shrapnel. That is to say, he traded *Maurice's* papers with McGinn's."

"Why?" said Flint.

"If the real Maurice Bailey regained his memory, it would be assumed that the wounded man with the damaged face was Rodney Edgecomb, and that the confusion had been caused by administrative error. Nobody would suspect a *second* switch had taken place. This would leave the real Edgecomb free to do as he wished. To build a new life."

"That sounds like a better arrangement," Flint observed.

"Yes," said Spector, "all except for one thing: the Aitken inheritance. Edgecomb had murdered his own brother to obtain it. He couldn't risk letting it slip through his fingers. That's why he needed to perpetuate the idea that Maurice Bailey was Rodney Edgecomb, that Will McGinn was Maurice Bailey, and that he—the *real* Edgecomb—was Will McGinn.

"In this new guise, he could keep track of the fake Edgecomb's progress. And once he was satisfied that the amnesia was total, he knew he was safe from justice. He went from inevitable conviction to inevitable acquittal. The man that you met back in 1918, Flint, the man who was presented to Barnaby Osgood as Captain Rodney Edgecomb, was in fact Maurice Bailey, an unwitting impostor. Osgood was unable to identify him as the man he saw the night Dominic Edgecomb died because this truly was *not* that man. And the real Edgecomb was now living under a third identity: Will McGinn's."

Flint was rubbing his forehead, his eyes screwed up. Like chewing on his pipe, this was a mechanical gesture into which he lapsed whenever the confusion was just too great. This happened often in Spector's soliloquies during a case.

"But there's a bleak irony to all this. Rodney Edgecomb, who had killed two men in order to obtain the Aitken inheritance, would now be unable to spend a single penny of it. Chess players call it zugzwang: a situation in which a player is compelled to move, and yet a move in either direction signals certain annihilation. Edgecomb traded his identity for his freedom from prosecution. But his *identity* was his only means of securing the inheritance. And so he was forced to give up the very thing which had caused him to commit his crimes in the first place. It must have seemed a bitter cosmic joke.

"Nonetheless, he persevered, and through intimidation and blackmail successfully turned Maurice Bailey into his puppet. And for two whole decades he lived off the spoils of the Aitken inheritance, while Bailey lived quietly as Edgecomb in Crook O'Lune Street.

"However, the looming threat of a second War made matters difficult for him once again. It became impossible to continue receiving payments in his new home on the continent. He was left with no choice but to return to England. It was a risk, but the exigencies of the global situation made it a necessary one.

"Meanwhile, the unthinkable had occurred. After two decades, Maurice Bailey's memory had begun to return. Do you recall what stimulated it, Flint? It was an incident while he was walking in Soho—a van rounded a corner and nearly drove straight into him. But remember the *precise* description. How did Lidia Rees tell it?"

"Uh . . ." Flint grunted. "Something about how the sun was in his eyes, how he came face to face with the driver . . ."[*]

"Precisely! In other words, he came face to face with his *own reflection* in the windscreen, superimposed over that of the driver. He saw a panicked face—his own—behind the wheel of a delivery van, and in an instant the moment of the explosion came back to him. Confusingly, he was not the passenger, as he had been led to believe, but the *driver*. And with that sudden realisation, other heretofore severed connections in his mind began to re-establish

***

[*]   *See Page 131*

themselves. He began to dream. Certain details—The Stepney Lad, for instance—were there in plain sight.* And there were also the fugues, those curious blackouts which took him to parts of London which he had never known before. At least, he had no *memory* of them. Once, he found himself on a bus heading for Bethnal Green.† Once, he was on the Underground's District Line, passing through Whitechapel.‡ And once, he was actually *on* the overground railway line, close to Cudworth Street.§ What do these locations have in common? They are all within a mile or so of Maurice Bailey's childhood home in Duckett Street, Stepney."¶*

"Wait a moment," said Imogen, "I hadn't put two and two together. But when Virginia Bailey—*grandmother*"—she spoke the word bitterly—"talked about the apparition she saw outside the house, under the streetlamp . . ."

Spector nodded. "She saw her son, Maurice, in the flesh. His fugues drew him back there, but left him in a state of bewilderment and distress. It was that expression she perceived on his face. His panic caused him to run away, seemingly vanishing into thin air before his mother could get to him. And yet she *knew* in her heart of hearts that he was dead. And so she pursued the path of spiritualism, interpreting what she saw as an apparition with a message from the Other Side."

---

*   *See Page 127*
†   *See Page 130*
‡   *See Page 130*
§   *See Page 131*
¶   *See Page 95*

"She was so close to the truth, then," said Flint. "When she went to visit 'Maurice' at Devil's Neck, how come she never once spotted the *real* Maurice? How come nobody at the hospital recognised Maurice's face when they saw the finished mask? Why did nobody realise he was alive and well under the same roof?"

"All excellent questions," Spector replied. "As for Virginia Bailey's visits to Devil's Neck, she was always ushered into the private wing where the most gravely injured soldiers were housed. She pointed out that the doctors did not wish her to see other, less-injured soldiers.*And as for why nobody recognised Maurice—the mask was made by facial reconstruction specialists. They would have no need to visit wards catering to other types of injury, and were therefore unlikely to encounter Maurice in the Edgecomb guise. The only ones who might conceivably have spotted the resemblance were the orderlies and nurses who saw hundreds of faces and for whom one injured soldier inevitably resembles another. Anyway, before too long 'Edgecomb' was discharged, and on his way to London. Meanwhile, 'Maurice' was wearing the mask of another man's face. It was such a cruel conspiracy of circumstance."

Spector sighed, then went on, "That is why I cannot bring myself to share what I know with Virginia Bailey. I think the realisation that her son had been alive and well all these years, and almost within reach, would be too much for her. At the same time, I knew that Maurice's daughter ought to be told."

---

* *See Page 94*

"I appreciate that, Mr. Spector," said Imogen. "It means a lot to me. And yet it's very painful to know that we all endured so much heartache and that he took his own life for nothing . . ."

"Not for nothing," Spector assured her. "I promise you, he did not take his life for nothing. Maurice Bailey was one of the cleverest and most industrious people I have had the pleasure of knowing. Cleverer than I. You know he built the automaton, The Stepney Lad, himself, piece by piece? Some might even call him a genius. However, the War robbed him of his memories, and the faculties that made him famous. But I think, as his memory began to return, so too did his ingenuity. He became the puppet master once more.

"Indeed, this elaborate plan could *only* have been the work of a mind functioning with clockwork precision. The Maurice I knew would have been capable of just such a plan. Maurice Bailey, who had believed himself to be Rodney Edgecomb, had begun to remember. The very name 'Maurice Bailey' must have borne uncanny resonances, shades of déjà vu. After all, he became preoccupied with 'Patient 217,' the moniker given to him at Fleurrière, which likely seeped into his unconscious via its repeated use by medics, nurses, and the like. I imagine he nonetheless perceived Maurice to be an 'other,' an external entity. That's why he hired Walter Judd. That's why Judd came out to Devil's Neck on his employer's ticket. Though he had been hired to trace Maurice Bailey, he now found himself on the trail of Rodney Edgecomb."

"But *why?*" said Flint.

"They say genius and madness are two sides of the same coin. I think Maurice Bailey's . . . *situation* had induced in him a kind of madness. He knew every detail of the Dominic Edgecomb murder, and indeed for a number of years believed that he himself was responsible for that murder. The eventual realisation that he was in fact blameless, and that he had been used by the real killer for all this time, must have driven him to the very edge. So he devised a highly ironical form of revenge.

"He knew Edgecomb was back in the country, most likely in London, though he did not know where. Perhaps Walter Judd had tried to find out, and was unable to do so. So Maurice decided to lay a trap; to snare Edgecomb for the murders he *had* committed by framing him for a murder he had *not*: Maurice's own. Maurice planned to create the inverse of the Dominic Edgecomb murder: a suicide disguised as homicide, with circumstances designed to recall those of 1914. And he was going to frame Rodney. Poetic justice, requiring all of Maurice's prodigious theatrical skills.

"Of course, the choice of Devil's Neck as a backdrop was both practical *and* highly theatrical. It ought to have been a clue enough in itself. The old hospital retained all manner of psychological associations for Maurice, and he likely assumed it would have the same emotional significance for Edgecomb. But, crucially, he knew that if he could guarantee Edgecomb's presence on an excursion to that isolated house—specifically, the three P.M. coach—then this would prevent Edgecomb from establishing an alibi elsewhere. It would enable Maurice to construct a posthumous narrative in which Edgecomb had visited Crook O'Lune Street, committed murder, then rushed off to catch that fateful coach. It would mean that Judd was there to apprehend him, and that Mrs. Lennox was there to identify him.

"Maurice was clever. He *thought* he had considered every possible eventuality. The night before putting his plan into action, he gave his bus ticket to Walter Judd, along with an envelope containing written instructions—not to be opened until Judd was on the coach. Judd knew he was on the hunt for a very dangerous man. What he *didn't* know was what the man looked like. That's why Maurice needed Mrs. Lennox. She had known Edgecomb back in the days when her name was Justine Lister. She had suffered because of him. This made her trustworthy in Maurice's eyes, and an unimpeachable witness to Edgecomb's identity, in case he should attempt further chicanery.

"The last part of Maurice's plan's initial phase saw him contacting Edgecomb by whatever means they had used in the past, and arranging to meet him on the Devil's Neck excursion. Likely he kept the reason for the meeting vague, but perhaps hinted the money was at stake. No doubt he knew just what to say in order to guarantee Edgecomb's attendance. All the same, he couldn't put the rest of his plan in motion until he knew with the utmost certainty that Edgecomb would be on that coach. And Edgecomb, it seems, was rather late in responding to him. The secretary, Miss Rainsford, spoke of how Maurice grew agitated, began to pace and peer out of the window saying 'not yet, not yet.'* Likely he was looking out at the darkening sky, painfully aware that with every passing minute his plan was inching closer to failure. And then—mercifully—the letter arrived. A reply from Edgecomb, confirming that he *would* in fact be on the coach. Maurice knew he didn't have a moment to waste—that's why he immediately burned

---

*   *See Page 46*

the letter, seized the revolver, and began the calculated operation of clearing the house and sealing himself in the locked study before committing his own murder.

"He made one mistake, however. A mistake that many others have made in the past: he took Rodney Edgecomb at his word. Edgecomb said he would be on that three P.M. coach, but in fact he had no intention of keeping the rendezvous. Instead, he attempted a double cross, sneaking out to Devil's Neck by car ahead of time, kidnapping the entirely blameless Clive Lennox, and forcing Mrs. Lennox to play along with his own charade.

"None of this mattered to Maurice Bailey, of course. He'd been dead for several hours by the time we arrived at Devil's Neck. But he had left those written instructions for Walter Judd. Both Imogen and I noticed Judd reading them on the coach,* though when we broke into his room after his death the papers were nowhere to be found. But we can make an educated guess as to their contents. I imagine they said something along the lines of: 'By the time you read this, I will be dead . . .'"

For the first time, Imogen began to show a little emotion at Spector's story; her eyes welled with tears.

"I'm sorry, Imogen," said Spector. "I'm sorry you never had the chance to meet your father, and that his life ended in such a bizarre fashion. But it must have seemed as though it were his only way out. For all these years, Rodney Edgecomb had been his tormentor, his 'wicked shade.' And while he knew that *he* was not Edgecomb, he was not entirely Maurice Bailey anymore either. He must have felt

---

*   *See Page 5*

like a kind of hollow man, with no identity to call his own. What he did must have seemed a neat and satisfactory end to his torment."

"But it didn't go to plan, did it?" said Imogen. "I mean, Edgecomb threw a spanner in the works."

Spector nodded sagely. "In some respects, the plan was a failure. In others, however, it worked better than even its creator could have predicted. Obviously, no one was supposed to die at Devil's Neck. Maurice thought that by offering up his own life he could prevent that. Unfortunately, he was mistaken. However, he could not have predicted the presence of his own mother, or of the infamous mask. It was the mask that drove Edgecomb to kill that night, but also brought about his downfall.

"We know he killed Judd because Judd recognised the mask. I can tell you now that he killed Madame La Motte for a similar reason—not because she recognised it, but because she *stole* it before she orchestrated the second blackout, and was likely planning to use it for a bit of skulduggery with Francis Tulp's camera during the night. You remember, of course, that *she* was the one who suggested the use of the camera."*

"That doesn't make sense," put in Flint. "How could Edgecomb have worn the mask in the corridor, then? He must have had it *before* he went into the room and killed La Motte."

Spector shrugged. "That was a presumption, based on the fact the photograph *appeared* to show the killer poised to enter the room. In reality, it showed him on his way *out* of the room, and on his way downstairs to fetch The Stepney Lad. He put on the mask

---

*   *See Page 151*

in the room and wore it when he deliberately triggered the camera. He knew where the pressure pads had been laid beneath the carpets, and so it was easy enough for him to step around them when he first approached the room." Another shrug. "The rest you know."

The trio sat in silence for a moment or two. Finally, it was Imogen who spoke. "So bizarre," she said. "So horrible."

"Indeed, both bizarre and horrible," Spector agreed. "But the nightmare has reached its end."

"Has it?"

"What do you mean, Miss Drabble?" asked Flint.

"Well . . ." She looked at their expectant faces, and debated for a moment whether to tell them what she had seen on the causeway that night. "Nothing," she said.

After Imogen was gone, Spector and Flint chatted for a minute or two without the previous air of formality.

"What's the matter, Flint?" asked the old conjuror. "You seem out of sorts. Not your usual chipper self—particularly bearing in mind the fact we've just concluded perhaps the strangest case of our respective careers."

"Have you seen this morning's papers? 'Never again,' we said. And look at this." He held up a copy of *The Times* so Spector could read the headline, which was so unpleasantly portentous on this sunny autumn morning.

Spector gave the printed words polite scrutiny, then smiled at Flint. "We weathered one storm, Flint. I dare say we shall weather another. Care for a smoke?" He clicked open his silver cigarillo case and extracted another, slipping it between his lips and lighting up with a flourish.

Flint shook his head distractedly, still chewing his unlit pipe.

For the first time, a shade of melancholy flickered across Spector's face. It was a strange and oddly intimate moment; Flint knew he was one of the few people in the world to whom Spector showed his "true" face, unadorned by the artifice of his vocation. Only when he was alone did he cease performing. He seemed to age perhaps two or even three decades in the space of a moment. But really, he might have been a thousand years old, this man who had seen so much strangeness and death. "I'll not insult you with platitudes, Flint. All the same, there was a certain inevitability to it, don't you think? No matter how much we might like to believe otherwise, the past always, always comes back."

Flint was restless. He got up from his chair and paced over to the window. There he stood with his hands clasped contemplatively behind him, looking out. London was changing, as great cities inevitably do, but even the view from this window was not quite the same as it had been the day before. The Thames was cluttered with supply boats. Earlier, aeroplanes had coasted overhead in grim formation; their thin vapour trails were still faintly visible in the otherwise unblemished sky. Flint wished he were at home with Julia, and that his daughters were with him.

He turned back from the window, and found he was alone. All that remained of Spector was a pungent wisp of cigarillo smoke.

"What a bloody awful mess," he said to the empty office. On the desk in front of him, the telephone began to ring.

ACKNOWLEDGEMENTS

Thank you for joining me on this little excursion out to Devil's Neck. I hope you've found it diverting, surprising, and amusing in the right places. My name is on the cover, but this was by no means a solo effort, and I owe a debt of gratitude to many people—too many to list here. But I've put together a few highlights all the same.

First, you wouldn't be holding this book in your hands if not for the following people:

The powerhouse team at Mysterious Press: Otto Penzler, Luisa Cruz Smith, Charles Perry, Julia O'Connell and Will Luckman.

The no-less-awe-inspiring team at Head of Zeus, particularly Greg Rees, Polly Grice and Sophie Ransom.

My fabulous agent, Lorella Belli.

Dan Napolitano for being one of my earliest readers, and for his invaluable advice and suggestions pertaining to the messy business in Crook O'Lune Street.

My dear friends Michael Dahl and Ana Teresa Pereira for being such enthusiastic early readers, and for their constant support.

The team at Mickleover Library, where a substantial amount of this book was written: Laura, Emma, Liz, Colin and Henry. And of course my sometime "library buddy" James Cornall.

Barbara Nadel, for continuing to champion the weird and wonderful side of things.

Paul Halter, "in locked-room fellowship"!

Michael Pritchard and Milan Gurung for their most excellent friendship.

Charlotte Lunn for her continued encouragement.

And in the wider world of writing and publishing, the following people deserve to be celebrated for all they do:

Martin Edwards, Douglas Greene, Kate Ellis, Jeff Marks, Lenny Picker, Ragnar Jonasson, Victoria Dowd, Gigi Pandian, Vaseem Khan, Tim Major, M.W. Craven and Matthew Booth, for championing all things mysterious!

The online community of bloggers, Bookstagrammers and BookTubers who have been so supportive, including Katie Lumsden, CriminOlly, @trwriteratwork, @reneesramblings, @mrsramsayreads, @nothing.beats.a.good.book, @mysterymanon, @travels.along.my.bookshelf, and too many others to mention.

All the reviewers, booksellers and librarians who continue to push the Joseph Spector mysteries, and of course the readers who have been with me every step of the way.

Last, I'd like to pay tribute to the memory of the great Phil Rickman, who was very generous with his support of *Death and the Conjuror*, and whose Merrily Watkins novels remain a benchmark for intelligence, sophistication and overall quality in the murder mystery world.